MONTANA UNTAMED

BEAR GRASS SPRINGS, BOOK ONE

RAMONA FLIGHTNER

*To My Family, Who Shows
Infinite Patience, Support
And Love as I Lose Myself
In the Worlds I Create.
Mil Gracias.*

WHAT READERS ARE SAYING

What Readers are saying about Ramona Flightner and her writing.

"...what makes Flightner so unique; she writes with depth and passion of characters who are human... flawed and overcoming, but not in a saccharine fairytale. They bring history alive in a way that leaves me yearning for more." Amazon Reviewer

"I love novels like this dealing with earlier times and how those before us paved the paths we take for granted." i-Books Reviewer

"Never have I followed a series as I have "Banished". Thinking at the end of each book that I will move on has proved fruitless. I am intrigued by your characters, the progressive plot and the historical aspects of your stories. A total enjoyment." Amazon Reviewer

CHAPTER 1

Montana Territory, March 1884

Annabelle Evans took a deep breath as She stood in front of the door to the General Store, or the Merc as the residents of Bear Grass Springs called it. She tugged on her wool navy-blue waist-length jacket that matched her dress as she fought panic. The man she sought information from would be inside. However, the gray day darkened the large glass windows on either side of the glass-paned door, as though curtains were drawn over them, preventing her from catching a glimpse inside. She ran a hand over her black hair pulled in a tight bun and pinched her cheeks.

After another deep breath, she entered the Merc, the tinkle of a bell heralding her presence, and she smiled impersonally at the man behind the counter. She glanced at the organized shelves of merchandise, ranging from foodstuffs to linens to farm equipment. She squared her shoulders as she walked with graceful measured steps and approached him.

"May I help you, miss?" the man behind the counter asked with curiosity and mild interest in his gaze. He was older, probably in his mid-forties, with broad shoulders, thick hands that reminded her of clubs, and an intent stare that missed little. His brown hair was shot with gray, and his beard held multicolored splotches.

"Excuse me. I'm looking for my sister, Fidelia Evans." She stiffened as the man looked her over from head to foot. She fought an instinctual blush as he focused on her bosom and hips, silently cursing that her prim clothes failed to hide her generous curves.

"And who would be askin' for her?" the man inquired, his thick eyebrows failing to hide a penetrating gaze.

Or, she suspected, a sharp mind.

"You don't sound like you're from around these parts."

"I'm Annabelle Evans, and I arrived yesterday." She met his implacable stare. "I'm from Maine."

Before she could continue further, he smiled, pulling at one of the suspenders holding up his pants. "Your arrival was heralded by all and sundry. We're just waitin' to see which way you'll go."

She frowned at his statement and barreled on. "I was advised by the front desk staff at the hotel that you've been in this town quite some time and that you're the man I should speak with about my concerns. I've been unsuccessful in locating my sister. She wrote, informing me that she's to be married to a Mr. Cailean MacKinnon. I've arrived in time for their nuptials as a surprise."

The inquisitive man appeared dumbstruck, the momentary silence broken by a deep, melodious voice with a hint of Scotland in it. "Like hell she is."

Annabelle spun to face the man who had been listening in. She had failed to see him, standing in the shadows, examining equipment for livestock.

But now he approached her, standing taller than her late father— over six feet—and exuding a lanky strength. His penetrating gaze met hers, his hazel eyes lit with anger while he slapped a dusty hat on his legs.

"Excuse me. Who are you, and why are you interrupting a private conversation?" she asked.

He leaned forward, his low voice more menacing than a bellow. "I'm Cailean MacKinnon, and I'm not marrying a whore."

"How dare you suggest my sister ..." Annabelle sputtered.

"*Charity* is what she goes by," the man behind the counter said, fighting a wry smile. "When she first arrived, she used her real name. But, for a while now, she's gone by Charity." He chuckled. "She's had plenty of charity for the men of this town."

Annabelle balled her fists, reminding herself she did not believe in violence as she took a deep breath. She jumped as Cailean MacKinnon slapped a list onto the wooden counter next to her.

"I'd appreciate you filling this while I finish my other errands," he said with a nod to the General Store owner. "My brother or I will be by to pick it up later today."

"Where will I find my sister?" Annabelle demanded of Mr. MacKinnon, backing up and preventing him from leaving. Her gaze darted from the amused storekeeper to the irate Scotsman.

"She'll be sleeping off her night's work at Betty's Boudoir," the General Store owner said. At Annabelle's blank stare at the name of the business, he half laughed then attempted to mimic her accent. "Just 'cause we're in the middle of nowhere doesn't mean we don't have culture."

Annabelle glared at him even while blushing beet red, unable to forestall her instinctive flushing. "And where might I find this ... this hotel?"

"Ha! That bawdy house of leisure is toward the end of Main Street. Near the bank, in case patrons think to overspend."

"Tobias ..." Cailean said with a touch of warning in his voice. He motioned for Annabelle to precede him outside and closed the door firmly behind him, causing the bell to rattle.

"Mr. MacKinnon," Annabelle began after she took a deep breath, gasping as he gripped her elbow and hauled her down the boardwalk a few steps, out of view of Tobias's avid gaze from inside the General Store. She opened her mouth to sputter a protest but clamped her jaw shut as she met Cailean's irate glare.

"Miss Evans, if you believed that lie you just told in there, why didn't you seek me out?" He vibrated with barely leashed fury as his gaze roved over her.

"I should have realized you lived in this town," Annabelle stuttered.

"What do you think you're doing, coming here and spreading your vicious gossip to a man like him?" Cailean asked, bending at his waist as he met her shocked gaze. "We don't need the likes of you here in our town. We've already your sister." He pushed past her, the tattoo of his boot heels sounding on the boardwalk.

She watched as he agilely jumped from the boardwalk and crossed the muddy street, entering the livery a little ways down on the other side of the main thoroughfare through town. She looked at the name above the establishment and sighed with resignation. *MacKinnon's Livery*. She shook her head at her ineptitude and jumped again as the door to the General Store opened.

"If I may, Miss Evans?" the man called Tobias said around a chuckle. "I'd wait 'til at least early afternoon afore seeking out your sister. She's bound to have had a tiring night."

Annabelle glared at him, not bothering to give him her thanks before she marched down the boardwalk. When she reached its edge, she noticed the Sunflower Café and stumbled inside. Gingham curtains hung alongside polished windows. She collapsed in a dazed stupor onto a chair at a round table covered by a checkered blue-and-white cloth and topped with an empty vase at the center of the table. Scattered framed pictures—torn from magazines—of far-off lands hung on the walls.

An elderly woman approached with a pot of coffee in one hand and a cup and saucer in the other. "You look like you need a cup." She set it down gracefully and smiled at Annabelle. The woman's gray hair was pulled into a tight knot, and her light-blue eyes shone with friendly interest. Her simple navy dress was covered by a white cotton apron. "I haven't seen you in here before."

Annabelle shrugged before she attempted to muster a smile. "I just arrived yesterday."

"Welcome." The woman stood there a few moments and then nodded. "I'm Mrs. Irene Tompkins. My husband and I run this café, and you'll meet my nephew, Mr. Sutton, at the General Store." When

MONTANA UNTAMED

she saw Annabelle grimace, she laughed. "I see you've already met him."

"He wasn't as welcoming as you are." Annabelle glanced around the empty room. "Can you sit for a moment?"

Irene beamed at her and settled into the chair across from her. "If there's one thing lacking in this town, it's female friendship. I hope you're not planning on up and leaving too soon." At Annabelle's blush, she frowned.

"I'm uncertain you'll want to associate with me when you realize who I'm related to." She blew out a breath and met Irene's curious gaze. "If your nephew is correct, my sister works at a place called the Boudoir."

Irene's eyes widened, and she murmured, "Oh my." After a moment, she patted Annabelle's clenched hand. "I'm afraid Tobias is rarely wrong. Or kind."

"I feared that was the case. I've never seen a man so angry as Mr. MacKinnon when I proclaimed he was to marry my sister."

Irene sputtered out a laugh. "Mr. Cailean MacKinnon?" When Annabelle nodded, Irene shook her head. "That man will never marry. And he's not one to visit the Boudoir with any frequency." She swiped at her eyes. "Whatever gave you such a foolish idea?"

When Annabelle blushed but remained quiet, Irene said, "I wish I had something other than coffee to offer. However, our baker recently quit, and I don't have the energy to run the café and cook meals, breads, and desserts too."

Annabelle watched Irene with interest for a moment. "There is need for a baker in this town?" At Irene's nod, Annabelle's look turned contemplative.

"I know the town doesn't look like much, but we're growing. And there's a sizeable miners' camp a few miles up the mountain and not far from town. It's called Obsidian after the dark cliffs bracketing the camp. Anyway, those men don't tend to cook much, which is why I started a café, even though I'd promised Mr. Tompkins I'd given up the business when we left Fort Benton. The only compromise was that it be in town rather than at the camp."

"Is he angry with you?"

Irene laughed. "Heavens no. It's more of a resignation to the fact I can't sit at home, content to care for just him." Her eyes sparkled with mischief. "Now I'm no gossip, like that nephew of mine. But I do like to know the goings-on in town—especially before I hear it from him —something that would be hard to come by if I were cooped up at home."

Annabelle laughed, the tension easing from her shoulders for the first time since she had left all that was familiar in Maine. "It seems you have a unique marriage."

"Oh, you'll come to know him well. He's a rascal but a good man. Nothing he wouldn't do for you if you needed help." She pinned Annabelle with a hard stare. "As long as he thought you worthy of it. Now tell me a little about yourself, Miss ... ?"

"I'm Annabelle Evans, and I'm from Maine." She paused a moment, picking at the tablecloth. "My father recently died, and I wanted to find my sister who I haven't seen in years. I thought she ... I thought she was a seamstress." She flushed at Irene's indignant snort. "I had no reason to doubt her letters."

Irene sighed and glanced down the street before shaking her head. "You keep in mind when you see that sister of yours again about what must have occurred for her to succumb to such a life. No woman dreams of working in a place like the Boudoir."

Annabelle nodded. "I'm afraid I won't believe it until ..."

"Well, I wish you luck, Miss Evans, for I fear you are bound to be disappointed." Irene rose when the door rang as noontime customers strolled in. She motioned for Annabelle to remain seated. "I like to think we'll be friends, Miss Evans. Come again when you want a good meal and a friendly ear."

Annabelle lingered a few minutes over her coffee as she thought about her sister. Fidelia was four years older, and she'd been a talented seamstress whereas Annabelle had enjoyed baking. Where she had black hair, Fidelia's gleamed a rich chestnut color in the sunlight. Annabelle smiled as she remembered her envy of her sister's beautiful blue eyes. She took a final sip of coffee as she refused to remember the last time she had spoken with her sister and stood to make her way to the Boudoir. Would five years have eased Fidelia's resentment?

~

Annabelle poked her head into Betty's Boudoir, her eyes adjusting to the darkened interior. The slightly faded burgundy walls showed their age as nicks in the paint highlighted the previously soothing yellow walls. The chips were most common in areas where chairs rested against the walls. A lone overhead lamp shone, enhancing the shadows in the corners. She imagined this was to give the room a sense of intrigue, but, to her, it made the room look worn and tawdry.

Chairs filled the entranceway, a few wooden and stiff backed, many plush and comfortable. Only one had arms. Annabelle frowned at that detail before she focused on an overly rouged woman walking on the faded, dilapidated carpet. A tall, burly man with a forbidding expression followed behind the woman, as though accustomed to his role as her silent shadow. Annabelle sneezed at the overwhelming combinations of perfume, cigar smoke, and sweat.

"May I help you?" the woman asked with an appraising smile.

Annabelle watched as the woman took in Annabelle's fine clothes, young face, and soft hands, and the woman's smile spread as though she had just struck an ore lode. Annabelle opened her mouth and then shook her head, her words momentarily silenced.

The older woman tapped Annabelle's hands clasped together in front of her, earning Annabelle's full attention. "Never fear. I understand your nerves. I had them too, the first time I stepped into such a place. However, soon this will seem like your home. You must call me *Madam.*" She attempted a French accent for the last word.

"I fear you're misinformed. I'm hoping *I've* been misinformed." Annabelle straightened her shoulders and disentangled her hands from the Madam. "I'm looking for my sister. Fidelia Evans." At the woman's blank stare, Annabelle ground her teeth together. "I've been told she goes by Charity."

"Ah, Charity. She's sleeping off another successful night. She is one of our favorites and is always quite in demand. I'm surprised you'd call so early." The woman's attempt at a cultured accent failed as her long vowels sounded forced. "And I'm disappointed you won't take the opportunity offered to you. I could make you the most popular woman in town."

Annabelle's jaw tightened as she met the Madam's beseeching gaze. Then she cringed. "I thought two in the afternoon was late enough."

"Considering she didn't seek her bed until after breakfast ..." The older woman smiled indulgently as she shrugged, her violet dress slipping off one shoulder. "You can understand why she'd be tired."

Glaring at the woman and ignoring the man hovering in the shadows, Annabelle gripped her hands together as she was unable to fight a bright blush on her cheeks. "If you would be so kind as to awaken my sister and advise her that I'm here?" She glanced around the interior again and raised her chin. "I'll wait outside."

The older woman laughed. "I'm certain the men of this town would be delighted to find two sisters at the Boudoir. I'll remain hopeful you'll soon come to see what a fine opportunity you have squandered. However, you must remain hopeful I'll be as welcoming when you return, asking for my aid."

Annabelle sputtered as she spun and pushed out the door. The door *thwack*ed behind her, and she took a deep breath in an attempt to calm her roiling anger. She breathed in and out, relishing the stench of horse dung, the sweetness of fresh rain, and the hint of pine trees rather than the cloying scents from inside the bawdy house.

She moved away from the door and sat on a bench halfway down the raised wooden boardwalk in the direction of the bank. Wagons moved up and down the street, and horses lazed in front of what she assumed was another saloon. Most of the wooden buildings had fake fronts, giving them the appearance of two stories, but the Grand Hotel, the Stumble-Out Saloon, and the livery were actually two stories tall. She jolted as a man stumbled out of the saloon, swearing at the occupants inside before he tripped and fell in a horse trough.

When he sputtered and pushed himself from it, he caught her witnessing his ignominious display, and he glared in her direction.

The slamming of the Boudoir's door distracted her from the drenched man, and she turned, then frowned. The woman standing with a shawl around her shoulders, her chestnut hair in ringlets and eyes darkened by kohl, was a stranger. When she turned to meet Annabelle's incredulous stare, she blanched a moment before glaring at her. "What're ye starin' at?"

Annabelle frowned as she studied the woman. Her hair color was correct, as was the color of her eyes, a light blue. Annabelle rose and approached her, frowning at the tight cobalt-blue dress with a flash of pantaloons showing. "Fidelia?" she whispered.

The woman's gaze cooled to the temperature of a glacier. "My name's Charity."

Annabelle shook her head and grasped the woman's arm before she could storm inside, away from her. "No, you're Fidelia. My sister," she breathed. "What happened to you?"

The woman wrenched away her arm, her glare filled with loathing and envy. "How dare you show up here! How dare you?" She tugged the shawl tighter about her, covering her bosom.

"I haven't seen you since I was twenty," Annabelle said as she fought, and lost, her battle with tears. "I thought you were happy with Aaron."

At the mention of Fidelia's old love, her sister froze. "He died."

"Why'd you write letters filled with lies instead of telling me the truth?"

"Why are you here?" Fidelia asked, losing some of the rough cant she had picked up in the brothel. She raked a dismissive glance over her finely dressed sister, not a button or hair out of place.

"Father died." Annabelle watched her sister for some sign of sadness. When Fidelia's deadened eyes failed to react, Annabelle frowned. "I was looking through his papers and found your last letter."

Fidelia rolled her eyes. "You always were the naive one." She snorted. "You believed, after all this time, I'd be gettin' married?"

9

Frowning in confusion, Annabelle watched her sister. "Why wouldn't I? You're ... you were respectable."

"A word to the wise, sister. If you want to remain out of such a place"—she nodded to the Boudoir—"I wouldn't spend much time loiterin' outside it or talkin' to the whores." She strode off and wrenched open the door and slammed it shut behind her.

Annabelle followed, then collapsed on a stool beside the door, suddenly faint. After a moment, she recalled her sister's words and rose, moving away from the Boudoir. She walked down the boardwalk, studiously ignoring Tobias's curious gaze as he stood outside, sweeping the boardwalk in front of his store.

She entered the town's only hotel, a more elegant establishment than she expected in rural Montana. The wooden two-story building was well built with decorative wallpaper in every room, crown molding in all public rooms on the ground floor, and comfortable furniture. Inside the front door, a staircase led upstairs to the private bedrooms. On either side of the entranceway was a parlor and a smoking room. The short hallway led to a large dining room, with a kitchen behind it.

The proprietor glanced up from a desk placed near the entrance of the dining room and beamed at her. "Miss Evans. I hope you enjoyed your walk around town. I'm certain you will discover this is a town you desire to settle in. There are many successful businesses, with numerous men interested in an accomplished wife."

She smiled impersonally. "Yes, well, I thank you, Mr. Atkins, for your kindness in suggesting I visit with the owner of the mercantile. He was most ... forthcoming with the information I sought."

Mr. Atkins, a short beanpole of a man, stuck out his chest with pleasure. "I'm only too pleased I was able to aid you, Miss Evans. Please inquire if you are in need of any other assistance." She accepted the key to her room from him and slipped up the polished pine steps of the hotel.

After she shut herself inside her rented room, she removed her coat and hat, setting them on the chair in the corner of her small room. The sole window looked out over the neighboring rooftops, and she glared at her view of the Boudoir. She washed her face in the clean water from the ewer on the bureau and then collapsed on the comfortable bed.

She swiped away a tear as she thought about the past few months. She remembered the hours she had spent, sitting beside her father on his deathbed, where he had admonished her to marry a good man and to remain in Maine. She shivered as she recalled his fervent prayer that she forget her sister. However, after her father's death, she had found a letter from Fidelia, describing an exciting, fulfilling life in a place called Bear Grass Springs in Montana Territory. After settling for her father's dreams her entire life, Annabelle had yearned for adventure and to reunite with her long-lost sister. Selling her family home and her own business before purchasing tickets to go west had filled her with purpose and exhilaration for the first time in her life.

She recalled her initial views of this valley yesterday as the train had trundled through the high mountain valley, its track one of the few blemishes to the unspoiled, wild beauty of the place. To one side, the valley sloped upward into towering snowcapped mountain peaks, pieces of granite glinting in the late afternoon sun. To the other side were rolling hills with scattered cattle herds dotting the landscape covered in a light coating of snow, with thicker patches in gullies. The valley in early spring showed little promise of what was to come. A creek covered with a latticework of ice resembling lace ran through the valley.

"What a fool I am," she whispered as she recalled the derision in her sister's eyes. Annabelle jumped as a gunshot sounded and then relaxed as she heard hoots of laughter from men outside on the street level. She pulled a pillow to her chest, hugging it to her as she attempted to banish her despair.

Cailean MacKinnon sat at the dining room table in the house he shared with his three siblings. The two-story house was next to the livery he owned and ran with his brother, Alistair. On the main floor was a large kitchen with an eating area, and on the other side of the stairs was a comfortable parlor. Upstairs were four small bedrooms.

He smiled appreciatively at Sorcha as she placed potatoes and a baked chicken in front of them, her shoulders back in defiance.

Her light-blue eyes shone with frustration.

"Not potatoes and chicken again," Ewan, the youngest brother at twenty nine, complained. He bolted as though he had been kicked, which Cailean suspected he had been by the glare sent from the second eldest, Alistair.

"Ye try cookin' in that monstrous oven. Then tell me what ye can produce," snapped Sorcha, their sister and the youngest of them all at twenty three. She slammed the butter onto the table along with a loaf of bread that appeared heavy enough to enter into a Highland Games competition.

"What in God's name did ye do to the bread?" Ewan asked. "Is it too much to ask to come home to an edible meal?"

"Ewan," Cailean said by way of warning, "until Sorcha arrived last month, we were taking it in turns. And, as I recall, your meals were only fit for the pigs." He winked at his sister and reached for the bread. He frowned when he was unable to tear off a piece and rose to retrieve a knife. He hacked up the bread, giving each sibling a large slice and glaring his brothers into silence.

"I hate this place. It's loud, dirty, and filled with unfriendly people," Sorcha complained. "I dinna understand why we canna go home."

Alistair sighed as he accepted his plate filled with potatoes and chicken. "There's no home on Skye. Ye should ken it better than the rest of us. Ye've been there, watching them kick the Scots off the land." He watched as his siblings frowned as they remembered the scenes of small family plots on Skye confiscated by wealthy English lords, their small subsistence farms replaced by hordes of sheep.

"I never thought the Clearances would come to our glen," Sorcha whispered. "I was glad ye three were spared seein' us thrown off our land. That mother and father were already dead by the time they came for our bit of land."

"Bloody sheep," Ewan muttered, earning a grunt of agreement from Cailean.

"Speaking of animals, did I see you washing with the horses today?" Cailean asked his brother Ewan. "I was on my way to the General Store when I thought I saw you take a tumble into a trough."

"A man has a right to enjoy his day off." Ewan, the second youngest sibling, flushed red. His blondish-red hair appeared redder as he shifted in discomfort on his chair, and his brown eyes were bashful rather than filled with mischief, as was more typical. He glared at his sister as she laughed. "Ye ken I only get one a month, other than Sundays."

"An odd way to spend yer time," Sorcha said around a giggle. "We have a fine tub here for washin' whenever ye want it."

Alistair rolled his eyes as he listened to his youngest siblings banter back and forth. "I saw ye talking to the new mystery woman who arrived in town," Alistair said to Cailean. Alistair studied his eldest brother closely. "Hadn't thought ye'd be eager to make her acquaintance."

"Why?" Sorcha asked. She grimaced as she took a bite of the bread but then continued to chew it when Ewan watched her.

"Seems she's familiar with those who reside in the Boudoir." At his sister's confused expression, he shrugged.

"The bawdy house, Sorch," Ewan muttered as he slathered butter onto his slab of bread. "She's friends with a who—" He bolted in his seat as he was kicked again.

"Those who are less fortunate than us," Cailean said with a glare at his baby brother. "Aye, I met her." He rested against the back of his chair and shared a chagrined look with his siblings. "She thought that her sister, who resides in the bawdy house, was to marry me."

Ewan choked on his piece of bread while Sorcha gasped. Her fork clinked on her plate as she dropped it. Alistair frowned at Cailean a second, then burst into laughter. Alistair threw his head back, his shoulders heaving, before he leaned forward and covered his face as he continued to chuckle. He ran his hands through his brown hair—on the verge of black—before he finally looked at his eldest brother again. "Oh, Cail, that's a fine tale. Did ye spend all day comin' up with that one?" Alistair asked, his Scottish accent thicker than usual with his amusement.

Cailean met his brother's amused gaze, and the levity faded in Alistair's countenance when he realized Cailean was serious. "Ye're jokin'," he sputtered.

"Not at all. Announced it in front of the likes of Tobias himself. Surprised the whole town hasn't heard the news I'm betrothed to a … a … a …" He broke off with a look at his sister.

"A lady of ill repute," she murmured, her eyes wide. "What a horrible trick to play on a person. I'll never like her."

He ran a hand over the tablecloth, flicking at crumbs and smoothing it down. "I believe there was no malice on her part."

Ewan, who had inhaled something down the wrong pipe, coughed continuously and finally gasped at his eldest brother's words. "I thought tumbling into the horse trough made for an exciting day."

Alistair watched his eldest brother. "That's why ye were fashed today when ye left the Merc without picking up the supplies we'd ordered."

Cailean nodded and then shrugged. "Mucking out stalls helped."

"What's she like? This misinformed sister?" Ewan asked. He took a long sip of water, his breath still catching from his near-choking.

"A little taller than Sorcha. Black hair, brown eyes." He shook his head. "Brave." He met his siblings' curious stares. "She stood up to Tobias and me. Neither of us were kind."

"A woman on her own must be brave," Sorcha whispered. "I canna imagine movin' here by myself." She frowned as she held up her fork and pointed it at her brothers. "Doesna mean I'm to like her."

"The last thing I want is for the women of this town to believe I'm eager to wed," Cailean muttered.

Alistair laughed and Ewan snickered. "Ye've treated them with such derision I doubt they'll look on ye with much favor due to one of Tobias's rumors."

Cailean inhaled and exhaled deeply. "I never meant to be rude."

"A blunt Scotsman is rude," Ewan muttered. "Ye ken that as well as we do. And when ye tell a woman that she'd have a better chance marrying the Pope, ye had to know ye'd start rumors."

Cailean ran fingers through his hair. "I wanted them to leave me be."

Alistair snorted. "Aye, they do for a whole host of other reasons." He laughed as Sorcha watched them, confused. "However, no matter how much ye wish they'd give up all hopes of ye, ye're still a successful businessman, and some mothers will always dream. What daughters they have, they'll want them to marry such men, rather than miners. An', ye're not getting' any younger. In a few years, ye'll be forty."

"Three," Cailean said around clenched teeth. "An' that doesna make me old and decrepit."

"Nae, but mothers want their daughters wed now, afore ye lose all yer faculties." Ewan laughed as Cailean threw his napkin at him.

Cailean groaned and stood, carrying his plate to the sink next to the hand pump for water. "Thank you for dinner, Sorch. It was delicious." He glared at his brothers, daring them to contradict his verdict about her cooking. He smiled as they mumbled their agreement and rose to carry their plates to the sink.

It was Alistair's turn to help Sorcha clean up after dinner, so Cailean followed his brother Ewan to the parlor. Cailean stoked the small fire in the potbellied stove and added wood. He watched as his brother sat on one of the chairs, an unopened book beside him.

"Whatever it is ye wish to say, I wish ye'd say it," Ewan murmured as he closed his eyes and stretched his legs in front of him.

"You already know what I'm to say."

Ewan grunted as he appeared to drift off to sleep in the warming room. When Cailean kicked his feet, Ewan glared at him. "Being the only experienced carpenter in this town is not easy work. I have every right to relax how I choose, Cail."

"You do. I don't comment on your visits to the Boudoir, although I hope you don't pick up a nasty disease." He raised an eyebrow as Ewan snorted. "However, you know how I feel about gambling."

Ewan rolled his eyes at his brother before closing them again, his hands crossed over his belly. "Aah, yes. Thrift and moderation are to be pursued at all costs, even the rejection of a little enjoyment." He shifted in the chair before looking at his brother again. "It's my money."

"I'd think you'd want more from it than to lose it to some idiot playing poker while being overcharged for a glass of watered-down whiskey." Cailean sat on the settee and studied his brother.

"Just as I'd think ye'd want more from life than courtin' ghosts and feedin' memories that will never bring ye joy." His eyes shot open to see his eldest brother stiffen. "I'm sorry, Cail. I didna mean that."

"I think you did. And I can see how my life appears to someone like you. You, who is determined to forget the regrets that haunt you." Cailean's hazel eyes glowed with intensity as he beheld his youngest brother. "You know I would have spared you the heartache if I had been able to."

Ewan's eyes flashed with momentary pain before he smiled his mischievous smile. "Life's meant to be lived, Cail." He watched as his eldest brother flinched at his words. "Ye must know by now that ye want more from life than this." He waved his hand around. "Mucking out stalls and carin' for others' horses. Livin' with yer siblings."

Cailean shook his head. "I will never have need for more again, Ewan. Nothing is worth the pain."

Ewan sighed. "I hope someone proves ye wrong."

Cailean rose, slipping out the parlor door, through the kitchen, and to the back porch. The cold early spring air acted as a tonic to the stifling warmth of the parlor and the overpowering emotions elicited during his conversation with Ewan. Cailean sighed as Alistair joined him and pulled out his pipe.

"I'll go to the front if ye'd rather."

Cailean waved away Alistair's offer, and the sweet smell of pipe smoke soon enveloped them. Cailean leaned against the wood railing while Alistair sat on a block of wood set on end. Cailean watched the multitude of stars and felt the tension seep from his shoulders.

"Seems as though yer discussion with Ewan didna go as planned," Alistair said, his mouth clamped around his pipe. He pulled air into it as he lit it again.

Cailean grunted. "He turned my concern about his gambling into a criticism of my life." Cailean sighed and tilted his head to look at the brother who had traveled with him from Skye twelve years ago when Alistair had only been twenty one and Cailean had been desperate to escape his sorrows.

"He never saw ye as I did," Alistair murmured. "And he wouldna have liked what he saw."

Cailean made another low sound in his throat as though in agreement and stared out into the darkness. "I know none of you understand. Not completely." He tapped his fingers on his thigh. "I've a horrible fear of not making it out of the darkness were it to happen again."

Alistair gave a soft grunt of understanding. "I've a better idea of what ye mean now that I've found Leticia and Hortence." He paused and listened to the soft evening sounds of distant laughter from the saloons and an owl hooting in a nearby tree. "She would have wanted more for ye than this."

Cailean froze at his brother's words. He shook his head and stuttered out a breath.

Alistair rose and shivered. He tapped out his pipe before he slapped his brother on the shoulder. "No grief should be clung to as though a shield."

He slipped inside, leaving Cailean to his thoughts as the evening's darkness deepened.

CHAPTER 2

$\mathcal{T}$he following morning Annabelle walked down the boardwalk in the small town of Bear Grass Springs. After crossing the street, she passed in front of the General Store, a barber-shop, and an Odd Fellows Hall. She made a wide berth around one of the most popular saloons in town, the Watering Hole, fighting her curiosity to peer inside. The most popular saloon in town, the Stumble-Out, was across from the Boudoir, on the opposite side of town as the school, church and livery.

After walking past the entrance to the café, she paused to sit on a bench placed outside—for times when customers had to wait for a seat—and studied her new home. She read the large signs over the businesses that lined Main Street, noticing that a few of the store-fronts were empty. There were numerous saloons, a butcher shop, and the hotel. The Boudoir and the bank were farther down the same side of the street as the café. When she left the hotel, she had heard a bell toll and then the delighted voices of children as they were called into the school that sat beside the whitewashed church with its short bell tower. The school and church were across the street from the livery, with the pastor's rectory behind the church

On the opposite side of the street, nearly across from the Merc, stood the livery with a paddock behind it, and a two-storied house. She heard the sounds of a blacksmith working at an anvil, his shop next to the livery. The train station was a short distance from town.

The overly friendly manager of the hotel had informed her that the doctor's office was in a small room alongside his private residence a few doors down from the hotel, should she ever be in need of one. A lawyer had an office along the opposite side of Main Street, and the sheriff and jail were nearby. She heard a bell toll and then the delighted voices of children as they were called into school. Behind each business and home stood an outhouse.

Although the most prosperous businesses appeared to line the town's main street, she had seen wagons weighted down with logs, as though to be delivered to a nearby sawmill. Between every third or fourth business, alleyways had formed, linking Main Street to the scattered rows of houses behind the main thoroughfare. Clumps of trees attempted to grow, although they appeared little more than shrubs on this cold March day.

The muddy streets had dried up, and a thin coating of dust rose with each wagon or horse that passed through town. The raised boardwalk on either side of the street helped with the mud—but did little for the dust—and allowed for greater ease of walking during inclement weather. Weak rays peeked out from behind the clouds, a shaft of light shining on the storefronts across the street. On the lower part of the nearby hills, snow had begun to melt with the day's milder temperature, and brown tufts of grass poked through the melting snow after lying dormant for the winter.

An idea nagged at her as she paused to study the vacant buildings along the boardwalk. A small building sat empty near the General Store and not far from the café, but a fair distance from the saloons and Betty's Boudoir. Annabelle smiled with purpose as she crossed the street, dodging wagons and horses, to enter the lawyer's office. She waited a few minutes until the attorney, Mr. Clark, was free to speak with her.

"It's highly irregular what you're proposing, ma'am," Warren Clark said as he leaned back in his chair. His white shirtsleeves were rolled up to his elbows, his black waistcoat well fitted, with a matching jacket slung over the back of his chair. A stove in the corner of the room pumped out heat, and a cup of coffee sat on one corner of his tidy desk. He stared at her a moment before glancing out his front window and down the street at the empty storefronts. "However, I know the owner is anxious to see the property in use. I will speak with him."

Annabelle murmured her thanks before pinning him with an earnest stare. "Would you be so kind as to only inform him that you represent an interested party and what I'm planning to do within the space? I would prefer for him to give me a decision *not* based on the fact I'm a woman."

The lawyer played with the edge of his mustache, his gaze unwavering as he studied her dressed in her finest clothes. "That's dishonest, ma'am, and I've known the people of this town for quite some time."

"I understand your concerns, but I hope you can understand mine. I would hate for the owner to deny considering my tenancy simply because I am a woman. Too often, rental rates are higher simply because the owner knows I am a woman. So I would prefer to be treated fairly." She met his cool gaze. "I have the money to open this business, and I am certain I'll succeed." Annabelle tilted her head up as she met his gaze filled with doubt and a touch of admiration. "I ran a similar business in Maine with success, and the town was devastated to see me leave."

The lawyer twirled the end of his mustache, his piercing blue eyes assessing her. "I assume you have some paperwork to give proof to such a claim?"

She nodded and extracted a letter from her purse. "This is from the mayor of the town."

Mr. Clark's eyebrows rose as he read the mayor's effusive praise of her character and of her abilities before setting it aside. "Here is what I am willing to agree to. I will negotiate on your behalf. However, if he asks, I won't lie to him."

"That's all I can ask for."

Warren studied her. "Will you do any improvements on the building or use it as is? In its current state, it is one large room."

Annabelle frowned. "I will need to build a kitchen, separate from the front area where I sell my goods. Why do you ask?"

"It seems to me that you will do improvements to a rather simple building. You should be compensated for such work." He paused. "If Dan is amenable to renting out the space, I'll attempt to negotiate a few months' rent in lieu of the costs of your improvements. Is that satisfactory to you?"

Annabelle beamed. "That is most generous and fair. Thank you." Annabelle rose and held out her hand to the lawyer.

He stared at it a moment before giving it a perfunctory shake.

"I will return in a few days to determine if you have any news."

She left the office, ignoring the lawyer's interested stare as she departed and wandered down the boardwalk, impulsively entering the café. She smiled at Harold who acted as a waiter today. He smiled when he saw her and rolled his eyes when his wife pushed him out of the way so she could attend Annabelle.

"Miss Evans. Wonderful to see you again and to see you weren't run out of town after your disappointment yesterday." Irene filled her coffee cup, leaving just enough space for milk if she desired it.

Harold bustled off to attend a few other stragglers in the café in between the busy mealtime hours.

"Do you want more than coffee?"

Annabelle shook her head. "This is perfect." She took a dainty sip. "I'm hopeful I'll be a part of your town for quite some time." She was unable to hide the excited glee from her eyes.

Irene set down the heavy metal coffee carafe with a thud. "Really? How wonderful. We always need new blood in a town like ours." She speared her with an intense stare. "Don't disappoint me and take up Madam's offer."

Annabelle blushed as red as a beet. "How do you know about a private conversation?"

"Word spreads in a town like ours. That's your first lesson about living here. Even what you want to keep private won't stay private long." She raised an eyebrow and laughed at Annabelle's distress. "I can't imagine it was much different where you came from."

Annabelle took a sip of coffee and spoke as though carefully choosing her words. "My town was well-established. If there was a … a place like the Boudoir, it was not advertised with pride."

Irene laughed. "I know all about you folk from back East. You think because you don't proclaim your vices, means you think you don't have 'em. We all have the same inclinations, Miss Evans. It's whether or not we're honest about it." She grinned as she watched Annabelle squirm in her seat. "How many saloons did your town have?"

"Alcohol wasn't sold in my town," she whispered as Harold joined them.

"Oh, this town must be quite a shock to you, with its four saloons," Harold said. He elbowed his giggling wife in her side. "She might laugh, but she don't countenance a frequent visit to the saloon."

Irene clasped Annabelle's fisted hand. "Did it keep men from drinking?"

Annabelle shook her head. "No. Nothing will stop a man from drinking if his thirst is strong enough." She flushed again and bowed her head as Irene frowned at her statement.

"Well," Harold said with a smile for Annabelle as he changed the subject, "what I'd like to know is why you were pesterin' Mr. Clark. Warren's a busy man, and he seemed right perturbed after you left him."

She let out a sigh, and some of the tension left her shoulders. "I have an idea for a business, and I asked if he would be willing to work as an intermediary for me. He said he would."

Irene snorted as she noted the few miners in the back were ready to leave. As she was about to heave herself up to wait on them, she said, "Warren would be a darned fool to turn away a new client. Anyone with sense can see you know what you're about."

Harold watched as his wife strode off with the carafe of coffee to refill coffee cups at a couple tables and moved on to chat a moment with the miners as they paid their bill. Then she headed into the kitchen, and a low singing was heard. "She's as curious as can be about what you have planned. If you take my advice, don't tell her." He winked at Annabelle. "A little intrigue would do her good."

He levered himself up, joining his wife in the back. Annabelle smiled, her tension disappearing upon realizing she was making friends in this town. The café was peaceful, and she enjoyed having it to herself in the midmorning lull. She watched as the door opened again, and she frowned. The man who entered reminded her of the man she had inadvertently offended the day before, but his hair and eyes were a darker brown. She paled as his gaze fixed on her.

"Ma'am," he said as he passed her table.

Harold bustled out of the kitchen area and gave a slap to the back of the man who had seated himself near Annabelle. "Alistair. I never thought to see you in here now that your sister's arrived."

"If ye tell my sister that I came in here, I'll never speak to ye again," he said, laughter in his voice.

Annabelle raised her gaze, surprised to see his serious expression, although his eyes twinkled.

"I take it her cooking isn't improving?" Harold poured the man a cup of coffee.

"Ah, heaven," Alistair said. "Nae, it's worsenin'. And today she somehow ruined the coffee. Tasted worse than burnt horse dung. I thought Cailean would have to put down a riot when Ewan tasted it and spit it out." Alistair took another sip, his eyes closing with pleasure. A chuckle emerged as though against his will. "Sorcha was this close to bangin' Ewan on the head with a fryin' pan. An' it was hot."

"You need a cook," Harold said as he chortled.

"No need soundin' so pleased with yerself." Alistair's lips turned up slightly at the corners. "Sorcha was to help us. I think Cailean's rethinkin' that plan."

"So we were informed yesterday. Seems he was to marry." Harold watched as Alistair covered his mouth as he choked.

He continued to choke and cough at the same time for a few moments. "Damn rumors," he gasped out as he glared in Annabelle's direction.

She made to rise but sat down as heavy boots sounded when Cailean MacKinnon entered the café. She saw the man note the café was virtually empty before he joined his brother and Harold.

"Damn it, Al. We can't have Sorcha knowing we hate her coffee too. It's bad enough she was about to bludgeon Ewan with the pan this morning." Cailean smiled as Harold handed him a cup with a wink. He drained it in two sips.

Her breath caught at Cailean's smile. Yesterday he had glowered at her and seemed foreboding. Today, with a lightened spirit and his focus on teasing his brother, she realized how handsome he was. Tall, with muscles in his arms rippling with movement under his flannel shirt, his light brown hair was cropped short. It enhanced his inquisitive eyes, sharp cheekbones, and the dimple in his chin.

When she realized she was staring, Annabelle slouched into her chair, attempting to become invisible. She knew she had failed when Cailean turned, and his gaze narrowed at the sight of her.

"Miss." His voice lost all warmth as he addressed her. His gaze roved over her pinned-up hair, flushed cheeks, and demure evergreen wool dress. "How is your sister?"

Her eyes widened a moment before she cleared her throat. "She is as well as could be expected." She frowned when she saw Cailean glare Harold into silence when he chuckled at her response. "It was a joy to see her after five years."

"I can imagine." He nodded at her and turned to focus on his brother. "Are you ready to head back to the livery?"

The two brothers departed, and Harold picked up their cups, depositing them in a small bin. "Those are two fine men," he murmured, as though to no one in particular. "Their dedication to family is legendary." When Annabelle raised a questioning eyebrow but remained quiet, Harold said, "Took out liens against their successful business to ensure their siblings were with them. Cost them a pretty penny to send for them all the way in Scotland. Sent first for their brother, Ewan, as the mother was still alive and they didn't want to leave their mother without their sister's aid. He's been here over two years now. The sister, Sorcha, arrived only a month ago. Wouldn't consider being separated from them."

"And their mother?" Annabelle murmured.

"She died nearly six months ago," Harold said. "Took them a few months to obtain the lien and send for Sorcha. But Cailean wouldn't have the family divided."

"How long have they been here?" She bit her lip as the question burst forth against her will.

"They arrived in 1881. Three years ago now. Although it seems as though they've always been here." He chuckled as he saw her fight her curiosity. "Of course Alistair is with the schoolteacher, but she doesn't seem interested in marrying. Makes me wonder how long he'll wait for her. But the eldest, Cailean, well, ... he has no one special." He hefted up the bin filled with dirty dishes and entered the kitchen, leaving Annabelle to her thoughts.

~

Annabelle twirled around the empty storefront, giggling like a girl. A chuckle sounded along with a knock on the open door as she came to a halt. "Oh, forgive me." She brushed at her hair and smoothed a hand over her skirt. She cleared her throat in an attempt to regain her composure. "How may I help you?"

"I'm here to help ye, Miss Evans." The man leaned his tall frame against the doorjamb, his brown eyes filled with mirth. His blondish hair seemed to shimmer in the light, and she realized it was due to fine particles of dust.

"Are you the carpenter?" At his nod, her blush deepened. "I hadn't expected you to arrive so early today."

He laughed. "I should think no." His voice held a hint of Scotland. "I'm Ewan MacKinnon." He held out his hand and shook hers. "Do ye have a vision for this space?" He looked around the large bare room as though seeing possibilities.

She motioned for him to follow her, and he shut the door behind him. "I have ideas sketched out." She led him to a table with two stools in front of it. "MacKinnon? Are you related to the livery owner?"

He smiled and winked at her. "Aye, and ye're infamous in our house." His laugh echoed around the room as she fumbled with the papers on the table. "It's been a long time since I've seen Cailean as flustered as the day he met ye."

"It was a terrible misunderstanding," she said as she pointed to her sketch.

"I should think so, advising a man he's to marry a who—" He caught himself just in time as he seemed to recall the woman in question was her sister. He focused on her drawing and frowned. "What in God's name is that?" He reached around her and grasped a pencil and a blank sheet of paper. "I've no idea what ye're hoping for by lookin' at that. Describe for me what ye want."

She looked around the room a moment before closing her eyes. At first her words were halting, but then she spoke with more fluidity as her vision emerged.

"So ye want to cut this large room into three spaces?" At her nod, he tapped her on the shoulder with her pencil, and she opened her eyes to look at his drawing.

"Oh, that's perfect," she breathed. "I'm afraid it will cost too much money though."

Ewan shrugged. "It willna be cheap, but, if ye're willin' to lend a hand with sandin' and paintin', it won't be too dear." He rose and slipped the pencil behind one ear. "I'll be by in a day or two with a quote."

He smiled and waved as he departed, shutting the door behind him.

Annabelle smiled, glancing around the large space that she would call home in Bear Grass Springs.

$\sim$

"What's this I hear about you being our competition?" Irene asked as she set a plate of chicken and dumplings in front of Annabelle. "And here I thought we'd been welcoming to you." Steam fogged the café windows on the dreary late March day, and many had ventured inside for a warm meal and some conversation. Annabelle sat at a small table at the front of the café.

Annabelle laughed at Irene's attempt to sound disgruntled. "You're a business woman through and through. You know as well as I do that a bakery is a good idea for the town."

Irene grumbled and moved into the kitchen as another dinner was ready to be served. Harold laughed as he joined Annabelle at her table. "She's just upset she didn't think of the idea herself. She's never happier than when she's setting up a new business. It's keeping the old ones going that she finds tedious."

Annabelle's smile held a hint of relief. "I'd hate to lose her friendship."

"If anything, you've risen in her estimation." Harold took a sip of water from a glass Irene had slapped down in front of him. "Having more businesses in town only helps us all."

"I'm eager to start work." Annabelle took a bite of dinner and sighed at the delicious flavors. "I've never been this long without working before."

Harold nodded to men entering for dinner and said a few words in passing. "I saw the young MacKinnon there yesterday. He's a good choice for you. Does excellent work but won't overcharge. He tapped his finger on the tabletop. "There are a few others who claim to be carpenters in town, but I wouldn't trust them as far as I could throw a cow pie. They barely know one end of a hammer from another." He grinned at her as she fought a giggle. "You'll be up and running soon."

Irene bustled over to her. "And, when you are, I expect a visit. Since our baker quit, I have no patience with rising at such an ungodly hour to make sure there are rolls and sweet breads for my customers. If you're as good at baking as is rumored, then we will expect to be customers."

"What rumors?" Annabelle gasped. "I haven't sold anything yet, and I haven't baked a thing."

"Small town," Harold muttered. "Seems one of the gents mentioned your plan to your sister, and she let it be known you were the best baker in Maine."

Annabelle flushed. "She exaggerates."

"Did you or did you not win first prize at the state fair for your pies three years running?" As her blush intensified, Irene nodded. "Exactly. We will expect a taste test. If you pass, which we expect you will, then you will have no shortage of customers clamoring for your goods."

Harold leaned in as though imparting a great secret. "There is a shortage of womenfolk in these parts. Many men are willing to pay good money for a little something sweet."

"As is testament to the success at the Boudoir," Irene muttered as she moved away.

"Never mind her. She likes to act affronted at times." He winked at Annabelle. "An' here we've been feeding you our inferior pie for weeks!" He chortled with laughter until his wife tapped him on his head.

"It's been delicious," Annabelle protested.

"It's barely edible, and I know it," Irene said as she sat next to Annabelle. "Baking has never been my strong suit. I can cook a fine roast chicken, but I've never had the soft touch for pastries."

Annabelle bit back a smile. "You gave me further incentive to consider my store." At Irene's interested smile, she said, "My first day here, you mentioned you'd lost your baker. It made me wonder if a bakery would survive in a town like this."

"If you're any good, you'll thrive." Irene heaved herself up to laugh and joke with miners who sat toward the back of the room.

"Good luck, Miss Annabelle," Harold said. "For all of us wishing you well, just as many are wondering if you'll fail."

Annabelle took a long sip of her coffee and nodded. "I'm tougher than I look, Mr. Tompkins." She shared a laugh with him as she nonetheless battled her nerves.

∼

Two weeks later, in early April, her bakery was on the verge of opening. After backbreaking days helping Ewan MacKinnon sand and paint the walls, she had worked as his assistant for the remainder of the construction. Her largest battle had been ordering provisions from the cantankerous Tobias. However, after negotiating a reasonable rate for her baking supplies and ensuring they would be ordered on a regular basis, her main worry was opening day. What if no one desired what she had to offer?

Annabelle swiped at her brow as she took a break from cleaning the outside of the front windows two days before she planned her grand opening. The inside of the store was hidden behind pale yellow curtains, adding a sense of mystique for the town's residents. She smiled at her weak reflection, her black hair tied in a braid down her back, her worn apron marred with splatters of paint around her waist. She grinned as she thought about the fair rental rate she had received from the building's owner before grimacing as she recalled the owner's shouts of outrage when he realized he had rented to a woman. She sighed. And to a woman whose sister worked at Betty's Boudoir.

She puffed out a breath, blowing away a strand of hair, before grabbing a rag to wipe the lower part of the glass door. She lowered her knees to the boardwalk to clean the glass, humming to herself while she worked.

"Well, if it ain't Miss Evans on her knees," a man said in a taunting voice from behind her. The man in rough miner's clothes laughed at her dismayed gasp. "You're famous in the mining camp." He waved to the mountains in the distance.

Annabelle rose and met the man's leering gaze. "Good day, sir." She kept a tight hold of the bucket of water she'd used to wash the windows and door. "I'm certain I've no reason for such infamy."

"I'd much rather a good night from a woman as fine as you rather than a good day. Seems to me you're wastin' your talents"—he raised and lowered his eyebrows—"with your foolish notion of this store. Many would like to make your acquaintance."

"When my store opens in two days, I'll be happy to meet all those who are inclined to purchase any of my baked goods," she snapped.

He tilted his head as he studied her. "I know you ain't slow, miss. You come from far away, and some folks say you're educated." He hooked his thumbs through his bright red suspenders. "I'd think you'd be eager for what a man could offer a woman like you."

"As a respectable woman, I'm certain I don't understand your meaning." She fought a flush rising on her cheeks.

He laughed before spitting out a wad of chewing tobacco at her feet. "'Course you do. With a sister like yours"—he watched her closely—"it's only a matter of time afore blood tells."

Annabelle took a step back from the man, and his eyes shone with triumph. She glanced from him to the splat of tobacco marring the previously cleaned boardwalk in front of her storefront. She backed up another step until she leaned against her door, before emptying the bucket in an apparent attempt to clean the area in front of her store. She smiled innocently at the man as she soaked him from the waist down. "Forgive me my clumsiness." She opened her door and shut it with a *click* of the lock behind her.

After she heard his boot heels and angry mutterings fade into the distance, she collapsed onto a stool as the shaking began. The bucket fell to the floor with a clang as she wrapped her arms around herself. After taking a few deep breaths, she swiped at her cheeks and rose.

The inside of the previously barren room had undergone a complete transformation. With the help of Ewan MacKinnon and another carpenter, she had turned the one large room into three spaces. The front room, now painted white with a mint-green trim, held glass-fronted cases awaiting baked goods. A doorway led to the kitchen area in the back while her small living space was set aside in one corner.

She walked into her private room, large enough for a desk, a comfortable chair, and a single bed. She sat on the chair, glancing outside to the distant mountains and attempted, but failed, to imagine the rough mining camp hidden in a canyon there. She jumped at a tapping on the back door to her store and rose.

"Who is it?" she asked, pressing her ear to the door.

"It's Leticia, Miss Evans."

Annabelle flipped the lock, opening it a hair's width to ascertain it *was* Leticia and then smiled her welcome. "I wasn't expecting you today!" Annabelle ruffled the red hair on Hortence, Leticia's five-year-old daughter, and motioned for them to enter.

Leticia Browne, the town's schoolteacher and girlfriend to Alistair MacKinnon, looked around the kitchen area of the bakery, although she was unable to hide her anxiety. Her blonde hair was tied in a severe knot at the nape of her neck. She stood about Annabelle's height, although her frame was much more willowy than Annabelle's curvy figure. Annabelle watched her newest acquaintance with curiosity, as she wondered what more was hidden behind her bright blue eyes.

"Have you thought any further about hiring help, Miss Evans?" Leticia asked. She kept a firm grip on her daughter's shoulder, who remained rooted in front of her. "Few children's parents are desirous of private lessons over the summer."

Annabelle sighed and moved into the kitchen area. "I have to admit I haven't. I like to believe I will be busy enough to need your help. However, I'm uncertain that is true." She watched as Leticia paled at her words. "At least not for an entire day's work. Why don't we start with you working for me in the mornings when I will be busy baking? It would be hard for me to bake, clean, and serve customers all at once. School will be out soon after I open, and I'm sure I will need your help then."

Leticia smiled, and her shoulders stooped with relief. "Hortence is a wonderful dishwasher." At her mother's slight nudge, Hortence nodded.

"I'm sure she is," Annabelle said with a smile. "However, let's see if her help is needed." Annabelle paused and glanced around the kitchen where sacks of flour, sugar, and spices were stored. Her icebox remained empty, although, starting tomorrow, she would have fresh milk, eggs, and butter delivered daily.

"If you're worried about being busy enough, I'd inquire at the Grand Hotel to see if they would like to purchase any of your breads. The woman who baked for them recently married, and they've struggled in the past months. Besides, I've heard the proprietor has been quite down in the mouth since you paid your bill and moved into your room here." She laughed at Annabelle's chagrined look. Then she covered her daughter's ears. "The same could be said of the Boudoir. I hear they eat poorly."

"I thank you for your advice. I'll inquire at each of those establishments." She motioned to her small room off the kitchen. "What do you think? Isn't it perfect?" she asked as she stood behind them as they stared at her tiny living quarters.

Hortence giggled. "It's like a dollhouse."

Annabelle laughed. "Yes, it is rather small. But it's mine. And I couldn't be more pleased."

Leticia smiled as she ran a hand over her daughter's head. "Then, as long as you're happy, nothing else matters." She squeezed her daughter's shoulder. "Come, love. We should head home for supper."

"Can we see the horses, Mama?" Hortence asked.

Leticia shared an amused smile with Annabelle before she brushed the hair out of her daughter's eyes. "Yes. I know Alistair would love to see you."

"'Bye, Miss Anna!" Hortence called as she raced to the back door. Leticia followed her, grabbing her hand. She waved to Annabelle before she walked hand in hand with her daughter toward the livery and Alistair.

Annabelle stood, watching them go, and took a deep breath. She nodded to a neighbor who walked along the dirt path formed behind the row of businesses that lined the main street and the homes behind them. She took a moment to enjoy the late afternoon sun before turning inside to prepare for her grand opening.

~

Annabelle left the Grand Hotel with a spring in her step. The manager had devoured her samples and had been eager to hire her to provide baked goods. She had had to deflect a dinner invitation, citing her busy schedule setting up her new business. He had barely haggled over her prices, and she frowned, wondering if she had set the prices too low. As she wandered up the boardwalk, she considered raising them but decided a price adjustment could wait until she determined if she was successful. "I don't want to discourage businesses from working with me," she muttered to herself. The café and Grand Hotel restaurant had agreed to a three-month contract with her, and she could barely believe her good fortune.

She took a deep breath as she stared at the closed back door of the final business she would offer to sell wholesale to. She walked up the steps and rapped on the door.

After a moment, a heavily rouged woman stared at her. "Yes?" she asked.

"I'm hoping to speak with the Madam," Annabelle said.

"You don't look like someone wanting to join us," the girl said, her dress sleeve falling over one shoulder and her petticoat ruffles visible.

"I have a business opportunity for the Madam."

The woman snorted. "Is that what you call it now?" She stared with interest at the covered basket. "We don't need no rouges or powders. An' we don't need no potions. The last ones nearly killed us."

"I'm afraid I don't know what you're talking about. I'm a baker, and I would like to see if the Madam would be interested in purchasing my goods for you and your colleagues."

A small tussle ensued, and the girl was pushed aside. "Blessing, stop your yammerin'." Fidelia appeared in the doorway and stared at her sister with frank confusion. "What are you doin' here?"

"I wanted to speak with the Madam," Annabelle said.

"You aren't working here." Fidelia's blue eyes hardened to the color of frozen sapphires.

"Oh, no. No. No," Annabelle stammered out. "As I explained to your colleague, Blessing, I wanted to ascertain if the Madam was interested in purchasing bread for you and your friends." She flushed at her sister's incredulous look and shifted on her feet.

"Well, come in then," Fidelia said, stepping aside to allow Annabelle inside.

Around a long trestle table with benches on either side, a dozen women sat in various stages of undress. Annabelle tried not to stare, but she was fascinated at their ease with their near nakedness and that of the other women's. "I beg your pardon," she stammered as she stared out the window while the women laughed at her discomfort.

"Come then. If you want to know if we'll desire your goods, give us a taste. We'll convince the Madam for you," Blessing urged.

"As long as Ezekial agrees," one muttered.

Annabelle nodded, pulling out a small plate filled with bite-size morsels of sweet breads, cookies, and basic bread. The women gobbled them down, moaning their delight and fighting each other for every sample.

The Madam stormed into the kitchen. "What in damnation is going on?" She swatted at one of the girls scratching another over one of the last samples and spun to glare at Annabelle. "Are you the one causing such chaos? How dare you storm in here, uninvited?"

Her shadow man, who Annabelle ascertained was named Ezekial, glowered at her. His black clothes made his forbidding look even fiercer and drained any color from his silver eyes. A billy club poked out of his back pocket.

Annabelle squared her shoulders, ignoring him to confront the Madam. "I *was* invited in. I made samples for you and the women who work here. I wanted to offer you the opportunity to be one of the few businesses I sell my products to in bulk."

The Madam stared at Annabelle a moment as though dumbfounded before her gaze moved among her girls. The Madam correctly interpreted the mood in the room. "I'm sure we can come to some arrangement that is mutually beneficial."

Annabelle smiled. "I have a fixed wholesale rate that must be agreed to. If you are unwilling to pay that rate, I will be unable to sell my goods to you. I have no need of any other arrangement." Her voice chilled as she and the Madam attempted to stare each other down.

"If you will follow me into my office?" the Madam asked. She motioned for Ezekial to remain in the kitchen with the girls and left the kitchen, assuming Annabelle walked behind her.

Annabelle nodded to the women in the kitchen—who had avidly followed her business discussion with the Madam—and then gave a small smile to her sister. Fidelia watched Annabelle with impassive boredom as she left the room.

The small office was dark, covered in velvet burgundy wallpaper with thick curtains covering the windows. Annabelle sat in the worn leather chair across from the Madam, who sat behind her desk. Annabelle balanced the basket on her lap. After a few moments of silence, she rose. "I see that was a display for your girls. If you will excuse me?"

"I want you here, Miss Evans. Working beside your sister." The Madam's gaze raked over Annabelle's perfect posture, her hourglass figure confined by a corset and covered by a demure sky-blue wool dress. "Do you realize what you could earn here?"

"The basic point is that I have no interest, now or ever, in working for you. I am smart enough to know that I would not be my own person, with the ability to make my own decisions, were I to work for a woman such as you." She tilted her head back farther in a show of disdain. "I bid you good day."

"I imagine you thought to inveigle your way into your sister's good graces with a few sweet buns. You truly are an innocent." The Madam smiled as Annabelle froze at the door, her fingers on the handle, but the door remained closed. "Your sister lost her innocence and her decency years ago. I wonder how long it will take you to learn that she will never be more than a whore in a small town. She is no more your sister than I am."

Annabelle turned to stare at the Madam. "You are a woman devoid of hope, decency, and charity. You are correct in that I am only here to offer my sister whatever support I can. If it also aids the other poor wretches working under you, I will consider it a bonus." She took a step toward the Madam, Annabelle's eyes lit with disdain and distrust. "I will never cease working for the day my sister is free of you."

The Madam laughed. "Even were she to leave, she'll never be free of me. No man will ever see her as more than what she is here." She rose and sauntered over to face Annabelle.

"You don't have that much power," Annabelle scoffed.

"No. But Charity believes it. And that's all that matters." The Madam nodded to Annabelle's basket, smiling as she saw Annabelle's white-knuckled grip on the handle. "I'll buy your buns. I'll help you create the little fantasy in your head that you're helping your poor fallen sister. And I'll enjoy watching your downfall."

Annabelle glared at her. "One missed payment and the deliveries cease."

True ire flashed in the Madam's eyes. "I pay my bills."

Annabelle turned, flinging open the door and marching out. She entered the now-empty kitchen and tripped down the back steps. As she made her way toward her bakery, she fought shivers and an overwhelming fear that the Madam's words were prophetic.

CHAPTER 3

$\mathcal{A}$nnabelle took a deep breath as she peered around the curtains covering the front of her shop. She read the backward stenciled words *Annabelle's Sweet Shop* in light blue on the front door and firmed her shoulders. She chastised herself for believing anyone would be awaiting her opening, as she drew the curtains, flipped the small sign to Open on the door, and unlocked it. She moved to the kitchen, listening for the bell to sound, heralding the arrival of her first customer.

She mixed together a final batch of cookies, hand-rolled individual balls, and placed them on a cookie sheet in the large oven to bake. She moved to the front of the store and smiled at those peering inside. When a half hour had passed, and no one had entered, she cut up a few of the warm cookies, put them on a plate, and moved outside her storefront. She cajoled passersby to try a bite of warm oatmeal cookie.

After a few minutes, customers were in her shop, eager to purchase more. One man leaned over the counter and whispered to Annabelle, "Don't tell my missus I was in here. She's angry you're selling to those in the Boudoir."

Annabelle nodded and handed him his bag filled with a half-dozen cookies. "I'd eat those up then before you arrive home."

He nodded and tipped his hat at her. She frequently replenished the sample plate, smiling at all who entered. Her smile faltered as Alistair MacKinnon came inside. He waited behind a small gaggle of women who muttered disparaging comments about Annabelle. A few perused her goods, proclaiming they were too expensive to consider purchasing and that any woman worth her weight could bake as well as Annabelle did. One woman stared at Annabelle with scorn. "I can only imagine what your parents think, what with two daughters in business."

Alistair cleared his throat, and the women tittered at the sight of him. "I'd think Miss Evans's parents would be proud. As should any family who had a member with enough resourcefulness to start a business." He stared at the woman. "How is yer son, Walter, Mrs. Jameson?"

She reacted as one slapped, then stiffened and composed herself. "Work for someone of his caliber is difficult to come by." She sniffed as she glanced at Alistair's dirty work clothes.

He stepped aside as the women marched out, the majority with heads lowered in mortification. He approached the counter and stared at the display of cookies, breads, and a cake. He frowned when he saw her pursed lips and fierce grip on her apron strings. "I wouldna let an old gossip like Mrs. Jameson ruin yer day. She's jealous of anyone who has better fortune than she does."

"Then she must hate most of the town." Annabelle gasped and covered her mouth.

A low rumbling laugh emerged, and he half smiled. "Ye're a sharp one." He pointed to the cookies. "I'll take half a dozen and a loaf of bread."

She packed them up and handed them to him. By the time he had set his coin on the counter, three more customers awaited her care. "Thank you, Mr. MacKinnon, for your business. I hope you'll be back." She watched as he nodded to her and slipped outside.

By midafternoon, she had sold out of her stock. She flipped the sign to Closed, pulled the curtains, and returned to the kitchen area to plan the next day's items for sale. The cookies and bread were fast sellers. If she offered sweet buns in the morning, she could entice otherwise busy men into her shop for a quick purchase. The cakes had barely sold.

"I'll have to advertise those as special orders," she said to herself as she moved to her living quarters, stripping off her apron. She untied her shoes, kicked them off, and flopped onto her bed, putting her feet up for the first time in over twelve hours.

"Heaven," she muttered to herself. She groaned at a knock at the back door. She pushed herself up and grimaced as she stood on sore feet. She eschewed her shoes and walked to the door barefoot. "Yes?" she called out.

"It's me, Leticia."

Annabelle let her in and moved to a stool. "Please forgive me. I was relaxing after a busy day."

Leticia smiled at Hortence who played marbles on the floor. "The boys at school said girls couldn't play marbles. Now Hortence insists she can play as well as any boy." She shared an amused smile with Annabelle. "How did today go?"

"It started out slow, and I was worried I had made a grave miscalculation. I decided to give out samples to those passing by, and I soon had customers in the shop." She frowned as she ensured Hortence was busy on the floor with her marbles before whispering, "Many said they had been reluctant to patronize my bakery because I sell to the Boudoir."

Leticia snorted. "Hypocritical if you ask me. The majority have visited it, and many of their husbands continue to partake of the pleasures offered there." She shrugged her shoulders. "I shouldn't worry. You'll have them addicted to your cookies and muffins, and they won't be able to keep away."

Annabelle fought a yawn. "Alistair was in today. Bought bread and cookies. He spoke rather harshly to a woman named Mrs. Jameson."

"Oh, she's the worst! She lives on gossip and will do whatever she can to make your life miserable so she doesn't feel so awful. Her husband left her a few years ago for a lady from the Boudoir, and so she has a special vendetta for anyone associated with the Boudoir. Her husband, Vincent, left her for a Boudoir Beauty."

"But I'm trying to extract my sister from there!"

"Yes, but you're making money off of the Madam by selling her your goods. Mrs. Jameson will see you as in cahoots with the Madam, even if you aren't." Leticia waved away Annabelle's protest. "Don't expect that woman to make sense. She's the most nonsensical woman you've ever met. But she's also got a tongue like barbed wire. When she fixates on you, others do too, and your life can become a living hell."

Annabelle studied her friend. "What did she do to you?"

"Oh, she worked harder than anyone to prevent me from obtaining the teaching post. Even though there were no other qualified candidates, and it meant the students would have no teacher for at least a year. She thought it would be better to forego education than to expose them to a widow of *dubious moral character*."

Annabelle laughed. "Oh, that's rich. Dubious moral character?"

Leticia flushed before laughing with her friend. "It was four years ago, but I'm still angry."

"As you should be. I could tell the woman is a menace, and I barely made her acquaintance today."

"If you are fortunate, you will have little to do with her in the future. However, she will watch you to see if you set a toe out of line and then crow about it to everyone if you do. I'd give thanks we have no newspaper, as Mrs. Jameson would write letters to the editor airing everyone's dirty laundry for every edition."

Annabelle took a sip of water. "Why don't we have a newspaper?"

"Well, we do of sorts, but we have no reporter. Thus, nothing is ever printed. The last reporter was shot over a hand of cards at the Stumble-Out two years ago. He was a cheat." She made a motion with her hand. "Palming cards. And those playing with him didn't appreciate it."

"Oh my," Annabelle breathed.

"Yes. The same men who Ewan plays with. You can see why Cailean is worried."

"I'd think you'd worry only if you were a cheat." Annabelle raised an eyebrow.

"Well, the problem is, it's one's word over another and, when one of the men is dead ..." Leticia shrugged. "Cailean is fearful of Ewan meeting the same fate." She shared a long look with Annabelle. "I don't know as Cailean could survive much more loss."

Annabelle looked up, startled, but refrained from blurting out her opinion. "I'm certain his brother will see sense before the worst happens."

Leticia tilted her head, as if considering whether to nod or not. "Anyway I hear that a search has begun for a new reporter. It will be interesting to see who decides to move here. It's not a hot bed of riveting news, like the big cities."

Annabelle giggled. "Reporting on the weather or the latest saloon fight would have its limitations."

"Or the number of cattle rustled. Or how the garden crops fared after a late frost." The women shared a laugh. "I can't imagine a big-time news reporter wanting to live here." A shadow crossed Leticia's gaze before she smiled at Annabelle and stood. "Come. Put on your shoes, and join us at the café for dinner. You should celebrate your first day before you fall exhausted into bed."

Hortence jumped up, cheering. "The café!"

"It's her favorite place, other than the livery. She loves the stories Harold and Irene tell." She watched her daughter pick up her marbles. "And she always hopes for a piece of pie."

Annabelle moved to her small room, donning her shoes. "I doubt they have pie tonight." She winked at Hortence as the young girl made a face. "But I'm sure they have cake."

She followed a laughing Leticia out the front door, locking it behind her.

⌒

A nnabelle entered the Sunflower Café behind Leticia and Hortence as Hortence dragged her mother by the hand. Annabelle laughed as Hortence danced around Harold while sharing a schoolyard story before she settled into a chair at a small round table. Annabelle joined them, ignoring the other patrons' curious stares. No one was seated near them, affording them privacy and the ability to speak freely.

After opting for the special of chicken fried steak with mashed potatoes and corn bread, Annabelle took a deep breath as the tension of the day slowly seeped away. "How is the end-of-school-year planning going for you?"

Leticia smiled. "Well enough. We are putting on a recitation for the parents, and I'm hopeful the students will remember their lines. I fear it will prove a challenge for some of the younger ones."

Annabelle smiled at Hortence who huffed out a sigh. "I imagine," Annabelle said, "it's hard even on the older students. I'd have trouble remembering lines!"

Hortence giggled. "But you're an adult. It should be easy for you."

Annabelle shook her head. "What's easy for one can be very hard for another. Now, if my recitation was a recipe, I'd be fine." That earned another giggle from Hortence.

They were served their meals and continued to chat as they ate. "What was Maine like?" Leticia asked.

Annabelle's gaze drifted to a spot over her friend's shoulder and became distant. "I lived in a coastal town. The sound of the waves hitting the shore was never far away, and the smell of salty sea air was ever present."

"Was there winter?" Hortence asked.

Annabelle half smiled. "Oh my, was there winter. Snowstorms with wind bursts so strong they'd about knock me off my feet. And, when the storm was over, there would be feet of snow to clear away." She sighed. "People were kind, especially as I'd lived there for years and known them since I was born."

Leticia tilted her head. "You don't realize you'll miss it until you no longer have that."

Annabelle nodded. "I never understood how hard it was to rebuild in a new place. I hate to admit I never gave it much thought."

"And alone, as a woman, can be a trying experience." Leticia ran a hand over Hortence's head before granting her permission to go to the kitchen to talk with Irene. "She's quiet, but, with Irene, Hortence talks a mile a minute."

Annabelle laughed. "She's a good judge of character." After a moment Annabelle looked at her friend. "How did you come to choose this town? It seems you could have gotten a job in Kansas, closer to your remaining family."

"I only have my great-aunt Maude, and we couldn't live with her. She runs a boarding house, and she didn't want to lose the rental of a room for us."

Annabelle winced. "That seems harsh. She's your only living family."

Her friend shrugged. "After I recovered from my anger, I have to admit that I understood. She has been on her own almost her entire life, and she was afraid of losing the income. I think she also feared she would become responsible for helping me raise Hortence."

"And Montana?" Annabelle prodded.

"I was out of my mind with ... grief and anger after my husband died. I wanted to escape all that was familiar." She glanced around the café and shared a rueful smile with Annabelle. "I succeeded." She took a sip of the coffee that Harold had set down along with a piece of cake for each of them. "I've been here four years, and this is more home to me than Kansas ever was."

"I imagine that the presence of a certain Scotsman helps with that sentiment." Annabelle laughed as her friend flushed.

"From the moment I saw Alistair, I wanted to know him better. I feared he'd be like his elder brother, uninterested in women. And few men are excited about a woman with a child. Especially a daughter. But he's wonderful with Hortence." Her mouth turned down in a grimace. "I had a few men proposition me, promising me that they were wealthy enough to send her away to boarding schools so I wouldn't have the inconvenience of raising her."

Annabelle gasped and dropped her fork. "They never said such a thing!" She clasped Leticia's hand after Leticia nodded. "I'm surprised they wouldn't understand how much you love her and that she is a reminder to you of your late husband and thus is doubly cherished." She frowned as Leticia squirmed a moment.

Leticia freed her hand and took a sip of coffee. "At any rate, Alistair has proven his constancy, as well as his patience." She bit back what more she was to say as Harold joined them.

He pulled out Hortence's chair, smiling at them as he cast a glance around the café to ensure no one needed anything. "How are the two loveliest women in town doing?" He winked at them. "Aside for my own Irene of course."

Annabelle laughed. "I'm exhausted. I'd forgotten how much work it was to bake and man the front of the shop. I can't wait for school to be out so Leticia can help me."

Harold nodded. "Sounds a smart plan to me. I know a few were reluctant to patronize your establishment due to your ties to the Boudoir. However, enough townsfolk are singing your praises that it won't be long before you'll need to hire more help."

"I thank you for your confidence, Mr. Tompkins. More than anything, I merely want today's success to continue." She stifled a yawn. "I should return to the bakery to prepare for tomorrow." Rather than rise, she sank farther into her chair as though a deep ennui had overwhelmed her.

Irene bustled from the kitchen, holding Hortence's hand. "It's a shame you weren't in here earlier. You could have met our grandson, Frederick. He came into town for supplies."

Harold leaned forward as though imparting a secret. "He was mighty impressed with your piece of cake we gave him. Thought his grandma Irene had been hiding a talent from the family all these years."

Annabelle shared a laugh with Hortence as Irene tapped him on his arm. "You keep that up, and I'll make sure I don't save any of Miss Annabelle's treats for you."

"Is he Mr. Sutton's son?" Annabelle asked.

Irene gasped before laughing. "Tobias's? Oh, heavens no. Tobias will never marry. He's our nephew, not our son."

Harold gripped Irene's hand a moment. "Our son died a few years back. Caught pneumonia. Left the ranch to our grandsons, but only Frederick lives there. The others are off adventuring."

Leticia tugged Hortence onto her lap. "In all my years in Bear Grass Springs, I've never met Frederick."

Harold winked at her. "If you did, that man of yours would have some competition." They all laughed and were momentarily silent, lost in their own thoughts.

Annabelle took a final sip of coffee before rising. "I must go if anyone is to have breads and sweets tomorrow. Irene, I'll be by in the morning with the breakfast and lunch rolls." She smiled at Leticia. "Thank you for insisting I join you for dinner. It was much better than what I had planned." She departed, her spirit light after a successful first day as the baker in her new town.

~

Cailean entered the bakery, frowning to see bare shelves, save for two cakes. He sniffed the air and closed his eyes as he attempted to name the scents. *Cinnamon. Vanilla.* He sniffed again. *Almond?* When a throat cleared, he jerked, his eyes opening.

"May I help you?" Leticia asked.

"Lettie, what are you doing here?" he asked, wincing when his words came out harsher than intended.

"I'm working here during the school break." Her slim shoulders straightened as though daring him to challenge her further.

He met her defiant gaze and smiled. "I'm glad. I know Alistair feared you'd leave town, looking for work over the summer months."

Leticia returned his smile. "I had no desire to uproot Hortence if I could help it." She bit her lip as she waved around at the empty display cases. "I'm afraid we've sold out of almost everything."

Cailean sighed. "It's my fault. I thought to surprise Sorcha with a loaf of baked bread tonight. Alistair came home with one last week, and Ewan can't stop talking about it." He shared an amused smile with Leticia. "Sorcha has yet to master the art of baking here."

Leticia watched him with fond amusement. "She's a young woman uprooted from all she knows, Cailean. You must be patient with her. I know Alistair worries about her too." She smiled. "As for a fresh loaf of bread, give me a moment."

He nodded, watching her disappear in the back. He roamed the room, noting the well-crafted cases. He spun to face Leticia, only to frown as Annabelle entered. "Ma'am." He was uncertain if she flushed from his cold tone or from having just been in her warm kitchen.

"Mr. MacKinnon, how may I help you?" She held her hands together at her waist, her apron covered in flour and bits of dough.

"I spoke with Leticia about what I needed." He nodded to the doorway as though Leticia were about to appear.

"Yes, well, she was called away with something to do with her daughter." She waited a moment in silence for him to speak and then huffed out a breath in frustration. "Well, as it must have been a personal call, I wish you a good day." She spun on her heel.

"Wait. She went to look for a loaf of bread," Cailean said, glaring at Annabelle's impatience.

"As you can see, we're sold out. I'm sorry, Mr. MacKinnon." She nodded toward the door, shifting from foot to foot as he remained in place, staring at her.

"Are you such a success then? Just like that?" he asked as though stupefied by the notion. "You waltz into town and seduce everyone with your buttered buns and sweetened tarts and—" He broke off as he reconsidered what he had said.

She bit back a laugh at seeing him flustered. "Yes, I am a success, as you can see. I have commissions from the hotel, the café, and other establishments, and I'm hopeful my business will continue to grow. I was a prosperous baker in my hometown in Maine, and I will continue to be one here too." She lifted her chin in defiant pride. "Success isn't only something for men."

He glared at her and nodded. "I'll bid you good day." He turned toward the door and then paused. "If you would be so kind as to save two loaves of bread for my family tomorrow?" The door shook as he slammed it behind him.

The following afternoon, Cailean entered the bakery and was again met with empty shelves. He waited a moment before tapping the bell on the counter. He bit back a smile as he heard a sigh and a groan and schooled his expression to one of bland impassivity as Annabelle entered the storefront.

"I see you've sold out again." He nodded his head in acknowledgment of the bare shelves.

"You should be a detective. You're very astute," she murmured. She pivoted to reenter the back area. "It's a good thing you had me save you two loaves." She returned with a paper bag containing one loaf of wheat and one of white bread. "Although you never said what type you wanted, so I improvised."

"Thank you, Miss Evans," he said. "My sister will be delighted with the surprise."

She watched him, unable to hide her amusement. "Did you advise her not to bake bread today?" At his blank expression, she giggled. "She'll have already started it as it must rise. You might find your sister aggravated with you because you haven't saved her any work."

Cailean scowled as he glared at the bread. "Darn it. I should have thought of that." He fished in his pocket for a few coins and paid for the loaves. "I thank you, Miss Evans. If you could save two loaves for tomorrow, I'd appreciate it."

She nodded. As he approached the door, she spoke, and he looked over his shoulder to meet her gaze. "I know we got off on the wrong foot, Mr. MacKinnon. I'm sorry you suffered any gossip due to my arrival. I hope we can be friends."

"We aren't ever going to be friends, miss," he rasped, yanking open the door and slamming it shut behind him.

~

The door to the bakery jingled as it opened, and Annabelle raised her head from her work in the kitchen. She listened, frowning as she thought she heard soft footfalls in the front of the store. Leticia had left earlier because Hortence was ill, and Annabelle still had a cake to decorate for the hotel restaurant and two pies to bake for the café. She swiped flour off her hands with a towel and poked her head out front. "Fidelia!" she gasped when she saw her sister staring around the small space. "How wonderful to see you."

Fidelia spun, a cream-colored shawl held high over her fuchsia dress, and her hair pulled in a loose knot at the nape of her neck. "I realize I should have come to the back door."

"Nonsense. Come into the kitchen. I still have pies to bake and a cake to decorate." She flipped the sign to Closed, locked the front door, and pulled shut the curtains. She waited as her sister watched her as though searching out a predator before walking with halting steps toward the rear of the shop. "I should have locked the front before now as I'm sold out. Come. I have a few cookies that fell apart. I couldn't sell them, but they're still good to eat."

She paused as Fidelia stared around the kitchen before poking her head into the small living quarters. "Seems like you've done well for yourself."

Annabelle cringed at the note of bitterness in her sister's voice. "I saved what I earned from the bakery in Maine. And I had the money I inherited from Father."

"Of course. He left it all to you." Rather than scurry out the back door, she pulled out a wooden stool and sat on the opposite side of the counter where Annabelle worked.

"Yes, he did." She waited a moment until Fidelia's defiant, angry gaze met hers. "However, I never considered it all mine. I always thought of it as ours. I have your half saved in the bank for you."

Fidelia flushed and then paled. "I've no need of that money. I do fine on my own." She glared at Annabelle when her sister appeared on the verge of arguing. "I will never take a dime of Father's money."

After a long stare-down match between the sisters, Annabelle resorted to tasting the frosting and deciding it needed a drop more almond flavoring, then glared at her sister. "Are you so hardheaded that you can't thank me for finding you? That you can't understand that I was misled all those years ago? I'm trying to do my best by you."

"What would you know about doing your best? You sit here in your little bakery open barely a month and already a roaring success. You have money and prestige and your honor. You have no right to act as though you've been wronged."

Annabelle took a deep breath and moved toward the icebox. She pulled out the milk, pouring her sister a cup before leaving it out to use in the piecrust. "And you have an inability to forgive." She shoved a plateful of crumbled oatmeal raisin cookies in her sister's direction. As her sister gobbled up the food, Annabelle frowned. "Don't they feed you there?"

"No one bakes like you," Fidelia whispered. "The girls fight over your bread and cookies."

Annabelle nodded in an abstract fashion, focusing on her sister. "I'll be sure to send some over, especially for you."

Fidelia shook her head. "No, don't do that. They already think I'm getting special treatment because you're in town. I can't receive nothin' from you."

"Special treatment?" Annabelle cocked her head to one side as she studied her sister.

"From the men. They're more interested in me because they're hoping to learn somethin' about you to earn your favor."

Annabelle tipped over the milk jar, spilling a little on the counter. "Oh my." She blushed. "I'd hoped their interest in me would wane."

Her sister watched her with avid speculation. "The longer you're in town and single, the more you'll have men clamoring to lead you down the road to sin." She shrugged. "It ain't a terrible road, but I doubt you'd like it."

Annabelle stiffened. "I'm not wholly disinterested in men."

Fidelia laughed and, for a moment, looked like the young woman who had left Maine all those years ago. "Of course you ain't. Although there are those interested in their own kind." She watched her sister frown in confusion and shook her head. "What I'm sayin' is that you are the type to want a primrose path, with a preacher to marry you at the end, and a home to go to."

"What's wrong with that?" She rolled out the pie dough and set it carefully in the pie plates. She then put in a sweetened rhubarb mixture before covering it with more dough. She repeated the process and slid both pies in the oven.

Fidelia sighed and watched as her sister pulled out a dulled flat knife to ice the cake. "There's nothin' wrong with that. It's just that most men I meet aren't interested in it." She looked away. "And Madam still wants us to work together." She grinned at her sister's snort. "I'm glad you ain't interested."

Annabelle frowned at her sister's sly study of her. "What?"

"I hear tell that a certain man has caught your interest." At her sister's headshake in denial, Fidelia laughed. "A man you thought had been intended for me."

Annabelle slapped the knife onto the counter and pointed at her sister. "Mr. MacKinnon and I are nothing to each other. He irritates me as much as I annoy him."

Her sister took a final sip of milk. "Seems like the courtship has already started." She rose and waved at her sister. "I'll see myself out. Good luck with your bakery, Anna." Before Annabelle could respond, Fidelia had slipped out the rear door and disappeared.

Annabelle tugged out a stool and sat on it, her mind spinning from her sister's visit and all that had been said and yet remained unspoken between them. She sighed, rising to finish the day's work before giving her kitchen a thorough cleaning.

～

A few days later, during a late morning lull in mid-May, Annabelle and Leticia worked together in the kitchen. Leticia washed pans while Annabelle was about to start on a cake for the café. "Leticia, why haven't you and Mr. MacKinnon already married?"

Annabelle asked. The question seemed to just pop out. "I beg your pardon."

"Why? You're only asking what the rest of the town whispers and snickers about behind our backs. Besides, I like to think you're my friend." She'd moved from the dishes to the cooling racks. She readied a tray full of rhubarb muffins to put out on display. "I can't wait until there's fruit other than rhubarb."

Annabelle laughed. "People talk nonstop about the huckleberry, trying to convince me it is as delicious as the Maine blueberry."

Leticia laughed. "You'll see we're correct, and you'll change all your recipes from blueberry to huckleberry. It's the highlight of summer for me when Alistair takes a few days off from the livery to take Hortence and me huckleberry picking."

Annabelle smiled at her friend. "I don't see why it should take a few days."

"We gather enough for the family. Besides, it's an excuse for him to get out of town for a few days." She sobered at her friend's worried look. "Don't worry. We only make long day trips. I've done nothing to jeopardize my reputation."

"Or your teaching position," Annabelle muttered.

Leticia set down a metal tray with a *thunk*, displaying snickerdoodle cookies.

Annabelle jerked her head at the sudden noise. "I shouldn't think you'd be worried. Everyone respects you."

"When I marry, I'll lose my position." Leticia frowned. "I hate that I can't continue to teach. I'm already a mother. I've proven I can be a mother *and* a teacher."

Annabelle winced. "I'm surprised they accepted a widow with a child as a teacher."

Leticia laughed. "I think a few were concerned I'd corrupt the minds of the children because I knew the secrets of the bedroom." She scoffed. "As though all but the littlest didn't have an inkling about what occurs at the Boudoir." She blushed as she saw Annabelle stiffen. "I beg your pardon."

"No offense taken. I know what my sister is and how she survives.

As does the town." Annabelle pulled a batch of cheese rolls from the oven. "Do you think these will sell?"

Leticia smelled them and smiled. "Yes, but why don't we tease them with an introductory price today and then raise it the next time you bake them? That way, they'll know how delicious they are and will be willing to spare another penny or two."

Annabelle laughed her agreement as she set them on the cooling rack. "How do you get along with the rest of Alistair's family?"

Leticia eyed Annabelle a moment before continuing her work. "Oh, they're all nice, although Sorcha is a bit hard to read. She's not as friendly as her brothers, which I find odd."

Annabelle shook her head. "I'm surprised you can say that the eldest is friendly."

"As long as he knows I have no inclination to marry him off to a relative, he treats me well. He was relieved to learn my only relative, other than an aged great-aunt, was Hortence. By the time she's old enough for marriage, he could be her grandfather." She laughed. "And I'm only exaggerating slightly." She studied Annabelle as she fidgeted. "I don't know as you'll ever live down your arrival and how you met Cailean with the MacKinnons. They still tease Cailean about his upcoming nuptials when they want to rile him."

Annabelle punched down a bowl filled with bread dough. "How was I to know my sister was lying? The last time I'd seen her, she was as honest as I am."

Leticia frowned. "I know you value honesty, as do the MacKinnons. However, there are always times in life when we must bend the truth." She shrugged and changed the subject. "As for Alistair, I think we'll marry next year."

Annabelle furrowed her brow at Leticia's lack of excitement and then smiled. "I can imagine he'll be delighted."

"After two years of courting me, the fact that I've agreed to a wedding next summer thrills him." She hefted one of the heavy trays. "He understands my desire to work one more year before marrying. Besides, his courting me has saved me from the miners' unwanted advances." She flushed at Annabelle's confused frown. "They believe, should they steal a kiss, that I would be honor bound to marry them."

"How ridiculous," Annabelle muttered as she shook her head at their circuitous conversation before focusing on measuring out the flour and spices she'd need for a cake for the café.

CHAPTER 4

cool breeze blew into the livery through the open door. Thick clouds hung over the town, threatening rain, and the livery was busier than usual. Horses snuffled and moved inside their stalls as they sensed the approaching storm. Alistair kept an eye on his eldest brother, thinking that the moody day matched his brother's temperament perfectly as Cailean worked tirelessly to outrun it.

"Awful nice of you to be so considerate of Sorcha. Buyin' bread every day rather than expecting her to learn how to use that stove," Alistair said, grunting as the horse whose hoof he worked on shifted and bruised his thigh.

"I'm a fool," Cailean muttered, swiping his forehead with his forearm as he leaned against the pitchfork and took a break. "If I didn't buy bread, we'd save money, and she'd learn an important skill."

Alistair chuckled, then crooned to the antsy horse. "Seems to me ye're more interested in yer daily meetings with the baker. Miss Evans is a bonnie lass." He crooned to the horse some more, although it was difficult to know if he was calming the horse or his brother. "A man could do worse."

"Don't start," Cailean said. "You know I'll never marry." He cleared his throat as he picked up the pitchfork and hurled it against the side of one empty stall. "Never again."

Alistair finished with the hoof, set down the horse's leg, and stood, patting the horse's haunch. "No, I don't. I think ye're actin' a fool." Alistair faced his brother. "Maggie died. She and yer bairn. Ye must move on."

Cailean's eyes shone brightly as he beheld his brother. "Just like that? As though it were easy, and I need only forget?" He fisted his hands as he stalked toward his brother.

"None of us will ever forget Maggie Mae," Alistair whispered. "She was as a sister to us all." He saw the agony in Cailean's eyes, and his shoulders stooped. "Ye must let her go. Find another to cherish." He raised a hand in defense, blocking his brother's punch. "I'll no' fight ye today, Cail. These are yer demons, no' mine." He pushed his brother away from him, frowning as Cailean spun and stormed from the livery.

∾

C ailean burst outside, seeing little in front of him. He barreled into the minister's wife, barely having the presence of mind to apologize as she toppled against the barbershop wall. He paused, taking a deep breath as the red haze of rage abated, and watched the normal daily activities of his town continuing around him. He sighed as he considered his brother's comment and glared across the street at the bakery.

His glare turned to concern and then irritation as he saw Miss Evans—for he refused to think of her as Annabelle—on her knees in front of her storefront as she washed windows. He leaned against the wall, now vacated by the minister's wife, and watched Miss Evans work. Her motions were economical yet graceful.

A wagon paused in front of him, blocking his view for a few moments. When he saw her again, he froze. She stood, her bucket toppled to the side, and a rag between her fingers as a man leaned forward and spoke with her. Her shoulders were stooped protectively, and she hunched farther into herself as though to render herself invisible. Cailean leaped from the boardwalk, easily avoiding the wagons and horse traffic, and approached her. "Miss Evans?" he called out, his boot heels clomping on the wooden boardwalk.

She jerked her gaze in his direction, beseeching him for assistance, yet embarrassed. She flinched as the man stroked her cheek, taking a step back, bumping into the plank wall of her store. Now trapped, he whispered something in her ear, causing her to shudder in revulsion. The man chuckled, tapped his hat, and pushed past Cailean. She stood still for a moment before whirling and grasping at the door handle to her shop. She tugged at it, in her agitated state having difficulty turning the knob, until finally it gave, and she burst into her store and home.

Cailean pushed on the door when she moved to slam it shut behind her, preventing her from locking him out. "I've come for the two loaves of bread, Miss Evans."

She glared at him before she marched to the back of the store. He heard clanging noises and then a soft *thud*. After a few moments, he tiptoed around the counters and peered into the kitchen area. He frowned when he didn't see her and moved toward the back door. He paused at hearing a stuttered breath come from a small side room.

He squinted at the bright light entering the single window to the room before he focused on her rocking herself on the edge of a cot, quietly crying. "Miss Evans," he whispered as he moved to sit next to her. "Nothing he could have said would warrant tears."

She buried her head in her hands as her shoulders shook with her sobs. He scooted closer and pulled her into his embrace, holding her as she cried. He made crooning sounds, like he and Alistair made to the horses, and sighed with relief as she began to calm.

She sniffled, her hands riffling through her pockets for a handkerchief. "I beg your pardon. All you wanted was bread, not my theatrics." Her voice broke on *bread*. She pushed away from him and rocked as though she would rise.

He settled a hand on one of her thighs, holding her in place next to him. "What did he say that unsettled you so?"

She swiped at tears that continued to fall. "It's of no importance. Not to you." When his grip remained implacable and his stare concerned, she shuddered. She plucked at a loose thread on the patchwork quilt covering her cot. "He wants me to join my sister at the Boudoir. He told me in detail about his evening last night with her." She dropped her face in her hands in shame.

"Bastard," Cailean rasped. "I beg your pardon. I shouldn't speak like that in front of you." He gripped her hand, prying it away from covering her face. "He should never speak to you in such a way. You are respectable. And he should know hearing of your sister's treatment would torment you."

A tear leaked down her cheek. "Because of who my sister is, there are those who will always see me as fair game." She hiccupped out a sob. "That's what he called me. *Fair game. Living here alone. Unprotected.*" She glanced around her small room, the sunlight streaming in the window, with a wildflower in a glass on her desk by the door.

"It's so unfair! I've felt safe and welcomed here, except for a few men like him. Why do they believe they can act like that?" She glared at Cailean and pushed his hand off her leg. "And you being in my private living quarters does nothing to help my reputation."

"I beg your pardon, Miss Evans. I was worried about you after seeing your interaction with that man today." Cailean rose. "I'll await you in the front of your store."

He inched out of the back room, flushing when Leticia froze as she entered the kitchen area. "Leticia," he said with a nod. "Could you find the two loaves of bread set aside for me?" He marched to the front of the store, his coins on the counter.

She brought them to the front but refused to hand them to him. "What did you do?"

He glared at her. "Nothing. A miner upset her, and I foolishly attempted to soothe her." He snatched the bag from Leticia. "I should know that she's not a woman who appreciates an attempt at comfort." He stormed out, noting that Leticia locked the door behind him.

Leticia poked her head into Annabelle's small room, frowning when she saw her sitting on the cot and swiping at tear-stained cheeks. "I've sent him on his way. What did he do to upset you?" Leticia whispered. She pulled out the small chair in front of Annabelle's desk and sat.

"Where's Hortence?" Annabelle asked as she held the handkerchief to her eyes.

"Sitting at the counter, composing a letter to my great-aunt in Kansas. It'll be more pictures than words, but it will keep her busy for a few minutes." Leticia smiled as Annabelle chuckled. "What happened? I've never known Cailean to be mean."

"He wasn't. He was remarkably kind for a man who doesn't like me." Annabelle sniffled and then blew her nose. "He was here when I needed someone." She bit back a sob. "I haven't had that in such a long time."

Leticia leaned forward to hold one of Annabelle's hands. "It can't be that bad."

Annabelle shook her head. "I've had to be the strong one. After Mother died, and Fidelia left, and my father drowned himself in a bottle ..." She took a deep breath and let it out. "It's been so long since someone worried about me." She shook her head again at the folly of the sense of wonder in her voice. "A miner was rude and propositioned me. Mr. MacKinnon arrived for his bread in time to aid me."

Leticia bit back a smile. "I think it's more than that. From what I hear from Alistair, Cailean doesn't know what to make of you. I think you surprise him as much as he does you."

Annabelle tossed her handkerchief in the direction of the hamper bin in the corner of the room. "I'm not here for romance. Why would I want romance after what has happened to my sister?" She glared at Leticia who watched her with kind concern. "I want to prove to the townsfolk that a woman can run a successful business. Alone."

Leticia shrugged. "There's no harm in wanting companionship. Or in acknowledging that life is easier with a good man by your side." Her gaze dared Annabelle to contradict her. "No matter how much you want to argue, you know Cailean is a good man."

Annabelle leaned against the wall, closing her eyes in resignation. "He might be. I hope for his family's sake he is. However, he takes great pleasure in irritating me."

Leticia laughed. "I doubt that brings him pleasure. I imagine it bothers him as much as it does you."

"Either way, it doesn't matter. I don't want or need a man in my life. I merely want a peaceful existence where I run my business and have a few friends."

Leticia watched her and smiled. "So you say. But there's no harm in wanting more from life."

Annabelle sighed and rose. "Come. Let's tidy up today's work and prepare for tomorrow." She attempted to put the afternoon's events firmly out of her mind with little success.

～

Sorcha sliced one of the loaves of bread Cailean had bought, setting it on the table next to the butter. She rattled pots and slammed the metal spoon a few times, glaring as her brothers wandered into the kitchen.

"What's got ye so fashed?" Ewan asked, his hair still damp from his evening wash.

She set bowls of stew in front of each seat and sat down with them. "All I do is cook and clean. There's nothin' to do in this town."

Ewan shared a long look with his brothers and made eyes at Cailean to speak.

Cailean shifted in his chair and raised his soup spoon. "What did you do differently in Scotland?" She glared at him, and he raised his hands in a placating manner. "I left when you were little more than a wee lass. I wasn't there to watch you grow. What did you do when you weren't helping with your chores?"

"I'd walk to the Fairy Pools or down to the Loch. I'd visit with

Maggie's family." She ducked her head at the mention of Maggie. "I was free to wander."

Cailean sighed. "I ken you believe I'm being unreasonable. But it's not the same here, Sorcha. You can't wander alone into the woods or around town. Men aren't always respectable." At her incredulous snort, he shared a confused expression with his brothers.

"I had to fend off a few men," she muttered with a roll of her eyes. "Ewan taught me what to do afore he left."

"Who?" Cailean demanded as he slammed his hand to the table, the silverware rattling. "Who would accost you?"

"One of the new landowner's hands. Out with his sheep," she said. "Ye wouldna ken him."

Cailean tore a piece of bread in half as though envisioning ripping the offending man limb from limb. "Did you tell Mother?"

Sorcha's bravado eased, and her brothers saw the echo of fear and relief at her escape. "Aye. I told Mother. I acted like a raving lunatic when I returned from my ramble, and it looked as though I'd rolled down a heather patch." When she raised her eyes to see her brothers' stormy gazes, she reached a hand out in reassurance. "I'm fine. Nothin' happened."

"Good of you to instruct her, Ewan," Cailean said with a nod of thanks to his youngest brother.

After a few moments of awkward silence, Alistair spoke. "Considerate of ye to continue to purchase bread, Cail."

Cailean rolled his eyes at his brother and continued to eat. After a moment, he lowered his spoon and looked at Sorcha. "Perhaps Miss Evans could aid you, Sorcha. She could teach you to make bread in that oven, and you'd have a friend."

Sorcha bristled. "I dinna want the likes of her as a friend."

Ewan raised an eyebrow at his sister's vehemence. *"The likes of her?"* She seems a nice woman with considerable skill."

"Her sister has skills too, but they aren't remarked upon." At her brother's shocked gasps, she barreled on. "I would think I could do better than to have her for a friend."

Cailean fisted his hand on the table, his meal forgotten as he glared at his sister. "You'd condemn one sister for the actions of the other?" At her mutinous stare, he leaned forward. "You have no right to judge, Sorcha. No one knows what drove that poor woman to live the life she leads, and you should show compassion to her and her sister." He nodded as his sister flushed. "I'll not be buying any more bread. I'll not coddle you further." He rose, striding from the room.

Sorcha glared after him before meeting the censuring looks from her brothers. "I refuse to believe my best option for a friend is that harlot's sister."

"What happened to ye?" Ewan asked. "Ye were the one who took in strays. Who believed the best in everyone. I don't know ye." He rose to follow his brother.

Alistair sat in quiet contemplation as he watched his sister. She continued to attempt to meet his gaze bravely, but her composure cracked minute by minute. "When did ye discover the truth?" he whispered.

She jerked. "I refuse to speak of this with ye. It has no bearing on anything."

Alistair took a long sip of water and crossed his hands over his flat belly. "I disagree. It affects everything. Until ye acknowledge that, ye will make yerself and everyone around ye miserable." He rose, carrying his dish to the sink. He returned to the table, resting his hand on her shoulder. "Thank ye for dinner, little sister."

After his footsteps receded, she pushed away her congealing stew and set her head on the table to cry.

~

E wan MacKinnon walked into the bakery and sniffed at the air. He smelled a mixture of cinnamon and cloves. He held a hand to his stomach as it growled and fought his embarrassment as Annabelle emerged from the back.

"Hello, Mr. MacKinnon. How may I help you today?" She wiped her hands on a cream-colored towel as she moved behind her largely depleted shelves.

"I'd like one of those cookies and two loaves of bread." He watched as she moved gracefully. He accepted the cookie and bit into it while she wrapped a piece of white paper around the loaves of bread. "*Mmm*, oatmeal with small chunks of chocolate."

She smiled as she accepted his coin. "I hope it's not your favorite, and you'll come back to try the other flavors of cookies I make."

He chuckled. "Talented and smart. It's no wonder ye are a success." He winked at her. "Cailean will be jealous as these are his favorite." Ewan watched her closely as she fought a flush.

"I'm surprised to see you here. Your brother made a point last week of informing me that he'd no further need of purchasing anything from my bakery."

Ewan chuckled as he scratched his cheek. "Cail can be a mite stubborn. He's insistent our sister learns to cook properly." He rubbed at his stomach as it growled again, and Annabelle fought a grin. "It's been a disaster."

"The café serves delicious meals."

"If my sister caught me eatin' there, she'd skin me alive." He shook his head as though he were long-suffering. "I've come to ask ye a favor, Miss Evans." He nodded for her to set the loaves of bread on the counter in front of him. "I'm buyin' bread because my sister is having trouble masterin' the new stove. I wondered if ye'd have a chance to help her."

Annabelle sobered and shook her head as she blew out a breath. "I'm quite busy with the bakery."

"Ye must have an hour ta spare for a starvin' man an' his family."

At his beseeching look and the thickening of his accent, she burst out laughing. "You're incorrigible." Her comment only seemed to make him preen.

"It was Cail's idea to begin with. Then he and Sorcha fought, and now he barely speaks to her."

After a moment she shrugged. "I could help her a few days a week, for an hour or so. Not enough to bake a meal but enough to set her in the right direction and prevent you from starving."

"Fantastic." He grabbed his loaves of bread and moved toward the door.

"Mr. MacKinnon."

He paused at the threshold.

"She knows I'm coming?"

"Ah, what Sorcha doesna ken willna hurt her." He saluted her with one of the loaves and departed with a jaunty step to his gait.

"I've been played for a fool," Annabelle muttered to herself. She forced a smile as other customers arrived and tucked away that worry for later.

~

T hree days later, Annabelle stood at the MacKinnons' front door and knocked. She waited until she heard soft footsteps approach before pasting on a pleasant, but informal smile. When the door swung open, she nodded to the woman standing behind the screen door.

"How may I help ye?" Sorcha stood a good three inches shorter than Annabelle. She was plump, with her red-brown hair tied in a loose braid. Her light-blue eyes shone with curiosity as they beheld Annabelle on the front step.

Annabelle straightened her shoulders. "I am Annabelle Evans, and I was asked to come here by your brother to help teach you to use your oven." After a moment, where Sorcha's expression transformed from one of mild pleasantry to disbelief, then to irritation, Annabelle reached for the screen door and eased inside. "I run the new bakery in town, and he thought I would be able to help you."

Annabelle waited just inside the threshold for Sorcha to speak before glancing around the small dark hallway. The walls were a thick pine that matched the floor. No artwork was displayed on the walls, although a coat peg hung near the door, with a horse bridle slung over one of the pegs rather than a jacket. A stairway led to the upper floor, and there was a doorway to the right and to the left in the hallway. A tattered, faded woven rug covered the wooden floor. She frowned as there was no evidence of Sorcha's feminine touch in the space. Annabelle raised her head and sniffed and tilted her head to the left. "I believe the kitchen is this way."

Sorcha heaved out a breath and stomped into the kitchen and dining area. "I canna believe Cailean thought a whore's sister would be an appropriate teacher."

Annabelle's momentary joy at hearing Sorcha's charming accent, heavily Scottish, died at her words. "I beg your pardon?"

"Why would ye think I'd want anythin' to do with the likes of ye? Ye cook bread, cookies, and cakes during the day, but who's to say what ye do at night? Ye could easily be offerin' other enticements to the men of this town that they'd find just as sweet." She smiled as Annabelle paled. "The name of your shop says it all. 'Annabelle's Sweet Shop.'"

Annabelle flushed red and balled her fists around the apron she'd extracted from a small bag. "Aren't you a vile little being. I had wondered why Leticia never spoke warmly about you, and now I know. It's because you have a core of venom."

"How dare ye come into my own home an' speak to me in such a manner?"

"And how dare you make such horrible comments about me and those I love?" Annabelle bent until she and Sorcha were eye to eye. "I'm here at your brother's request so that they no longer have to sneak food from establishments around town. They are at the point of desperation due to your inability to serve an edible meal. If I were you, I'd cease antagonizing the one person in this town willing to help you."

She slipped the apron over her head and tied it around her waist. She approached the stove and sighed. "What a lovely stove."

"Ye call that hideous contraption *lovely*?"

Annabelle rolled her eyes. "I imagine you prefer cooking over a peat fire, but this is a modern stove. If you haven't thanked your brother for it yet, it's high time you voiced your gratitude."

Sorcha broke eye contact. "I told him it was an old piece of junk, worse than anything he could ha' bought in Scotland."

Annabelle laughed. "Oh, I imagine that burst his ego. Few can afford to buy such items, and yet he bought it for your arrival, I presume." She smiled as Sorcha nodded guiltily. "Well, today, I won't teach you anything about cooking. But I will teach you how to use this."

She motioned for Sorcha to stand next to her, and she reviewed how to build the fire, control the heat in the different sections, and how to ensure the fire never went out. When she departed an hour later, Sorcha continued to watch Annabelle with disdain and mistrust but a glimmer of respect fought to emerge.

"I'll see you next week, Miss MacKinnon," Annabelle called as she walked down the steps. "Please attempt to cook something for your brothers. I'll be curious to hear how it goes."

～

F our days later, Annabelle stood at the front door to the MacKinnon residence and knocked. She stared at the closed door, listening for approaching footsteps. When none sounded, she raised her hand and pounded on the door with a bit more force. The door lurched open, and she sprang back as Cailean glared at her. "I beg your pardon. I'm here to see Sorcha."

He waved her inside, following her into the kitchen. Slabs of bread slathered with butter lay on a plate by the sink. "I forgot about lunch, and I'm here for a snack." He motioned for her to sit, but she shook her head.

She rummaged in the icebox, frowning to find little besides butter and milk inside. "What are you to eat for dinner tonight?" she asked as she turned away from the barren icebox.

He shrugged. "I hope Sorcha's at the Merc and the butcher's now. Her cooking's improved and so has our appetites." His stomach growled again.

"Please, eat," Annabelle said.

He sat at the table with a glass of milk and his slices of buttered bread.

"I would offer to start preparations, but I can conjure up nothing with what is at hand other than the bread and butter you now eat." She sighed, leaning against the counter.

"Why are you here?" He furrowed his brow as his gaze dropped momentarily to her curves, poorly concealed in a plain light-green dress with no adornment. Rather than hide her lush figure, it enhanced it. He shook his head and focused on the plate in front of him, his ears reddening.

She turned, rummaging for an apron, and tied that around her waist before she sat across from him.

"If you believe an apron will save you from a man's gaze, you're a fool," he muttered.

"I beg your pardon?" Annabelle asked.

"I meant no offense," he said with a shrug.

"I don't go around staring at men who I find attractive," she sputtered. "There's no reason men can't control their gazes as I'm expected to control mine."

He opened and closed his mouth a few times, finally opting to drain his glass of milk. "You're right in principle, but you must know that's not how things are." He grinned as she shook her head in consternation. "I hear your bakery continues to be a roaring success."

She nodded. "I almost have too much work." She attempted and failed to hide a triumphant smile. They sat in companionable silence for a moment. "Why don't you have an accent like your siblings?" She flushed as the question burst from her as though out of her control.

He laughed. "In my mind, I think like a Scotsman. Like a High-lander. But I found that, when I emigrated, I was accorded more respect—and fewer tried to fleece me—when I sounded more like a typical American. Now it's second nature." He shrugged. "My accent tends to reappear when I'm angry."

"I doubt I'll ever talk like the locals." Her shoulders stooped as though crestfallen.

"Why would you want to? You've a lovely accent." He smiled at her. "And in Bear Grass Springs, it's all yours." He rose, depositing his dish in the sink. He turned to face the doorway as the front door slammed shut. "Hello, Sorcha. You've kept Miss Evans waiting."

Sorcha entered, her basket nearly overflowing. She smiled appreciatively as Cailean grabbed the basket and set it on the table. "I was waylaid by that horrible Mrs. Jameson. She attempted to ascertain why Alistair and Leticia have yet to set the date." She shuddered. "I can't stand that woman." She focused on Annabelle. "Did Cailean tell you my cooking is becoming edible?"

"Aye, she's finally learning to use the stove." He grunted as Sorcha elbowed him in his side. He nodded to them and departed out the back door to return to the livery.

"Why was he here?" Sorcha demanded after he left, spinning to glare at Annabelle.

Annabelle scrubbed at her forehead. "He answered the door. He told me that he forgot to eat lunch, and so he ate a snack of buttered bread while I waited for you."

"I don't need your help anymore. I know how to use the oven. I can cook all I need." She thrust her shoulders back, her glare transforming into a glower. "I'd think you'd know Cailean wouldn't want anything to do with a woman like you."

"A woman like me? A successful businesswoman who knows how to cook?" Annabelle smiled as she met Sorcha's frown. "A woman able to care for herself without relying on her brothers? Is that what you mean?"

"Get out," Sorcha hissed. "Ye are no' wanted or needed here. I'll never understand why Cailean asked ye to come here."

Annabelle opened her mouth to correct Sorcha and then shook her head. "Good luck with dinner. I hope your brothers don't end up at the café, looking for a decent meal." She spun on her heel, slamming the front door behind her.

CHAPTER 5

*L*eticia studied Annabelle. "What's got you so riled?" Leticia swiped at her sweaty brow and continued to wash a pan in the sink. An early warm spell had hit on the first Friday in June, and the front and rear windows were open to allow any cooling breeze to enter the confined kitchen space as the large ovens overheated the room.

"Sorcha MacKinnon is the rudest person I've ever had the displeasure of meeting."

Leticia laughed. "She goes out of her way to make enemies rather than friends. What did she say to you?"

"Ewan MacKinnon begged me to teach her to cook. It seems the brothers were near starving. I helped her almost a week ago, teaching her how to use the gorgeous stove her eldest brother bought her." She glared at the baking supplies set out in front of her. "Yesterday I returned to help her, in the free time I don't have."

"And she was rude again?" Leticia asked, biting her lip to prevent from laughing.

"There is no word to describe the insolence of that woman!" She stopped and took a deep, calming breath. "Can you believe she accused me of attempting to entrap her eldest brother, when all he did

71

was answer the door?" She sighed. "I admit I was in the kitchen with him as he ate a snack while I waited for her."

Leticia's eyes gleamed with amusement. "You must guard against such gossip. You never know what he could be accused of doing in the kitchen." She burst out laughing as Annabelle blushed. "Did you set Sorcha straight that Ewan, not Cailean, had arranged for you to help her?"

"Of course not. After she declared she was competent and needed no further help, why should I correct her misconception?" Annabelle sighed. "I resent how she judges me without knowing me."

Leticia nodded, sobering. "Alistair is frustrated with her too. Something happened in Scotland, but he won't say what." She met Annabelle's questioning gaze. "I suspect he knows."

"She should be thankful for discreet brothers. If that Mrs. Jameson were to catch wind of any hint of scandal ..." Annabelle shuddered. "I swear, she visits the bakery most days just to ensure I'm still open and to see if there is anything to report to her friends."

A few minutes later, as Leticia wiped dry the pans on the drying rack, she asked, "What are you wearing to the event?"

Annabelle looked at her friend with confusion. "What event?"

Leticia rolled her eyes. "The event celebrating the town's founding. *Tonight.* You can't have forgotten about it as that's all anyone has talked about for weeks."

"Oh, I'm not going. I'm too tired, and I have to bake tomorrow."

Leticia glared at Annabelle, muttering about hardheaded women before entering the storefront to attend customers. When she returned to the kitchen area, Annabelle was occupied, measuring flour and sugar, so Leticia remained quiet so as not to interrupt her count. When Annabelle mixed her ingredients, Leticia began her persuasion campaign. "It would appear snobbish to the townsfolk if you didn't attend the celebration."

"They'll understand. They'd rather have their breads, cakes, and cookies for Saturday than my presence tonight."

"How can you say such a thing?" Leticia held her hands on her hips as she glared at Annabelle. "You're new to this town, and you are denying them the chance to show you their hospitality. It's rude."

"I don't want to appear rude. However, I've never been one to enjoy such festivities."

"Why? I'd think you'd enjoy dancing." She smiled as her friend flushed. "That's the problem, isn't it? You *do* enjoy dancing, but you were told you shouldn't." At Annabelle's nod, Leticia smiled. "Well, no one here will be upset that the pretty single baker has an inclination to dance. There aren't enough women here, and most men spend the evening on the side of the dance floor, dreaming of holding a woman in his arms, if only for a dance."

"I'm not attending to fulfill some man's dream." She clapped a hand over her mouth as Leticia chortled. "That didn't come out right."

"No, but maybe you should attend so you could fulfill your own." She met her friend's hesitant gaze. "You've lived long enough under the expectations of others. Now's the time to determine what it is *you* want."

Annabelle rapped the wooden spoon on the bowl. "Did it ever occur to you that I am doing what I want? That this bakery is my dream?" She swiped the back of her hand over her forehead, smudging it with flour. "I don't need anything else."

Leticia sighed. "I can see that you wish that were true. But even you hear the lie in your words." She met Annabelle's glare. "If you decide to come, you'll hear the music start around five."

Annabelle muttered about interfering friends and then turned her back to focus on baking.

That evening, Annabelle ran a hand over her light-blue calico dress before ensuring her hair was in place. She huffed out a breath as her nerves nearly failed her before she straightened her shoulders and marched into her kitchen, picking up the basket of cookies she had made for the town dance and celebration. After pocketing the bakery key, she walked with measured steps toward the sounds of the festivities in a field by the schoolhouse.

"Annabelle!" Leticia called out. "It's wonderful you arrived." She beamed at her friend, and Annabelle relaxed at the warm welcome. Handing over her basket to a gaggle of women intent on presenting all food in an equally favorable manner, Annabelle slipped to the side, hoping to remain an observant wallflower as she stood against the wall of a barn on the property.

She stood, watching Leticia laugh and joke with the women behind the food tables. A low voice caused her to jump.

"I thought ye'd join Leticia. Ye are our town baker."

She turned to meet Alistair's teasing, curious gaze. "I'll let you in on a secret. I tire of being around food." Her ease disappeared as she watched the women. "Besides, most of them tolerate me at best."

"Tolerance is always a good place to start," he murmured. "And now I'll let ye in on a secret. They set the food out in two rows, one in front of the other. The edible food is in front. Only those who are truly daring or don't ken any better will eat food from the back row."

He raised his eyebrows as Annabelle stifled a giggle. His glance roved from Leticia talking with the town's womenfolk to the play area in front of the school where many of the children gathered. He seemed to relax when he saw Hortence running around, playing tag with her friends.

"You're wonderful with Hortence."

His startled gaze returned to her. "Of course." He studied her a moment. "Are ye glad to finally have some festivities in this town, Miss Evans?"

Annabelle forced a smile as she bit back a grimace. "I'm so very ... *delighted.*" His bark of laughter sparked a few curious glances, and she blushed.

"Never take up poker, Miss Evans. Ye'd lose all ye own." He shook his head. "Why wouldn't ye want to celebrate the town's founding?"

She shrugged before nodding her thanks to a man who approached and offered her a glass of punch. After he wandered away, and she had taken the requisite sip, she sighed. "I prefer to live a quiet life."

"Ye mean, hidden away in yer bakery, yer only contact with others when ye sell 'em yer goods an' take their coins?" He shook his head. "Which ye rarely even do as ye have Leticia runnin' interference on that. I don't see playin' with flour and sugar satisfyin' ye for long."

She stiffened next to him, any sense of ease disappearing. "What gives you the right to contemplate my life?"

He sighed. "Ye've made a friend of Leticia. She'll be my wife. No' as soon as I'd like, but she will be." He shared an intense look with Annabelle. "I care for those close to me and mine, Miss Evans."

Annabelle shook her head in confusion before smiling at another man and turning him down for a dance as the fiddlers began to play. "I don't understand."

"With Leticia and Hortence spendin' so much time at yer place, I've been keepin' an eye out for ye too. I've listened to her stories about ye. And I've come to my own conclusions."

Annabelle rolled her eyes. "And by your extraordinary deductive abilities you've decided I'm not content? That I'll become wild someday?"

He frowned at her words and shook his head. He glared as another man approached, and the man slunk away before he asked Annabelle to dance. "Nae. That's no' what I'm sayin'." His accent thickened as he became more agitated. "Since ye arrived in town and met Cail in the Merc, ye've lived a buttoned-up life, afeared ye'll put a foot out of step, an' be forced to live a life like yer sister." His gaze roved over her. "Ye've squashed out any chance for joy."

She vibrated with fury next to him. "You have no right to stand here and pass judgment. You who can't even convince the woman you want to marry you." She hissed as she saw him flinch at her words. "I beg your pardon. That was uncalled for."

Alistair fisted his hand and rapped it against his thigh a few times. "What ye said was no less true than what I said." He sighed before half smiling. "Ye wouldna have felt a need to act like a cornered cat if my words were no' part true."

Annabelle forced a smile as Irene and Harold approached them. Irene was called away to the food tables, and Harold ambled over, his eyes gleaming with interest as he noted the tension between Annabelle and Alistair. Although he stood at least half a foot taller than his wife, he was still inches shorter than Alistair. Harold's eyes seemed to twinkle with constant mischief. Annabelle found her smile became genuine as he joined them.

"I've always wondered why the town goes about celebrating such a day. And in such a fashion. Never seemed like there was much to celebrate." Harold took a sip of his punch and sighed in contentment.

Alistair frowned as he tasted it. "Sickly sweet."

"Why shouldn't a town celebrate its beginning?" Annabelle asked, ignoring Alistair and the sweet punch.

"Well, any excuse for a party is a good one. An end to winter or beginning of summer celebration would make as much sense. Or a lilac party." He swept his hand out to the end-of-season lilac bouquets on each table. "But to celebrate those two ornery ba ... men seems sacrilegious."

Alistair sighed. "Since yer near burstin' with the need, tell us about 'em." He hooked one foot across the other and leaned against the wall of the barn.

Harold raised his cup to Alistair as though he were astute and then grinned at Annabelle. "I had the misfortune of meeting them both when their paddleboat came into Fort Benton. I'd hoped the Indians had gotten them. Or their own stupidity." He smiled apologetically at Annabelle's shocked gasp. "Mr. Bachman was a miserly, miserable man. A visionary with no grace, charm, or charisma. He could have found the way to the Promised Land, and I would have given any excuse not to travel there with him." Harold chuckled. "His partner, Mr. Erickson, was a snake-oil peddler. I always patted my pocket to ensure my billfold was still inside as I feared I'd been swindled of it by his smooth talking."

"Sounds as though Mr. Bachman didn't need charisma if he had Mr. Erickson," Alistair said, his curiosity piqued against his better wishes.

Harold cackled out a gleeful laugh as Irene joined them. "Oh, they hated each other. Yet they needed each other to survive as Mr. Erickson had no head for business or ideas but could peddle what was put in front of him."

Irene sighed. "I was always thankful I had no daughters. That man was too charming for his own good. Then, one day, I heard they'd bought a wagon, and were headed out of town."

"No easy feat when you have to climb those bluffs and venture into the scrub grass." Harold rubbed at his head.

"Imagine our surprise to realize we'd settled in the town they'd founded," Irene said with a wide smile. "Seems they wanted the notoriety of a mining town, with plenty of men to swindle."

"It's why they had to leave Fort Benton. Too many men had lost too much money to them, and they knew they had to move on."

"Then why is the town called Bear Grass Springs rather than named after them?" Annabelle asked.

"Well, the name changed not long after their demise. Bachson doesn't slide off the tongue as easily."

Alistair chuckled as he looked at Harold, appearing to bite back words as Annabelle was enthralled by the tale.

"If rumor is correct, and I fear they are when it comes to those two, they planted the fine metal that was 'discovered,' then yelled for all and sundry of the discovery of gold and silver in the creek." Irene nodded toward the placid waterway, weaving its way in the distance through the meadow.

"Their dumb luck was that actual silver was to be found up in the hills." Harold shook his head in wonder.

"What happened to them?" Alistair asked.

"Got so drunk they could barely tell up from down and then started a pissing match." Harold grunted as Irene dug her elbow into his side. "Beg your pardon, Miss Evans. Shot each other in a duel. Rumor has it that Bachman got it right through the temple. Erickson lay on the ground as he bled to death from his wounds."

"Too stupid and too drunk to have a doctor around." Irene shook her head. "An' the few scraggly whores who remained in town didn't care to look after either of them."

Harold sighed and nodded as he looked over the prosperous town. "That's who we celebrate today." He raised his cup. "Never met a worse pair in my life, and that's saying something." He called out a greeting to an acquaintance, and Irene moved with him to meet friends and neighbors.

Alistair watched them go and shook his head as he studied the older couple.

"What is it, Mr. MacKinnon?" Annabelle asked.

"I've been here three years, and I've yet to understand them. They just twirled some fantastic tale riddled with half-truths, failing to tell ye about the real founding of this town." He shrugged. "Perhaps those men existed. But this town never thrived because of them."

Annabelle frowned. "Why would they do that? And who really started the town?"

He nodded in Irene's and Harold's direction. "They and their family helped to settle the area." He met her shocked gaze with a smile. "I'd guess they don't want ye to know they are the richest people from here to Butte." Alistair laughed at her confused expression. "What's the most profitable business in this valley?"

She shook her head.

"Ranching. And they control almost half the valley. Their family was some of the original free-herders. Came here from Fort Benton on the Mullan Road and thought this looked like a good place to settle. One of their grandsons runs cattle from Texas to Montana now."

He half smiled as he murmured, "Those would be the tales I'd want to hear." He nodded his hello as his younger brother approached. "Ewan, I thought ye'd spend the evening at the Stumble-Out."

Annabelle bit her lip as she fought a smile at the town's name for the popular saloon.

Ewan laughed and slapped his brother on the back. "Not when I'd miss the year's best celebration in town. The Fourth of July party next month does no' match this." He took a sip of punch and grimaced.

"Too sweet. How is it always too sweet?" The fiddlers began to play again, this time a slow waltz. "Miss Evans, would ye honor me?" He winged out his arm and smiled at her as he handed his punch glass to Alistair.

She laughed, slipping her arm through his. He led her to the floor, swinging her into motion as the fiddlers played and the dance area of flattened-down grass filled with dancers.

"Alistair can be almost as serious as Cail at times," Ewan murmured as he maneuvered her around.

"He's worried I keep myself separate and that I don't enjoy life enough."

Ewan burst out laughing. "Ah, the irony. He worries I enjoy it too much." He grinned at her, and she giggled as they found their rhythm. "Thanks for savin' me from the town lasses." He met her confused stare. "The likes of Helen Jameson are a bit too forward for me."

Annabelle squinted. "Is she the daughter of that horrid Mrs. Jameson?"

"Aye, her mother is insistent she marry an upstandin' man. Since Cailean's rudeness at last year's Founder's dance and Alistair's attachment to Leticia, I fear she'll set her sights on me."

Annabelle followed his gaze to a curvy woman in an indigo dress dancing with a miner. Her wheat-colored hair was pulled back in a style resembling a coronet.

"I hope she's unlike her mother in every regard," Annabelle murmured.

He shrugged. "I fear she doesn't ken who she is. Her mother dictates her life for her." They settled into a quiet camaraderie as they listened to the music. Swallows swooped and dove above them; children squealed and laughed in the distance, and the early evening light cast a gentle glow over them.

"I love it here," she whispered, forgetting herself and resting her head on his shoulder.

He chuckled. "Ye havena lived through a winter yet. I'll ask ye in January how ye feel."

She laughed and continued to sway around the dance floor with him. When the song ended, she smiled at him. She stiffened as a line of men had formed to ask her to dance. She looked at him helplessly, before agreeing to dance with the first in line. She watched Ewan depart to join his brothers on the side of the dance area by the food, Leticia now arm in arm with Alistair.

~

"What could she be thinkin', dancin' with all those men?" Cailean muttered to his brothers after Leticia moved away to mind Hortence.

Alistair chuckled. "I'd think she's finally decided to enjoy herself. She's earned it after the hard work of the past few months." He nudged his brother in the side. "And I ken ye're talkin' about the baker and not yer sister. Although ye should be just as worried about her. Men are fightin' over the both of 'em."

Cailean glared at his brothers as Ewan grumbled his agreement to Alistair's words. "Miss Evans shouldn't give rise to talk. She doesn't have brothers to look out for her."

"It's dancin', Cail. Everyone except ye has danced. Asides, she's single, attractive, and kind." Ewan eyed his brother with a wicked gleam. "Maybe ye're jealous."

Cailean stiffened. "Of course not."

Alistair bit back a snicker. "Seems to me ye spend an inordinate amount of time worried about the town's baker. Perhaps ye should spend a little time with her. Other than buying loaves of bread." He flashed a rare grin and winked at Ewan. "Or Ewan could dance with her again. She seemed partial to Ewan."

The three men glanced to the dance floor where Annabelle twirled on the arm of one of the miners. She smiled impersonally to the miner and kept him at arm's length as they moved to the music. Her answers to his questions appeared short and stilted.

"That's 'cause she kent charm when she heard it," Ewan said, laughing when Cailean poked him in the side with an elbow.

"I'd take my chance if I were ye. The song's gettin' ready to wind down," Alistair murmured to his eldest brother. He watched Cailean's jaw tic before he nodded curtly and marched to the dance floor.

Cailean eased around two chattering matrons and men sipping beer from glasses near a keg rolled down from the saloon. He sent a severe stare at the men circling the dance floor, and they backed away as Annabelle was led to the side of the dance area. "Miss Evans." He watched as she jerked in his direction, not noting his presence. "If I might have the next dance?"

He glared at the fiddlers and then glowered at his youngest brother who slipped them a few coins. A moment later, a waltz started, and he shook his head.

"Do you not want to dance?" she whispered, standing next to him and flushing as a few of the townspeople watched them curiously.

He grabbed her hand and tugged her onto the grass, pulling her close with a hand at her waist. She stumbled over a piece of uneven ground and fell against his chest. "*Oomph*," she grumbled. "You don't have to act like such an oaf."

"I imagine you believe the miners have better manners." He twirled them around, joining the others dancing. The faint scent of almond clung to her, and he breathed in the elusive smell.

"In fact, they do." She eased away from him but was still held close against him. "They understand I don't wish to be manhandled and towed around like a prized heifer."

"I'd think you'd be more valuable than a heifer," he muttered as humor lit his eyes. He grunted as she miscalculated their dance moves and stomped on his instep.

She glared at him, her chin tilted up as she refrained from responding to his question. "You are a boor."

"Aye." He sighed. He looked over her shoulder to see his family and Leticia watching him dance with the baker. "We've an audience. We don't want to disappoint."

"Who says we're disappointing them?" She tripped again. "Slow down. It's a waltz, not the galop." She glared at him as he continued to dance in the 2/4 time of the country dance called the galop rather than the 3/4 time of the waltz.

"I'm no' the most adept dancer," he muttered. After a moment of stilted silence, where she tensed further in his arms, he blurted out, "Thank you for attempting to help Sorcha."

She laughed. "Your sister has less charm than a viper." She bit her lip as she flushed as red as a ripe stick of rhubarb. "I beg your pardon."

"I know she has strong opinions and isn't always kind when she shares them. I apologize if she offended you." He watched as she broke eye contact and studied the buttons along his shirtfront. "You should know my brothers and I don't share her sentiments."

She shrugged. "She must have her reasons for spewing her venom."

Cailean waited until Annabelle met his gaze. "Aye. She does. And it has nothing to do with you. Or your sister." He sighed as the waltz ended. "I thank you for the dance."

He watched as she nodded and scurried off the dance floor. The evening turned toward dusk, and he saw the women of the town cleaning up the food while the musicians announced they'd play only two more songs. He rejoined his brothers who now stood near the fence by the schoolhouse.

"What did you say to make her run off?" Ewan demanded before he moved away to chat with men who worked for him.

Alistair rolled his eyes as he watched his other brother shrug. "The festivities are about to end. We should ensure she makes it home safely." Alistair's eyes lit up as Leticia joined his side, and he hefted Hortence into his arms, where she almost immediately fell asleep against his shoulder. At Alistair's encouraging look, Cailean sighed.

Dusk had begun to fall, and the swallows now circled around the eaves of the schoolhouse and the nests they had built out of mud there. A light pink tinged the peaks of the distant mountains, and the air cooled. Cailean walked around the back of the schoolhouse to trace the path Annabelle had taken. He came to an abrupt stop to find her sitting on the school's back steps.

She shivered in the cooling night air, her arms hugging her dress around her legs as she stared at the mountains in the distance. From her vantage point, it appeared that they were dressed in a thick blue-green velvet as the light softened. Only the highest peaks retained any snow.

"Miss Evans," Cailean murmured. "I hope I didn't offend you during our dance." He shifted as he saw her rub away a tear.

"I'm fine." Her voice emerged as a croaking frog, and she ducked her head. When he crouched in front of her, she did not lean away from him.

"Don't cry. I'm not worth crying over." He grinned as his teasing elicited a smile.

"You've a big sense of yourself to believe I'm crying over you." She let out a stuttering breath. "I'm being foolish is all."

He watched her as he settled into his crouch, his fingers rising to trace her hands clasped around her elbows. "You're one of the least foolish women I've ever met." His gaze gentled as he saw her take pleasure from his words.

"Why are you here? You barely tolerate my presence in my bakery, and you've avoided me since I arrived in town." She watched him with detached curiosity. Night continued to fall, and the distant sounds of children playing and townsfolk chattering faded away as the party broke up.

"You're friend to Leticia, and she's important to Alistair." He rose when she pushed against his arm and stood next to him. "I think you could be a good friend to us."

She nodded and wrapped her arms around her middle, watching the distant outline of the mountains darken and become less distinct. "I've never been much good at friendship." She spun to face him at his amused chuckle.

"I see how you are with Leticia and Hortence. How you'd be with Sorcha if she'd let you. Whoever filled your head with such thoughts was a fool." His hand rose as though of its own volition and traced over wisps of hair that fluttered around her face.

She watched him, mesmerized, as his hand dropped and cupped her cheek. The cautious wariness in his gaze faded as a passionate intensity smoldered. He studied her with a fierce ardor as she stilled under his touch, neither moving toward nor away from him.

After a long, searching glance, he leaned forward, sealing her mouth with his. At the gentle slide of his mouth over hers, she moaned softly and canted forward into his embrace. He slid a hand around her lower back, tugging her toward him, and she stumbled into him. He huffed out a laugh before deepening the kiss, one hand caressing her neck. She latched onto his shoulder, arching into his kiss and touch.

A loud gasp rent the quiet evening air, and they broke apart. "Well, I never," Mrs. Jameson uttered as she attempted to cover up her delight and yet appear appalled. She relished her role as the town gossip, and this was the first noteworthy event from a rather uninspired evening. She glanced from Cailean to Annabelle, and a sly smile spread. "My mama always told me the apple didn't fall far from the tree." She skewered Annabelle with a look as sharp as a dagger. "If you'll excuse me?"

A subtle quivering worked through Annabelle as she saw Cailean swipe at his mouth and then run a hand through his thick brown hair. He spun as footsteps approached, his hazel eyes daring anyone else to disparage them. His stance relaxed when he saw Ewan. "Take her home."

Annabelle flinched at Cailean's sharp tone and flat command. "I can walk there on my own."

"No, Miss Evans. Cailean is correct, even if he is living up to your assessment and acting like a boor." He winged out an elbow. "Let me escort you home."

Cailean speared her with a fierce frown as she took Ewan's arm and meekly walked beside his brother. He spun and kicked at the side of the schoolhouse once before storming off to return to the livery.

E wan clasped her hand slipped through his arm and glared at those who muttered uncomplimentary comments. Mrs. Jameson's gossip had spread like wildfire among the few who had lingered and not ventured home or to the saloons or to the Boudoir. He pushed through the small crowd gathered in front of the schoolhouse, shielding her as she leaned against him. "'Tis all right," he soothed. "Nothin' to worry about."

Annabelle choked out a laugh. "Even you, the perpetually jolly man, can't lie convincingly. I know I'm ruined." They walked with alacrity to her bakery.

"Hush," he whispered as he followed her into the back room of her bakery. "Ye ken no such thing."

She swiped at her tears. "Of course I do! With my sister and this town's obsession to determine if I'll follow in her footsteps, I can do little now to save my reputation and continue working here." She swung her arm around. "We were discovered by the biggest gossip in town. Everyone will know of my actions by tomorrow. I'll be surprised if I have any customers."

Ewan pushed her onto a stool and roamed around the kitchen. He picked up a kettle, setting it on the stove to heat. After following her instructions, he found the teapot and tea, and set out two cups. "I never thought to have a tea party on the night of the town's anniversary dance," he mused.

She rubbed at her eyes. "Go home, Ewan. There's no reason for you to stay." She jerked at the loud knock at her back door and the sound of someone fiddling with the lock.

Ewan stormed over to the door and flung it open. "Ye'd better leave afore I lose my temper," he growled. Sounds of retreating footsteps could be heard before only the distant revelry from the saloons carried on the wind. He slammed the door shut again and flipped the lock. "That's why I'm stayin' for a while."

Her shoulders stooped, and she shivered. "Thank you."

He slammed a fist onto the butcher block. "I'm sorry Cailean's a fool. I fear I'll be sayin' that to ye many a time afore this is over."

She shook her head. "I'm the fool. I knew better." She brushed at her tears. "I've proved too many in this town right tonight."

"Only those who have no sense. Many snuck away to steal a kiss." His soft smile did little to ease her tension.

"Perhaps. But we were the ones who were caught." She swiped at her disheveled hair.

Ewan sighed. "From what I hear, those who are caught are teased but never ridiculed for long. There's always another wee scandal to come along."

She moved around her kitchen area, wiping down the already clean counters and setting out bowls for the morning. "Somehow that fails to reassure me." She opened a tin and pulled out a few oatmeal raisin cookies, setting them on a plate for him. She poured him a cup of tea, holding her cup so that it warmed her hands. "If you insist on waiting with me, you might as well eat something."

He laughed, closing his eyes with pleasure. "Dinner was hours ago, and I'm always hungry." He gobbled up a few more before finishing his cup of tea. He tilted his head, listening as the sounds coming from the town had quieted. "I think it's safe to leave ye now. I want ye to lock up after me, and no' let anyone in until ye open tomorrow."

Annabelle nodded. "I can't thank you enough for your help tonight, Mr. MacKinnon."

He waved away her thanks and exited the back door, waiting until he heard the lock sound before he departed. He looked around to ensure no one hid in the shadows, stayed for a bit more, and then headed for home.

"Por God's sake, Cailean, see sense. Ye canna leave her to the wolves," Alistair snapped as he slammed a stable door shut in the livery. A horse whinnied in indignation at the sound. "Or to some of the men of this town."

"I'm no' marryin' her," Cailean said, his accent momentarily as strong as Alistair's. He took a deep breath. "If ye're that worried about her, ye can have her."

Alistair grabbed Cailean by the shirtfront and pushed him against a wooden post. "Ye know I'm promised to Leticia. I'll no' betray her for a woman I barely ken. Besides, ye're the one fascinated enough to stalk her bakery and kiss her tonight."

Cailean pushed at his brother and strode to the far end of the livery. He glared at Ewan as he eased into the barn. "No one's making me marry."

"She's safe for the night in her bakery," Ewan whispered, meeting Alistair's worried look. "I escorted her, scared enough away until I was sure she was settled, and then stood outside long enough that I'm certain she'll be left alone." His worried gaze met Cailean's. "She'd be better off if she left this town and started afresh somewhere else."

"Or married," Alistair said with a glower at his eldest brother. Alistair watched Cailean pace, his panic and rage easy to see, and Alistair's own ire eased. "Cailean, ye have to have known ye'd marry again."

"Don't," he rasped. "I swore on Maggie's and … and …" He swallowed, unable to speak. "I swore I'd never marry again. I promised Maggie."

Alistair shoved Cailean back a step. "Ye ken Maggie'd not want ye alone. She'd want ye happy, with bairns." He flinched at his brother's tortured expression. "Besides, if what ye say is true, then what were ye thinking, kissing Annabelle? On the other side of the schoolhouse, with bairns running around and curious parents searching for their own? If ye wanted to blacken her name any further, ye couldna have done a better job." He shook his head in disappointment at his brother.

Ewan sighed. "Unless ye want to see her suffer a similar fate as her sister, ye have to marry her, Cail. I had to scare away two drunken men."

Cailean shook his head as he sank to his haunches. "I can't. Not again."

Ewan swiped at his mouth. "Whoever marries her is a lucky man. While I waited with her, she fed me some of her day-old cookies." He winked at Alistair. "She must keep a stash for herself. Served me a cup of tea too." He sighed with pleasure.

Cailean growled at him and paced away.

"Ye have to know, if ye dinna want a woman like her, many will."

Ewan met his eldest brother's glare. "An' I don't mean like her sister. She's smart, funny, an' a businesswoman. Any man with sense would want to marry her."

Alistair shared a long look with Ewan as Cailean remained silent. "Think about it over tonight. Come tomorrow, ye need to have a plan."

CHAPTER 6

*C*ailean stood on the back porch as the dusky rose of dawn
lightened the sky and brought the subtle curves of the mountains into focus. Low-lying clouds glimmered with the changing light
as the sun attempted to peak over the horizon. Soon a soft golden
glow lit the sky.

He took a long sip of coffee as his mind drifted to a red-haired
woman, fiery yet patient, curious yet cautious, who had loved him
since he had first been able to consider himself a man. "Maggie," he
whispered to the soft breeze. His eyes fluttered closed as he thought
of her laughter, her teasing, her indignation, her anger, and her
passion. Her steadfast love for him. Her absolute honesty in
expressing how she felt. "God, how I miss you." He rubbed at his chest
and bowed his head.

After a few more minutes, he took a deep breath and squared his
shoulders. He tossed the remnants of his coffee into the yard and left
the cup on the windowsill. He walked down the steps and into town,
thankful that many of the townsfolk were still asleep after the night's
festivities. He cut down an alley behind Main Street to knock on her
back door.

After a minute, he knocked louder. He squinted as he thought he heard movement inside. "Miss Evans, it's Cailean MacKinnon." He glared at the door as it remained shut and was about to try the handle when it creaked open.

"What are you doing here?" she whispered through the small opening.

"I must speak with you. Would you prefer to speak in your shop, at my livery, or somewhere else?"

She opened the door a little wider and glared at him. "Seeing as you've already traipsed over here for all the townsfolk to see ..." She sighed as she motioned for him to enter. She shut the door after him.

He stood, holding his hat between his fingers and studied her. He frowned at the dark circles under her eyes, the faint lines by her mouth that he feared were from frowning rather than laughing, and the distance she maintained between them. "I'm sorry to have caused you difficulties last night, Miss Evans."

She snorted. "I caused them for myself. Haven't you noticed that society never blames the man but always the woman? Don't worry about me. I'll find a way to survive this."

"Will you?" he asked. A sharp rapping on the glass door at the front of the store interrupted their conversation.

She motioned for him to stay hidden in the kitchen, out of sight from the front windows, and to remain quiet as she moved toward the insistent knocking. Low murmurs and then indignant protestations were heard before the front door slammed shut.

"What was that all about?" he asked as she entered the kitchen area. He watched as she plopped onto a stool, her customary determination and optimism absent.

"That was the owner of this space. It seems he no longer wants a woman, especially a woman of questionable reputation, to rent his storefront." She rubbed at her forehead. "He says he'd rather have it empty for the next ten years than to live with the infamy of a woman such as me living and working here."

Cailean snorted. "Seems small-minded of him when he has three bastard daughters from his mistress." He shared an amused smile with Annabelle. "His wife hated Montana and returned to Philadelphia a month after they arrived six years ago. His so-called wife here is really his mistress as he's too miserly to have divorced his first wife and given her any settlement."

Annabelle's shoulders stooped. "I know you think that story helps me in some way. All it does is highlight that the world is unjust. Especially toward women."

Cailean watched her with an intense light in his eyes. "You're right. It is unjust, and I fear it always will be. Women will be held to a different standard than men for as long as we're alive. There is no getting around it." He gripped the edge of his hat with such strength he feared he'd rend it in two. "It's why you must marry me."

Annabelle gaped at him and then laughed. "Oh, Mr. MacKinnon, thank you for that joke. It's just what I needed to lighten my spirit."

He crossed to her in two strides and gripped her jaw in a firm grasp, yet caused her no pain. Her wide startled eyes met his earnest ones. "I'm deadly serious. You must be protected, and I can protect you. Due to my actions, you are in this predicament. You need to marry."

"I refuse to marry out of necessity." She glared at him. "I barely know you, and, whenever we are together, we argue."

He chuckled. "I'm not saying it will be easy, and I'm certain we'll drive each other daft." He looked at her in a challenging way. "Can you deny there are times you haven't felt safe here?" At her flush, he nodded. "Can you deny that a husband wouldn't ease your acceptance into the town?" At her glare, he smiled. "Can you deny that there isn't a speck of attraction between us?" At her gasp, he laughed.

"How dare you turn this into a … a … farce. This is my life. If I marry you, I'm bound to a man I barely know." She shook her head in defiance, freeing herself from his grasp. "No, I will not marry you."

He now gripped her shoulders. "Listen to the reasons we should marry. As a married woman, you can continue to work here in the bakery. I have no objections to you working. The extra income is welcome. You'll have your own home. A family."

Her gaze lit with disappointment. "It's *your* family. *Your* home. I'll just be living there." She bit her lip. "My sister will always be seen as an embarrassment to you and yours, and I can never see her that way. She's my sister."

Cailean released her and rubbed a hand over his face. "I understand loyalty to family, Annabelle. I understand wanting to see them well." He speared her with an intense stare. "It's why we're living here rather than in Scotland."

She fidgeted on her stool and stared at him. "In all of this marriage talk, you never mentioned that you'd come to care for me."

He froze, his gaze shattered for a moment before he masked the deep emotions. "I will never love you. Not as a woman would wish to be loved. I'll care for you. Ensure you have all that you need. But I will never love you."

Annabelle nodded at his emphatic words. "Of course not," she whispered, hugging her arms around her waist.

"That doesn't mean we shouldn't marry," he murmured. "If you don't, you'll have no reason to remain in town near your sister."

Her eyes widened, and she took a deep breath. "I can't lose her, not now that I've finally found her again." She swiped at a tear. "I know you think I'm foolish. That the townsfolk think I'm delusional in my belief that I'll have a relationship with her. That there's any reason to have a relationship with a fallen woman." She jutted her chin up in defiance. "But she's my sister."

He nodded. "As long as you keep my sister away from her."

Her bravado faded to disappointment as she watched him. "It's not a catching disease." She swiped at her cheeks. "And I notice you aren't worried about your brothers." At his silent stare, she shook her head.

"Well, what will it be?" he asked. "Will you remain here, to be evicted and to suffer the town's ridicule before you're eventually run out of town, away from your sister, your family? Or will you marry me?"

She slid off the stool and stood tall, looking him in the eye. "I have money of my own. Money from my father. I want ..." She faltered a moment. "I want a written agreement from the lawyer in this town that my money will remain under my control after we wed." She met his shocked glare with one of defiance.

"That's not how it's done! And I won't have you shaming me in front of the townsfolk when word leaks of our agreement." He ran a hand through his hair and slammed his hat onto the kitchen counter. "I give you my word, as a MacKinnon and as a Scotsman, that your money is yours. I won't touch it. I refuse to see a lawyer."

She studied him for a long moment. "How do I know you are just saying that so, when we wed, you can do what you like?"

His nostrils flared as he exhaled sharply. "My word is my honor. I'd thank you not to impugn it in the future." His expression softened when he detected the fear and desperation she attempted to conceal. "I can promise you that I will never attempt to use your money. It's yours, to do with what you like." His anger fully eased when he caressed her cheek, and she leaned into his touch.

"I'll marry you," she whispered, her eyes widening as though shocked at what she had said. She watched him with a touch of wonder and trepidation. At his curious look, she squared her shoulders. "I will. I will wed you."

He swooped forward and kissed her. Rather than the tentative, gentle kisses from the night before, this kiss was passionate and demanding. He bracketed her face with his palms and pressed his body to hers until she backed up against a far wall. He slanted his mouth for a better angle, deepening the kiss when she gasped.

He groaned with delight when she gripped the back of his shirt and then raised a hand to his nape, tugging him tighter. Her tongue dueled with his, and he gripped her hips to lift her when the distant sound of a door slamming broke them apart. He spun away, muttering a curse as he panted. He walked toward the counter and grabbed his hat, holding it in front of him as he turned to face her. "We'll wed as soon as it can be arranged, Annabelle." He nodded to her as she leaned against the wall, also panting. "There is little doubt we'll suit in at least one department." He watched with masculine delight as she flushed and then nodded her agreement.

"Good day, Annabelle," he said with a last long look. He slammed the door behind him.

~

L eticia arrived at her usual time with Hortence at her side. Little Hortence played in the corner with a doll and a cracked teacup and saucer while her mother worked with Annabelle. After assuring herself that Hortence was settled, Leticia focused on her friend.

"What happened?" she sputtered as she looked at the chaos present in the usually pristine kitchen. Oatmeal bread was rising; sweet buns were still in the oven, and Annabelle had a wild look in her eyes as she stood wrist deep, kneading dough to be turned into rolls.

"I'm behind. I got a late start." She shook her head as though in self-recrimination and blew at a strand of loose hair that fell in front of her eyes. "I should have some sweet buns ready in about ten minutes for those who show up on time. Otherwise, everyone will have to come back later for bread."

"Are you making anything else today?" Leticia asked, wrapping an apron around her waist. She sighed when she heard a tapping on the front door. Rather than move to answer the door, she entered Annabelle's small room. After a moment she emerged with a piece of paper in her hand. She walked to the front door where a few people mingled and smiled broadly.

"I'm afraid we are running behind today, and you will need to return in about an hour," she called through the glass and smiled vaguely. She crammed the piece of paper, stating *Opening Delayed* in the space between the door and glass and retreated to the back of the shop.

When she reentered the kitchen, she smiled at Annabelle who stood staring into space. "I've bought us an hour, but, if that's all you're going to do, it won't be enough time."

Annabelle jolted and began kneading again with vigor. She gave the dough a pat, then placed a cloth over the top of it. "With a shortened day today, I won't plan on much besides the sweet buns, bread, and rolls."

Leticia washed the bowls and set them to dry. "Did something occur last night at the dance? I had to leave early due to Hortence."

Annabelle smiled at Hortence playing in the corner. "I saw Mr. MacKinnon carrying her as she slept on his shoulder. He seems like a nice man."

Leticia's smile bloomed, unable to hide her delight. "Alistair's a wonderful man and doesn't mind that I have a child."

"Have you set the date yet?" Annabelle asked as she joined Leticia at the sink to wash her hands free of the bread dough.

"I … I want to wait just a little longer to ensure that we suit," Leticia murmured. "However, I heard there was a scandal last night. Do you know anything about it? Townsfolk were uncharacteristically closemouthed with me today."

"I'm sure that was out of their regard for you and concern for Hortence," Annabelle said as Leticia stared at her. "It might also have been due to the fact you work for me. Mr. MacKinnon, I should say, Cailean, and I were caught in a compromising situation."

Leticia gaped at her friend with wide eyes. After a moment she clamped her gaping jaw shut before battling a grin. "You and Cailean?"

Annabelle glanced over her shoulder to ensure Hortence was not listening and then whispered to her friend. "I went around the side of the schoolhouse to escape all the men requesting a dance, and Cailean followed me to ensure I was all right. I was foolish." She closed her eyes. "And lonely."

"You kissed him," Leticia breathed.

"Yes," Annabelle admitted, opening eyes filled with shame. "And it was glorious. I've never felt so alive before or felt such a desire."

Leticia frowned as she saw her friend battle her emotions. "There is no shame in feeling passion for a man who feels the same for you, Annabelle."

"I know he'll never feel anything for me but passion or desire, and that makes the entire encounter sordid." She wrapped her arms around her waist and leaned against the counter. "He came here this morning. To propose."

Leticia gasped. "I never thought Cailean would marry again."

Annabelle's head shot up in confusion as she looked at Leticia. "*Again?* He was married before?"

Leticia bit her lip. "I shouldn't have said anything. I thought you knew, that he would have told you." When Annabelle shook her head before moving toward the large oven, Leticia sighed. "He was married before he left Scotland. All I know is that she died, and he vowed to never marry again."

Annabelle nodded as she removed the heavy tray of buns from the oven. She set them on the wooden countertop and sprinkled sweet syrup over the top. "And now I've acted in such a way that he's been forced to break that vow. No wonder he resents me."

Leticia frowned. "It seems to me that he acted the same as you. That his actions are as much at fault, if there is any fault in this." She attempted a reassuring smile for her friend. "You are to marry, and you will marry an honorable man. I would give thanks, for few women are as fortunate as you."

Annabelle shuddered before she tamped down her emotion. "I'm not fortunate. I've agreed to tie myself to a man who can barely tolerate me." She blinked away tears. "I would call that a grave misfortune."

Leticia watched as her friend focused on setting the buns on a plate for her customers and then placed one batch of bread in the oven. She understood the tumultuous emotions roiling through her friend and gifted her with silence as she worked alongside her before she moved to the front of the store to ward off impertinent inquiries with a smile and a sale.

Cailean entered his home and headed to the kitchen to find his siblings already seated and eating breakfast. A glance at the wall clock showed it was a little past eight. Ewan clutched a cup of coffee as though it provided the elixir of life while Alistair watched Cailean with abject curiosity. He helped himself to a fresh cup of coffee and sat.

"Seems you were up early this morning. Coffee was made before I rose," Sorcha said with a yawn. At Cailean's distracted nod, Sorcha filled a plate for him. "I never thought a small town dance could be so intriguing."

"Where there are people gathered, there's bound to be something of interest," Alistair muttered. He glared at his sister to cease her prattling, but she ignored him. "Ye ken it was the same in Skye."

"Imagine my surprise to learn that the baker is as wicked as her sister! I heard she was caught outside with a man." She smiled with delight to her brothers, belatedly frowning when she saw Ewan and Alistair glare at her. "Serves her right after her show of airs and graces to be proven no better than the women at the Boudoir."

Cailean cleared his throat, and her gaze darted to him. "That man you speak of was me." He met his sister's shocked gaze. "If anyone acted dishonorably last night, it was me."

Sorcha rolled her eyes. "She knows the ways of a seducer. She had a wonderful tutor in her sister. You were ensnared by—"

"Enough!" Cailean roared. "She is an innocent woman, who was caught in a compromising circumstance. With me." He took a deep breath. "Which is why we shall marry. As soon as possible."

"Ye can no' be serious," Sorcha sputtered. "Ye expect met to accept such a woman into this house? To live here with her?"

Cailean nodded.

Sorcha continued to sputter but had finally found the good sense to cease speaking.

Alistair grinned, and Ewan dropped his cup of coffee, splattering the table and floor with it.

"She will be your sister-in-law, and I want her to feel welcomed here." Cailean stared at his sister until she nodded her agreement.

"What about Maggie?" Sorcha whispered.

Cailean stiffened. "She's been … gone for twelve years," he rasped. "It's time I moved on." He stood abruptly and strode from the room.

"How could ye?" Ewan glared at his sister. "How could ye bring up Maggie after he tells ye about his new wife-to-be?"

Alistair shook his head in disappointment as he watched his sister and rose to follow his brother to the livery. He found Cailean there, picking up a bucket to haul water. He stood in front of his brother, impeding his progress. "Give me the bucket."

"Get out of my way." He shoved at Alistair with little success.

"Ye are dressed too well to be in the livery. Run the errands ye must. Speak to the preacher. Do whatever must be done this morning to ensure ye keep Miss Evans safe. There's nothing urgent for ye to do here." He held out his hand for the bucket, waiting for Cailean to hand it over to him. When he hesitated, Alistair furrowed his brow as he met his brother's tormented gaze. "I ken ye want to act as though nothing has changed. But everything has."

After a moment, Cailean gave him the bucket and brushed past him, walking aimlessly down the boardwalk for a few minutes. He nodded and spoke pleasantries to the few townsfolk who were about, ignoring their curious looks or pointed stares. As he walked down the boardwalk, he passed in front of the General Store. Tobias swept the area in front of the store, the store empty of patrons on the early morning after the dance. Unable to avoid speaking with one of the town's gossips, Cailean paused to comment on the fine summer weather.

"Why would I want to discuss the weather with the man who's finally induced that harpy to act like the woman we know she is?" Tobias said as he nudged Cailean in the shoulder. "Many miners will be mighty happy with what you accomplished last night!"

"And what was that, Tobias?" Cailean stared out at the empty street rather than focus on Tobias.

"You showed she is open to temptation." His lascivious grin widened as Cailean spun to glare at him. "And I know there'll be plenty to take advantage of such an opportunity."

"Miss Evans is my fiancée, and I'd appreciate you speaking of her with respect," Cailean snapped. "For when you speak against her, you are speaking against me."

The broom clattered to the boardwalk, unnoticed by Tobias. "Well, I'll be damned. Never thought the eldest MacKinnon would marry. Thought you were a more solitary man." He nodded as Cailean canted forward in warning. "Miss Evans is a most fortunate woman."

"She is, and when she's Mrs. MacKinnon, your attempt to disparage her success at her bakery will cease." When Tobias began to sputter, Cailean smiled. "She'll continue her work, and you should stop your whining that she's stolen business from you. Anyone with a memory knows your short-lived attempt at providing baked goods at the Merc was a disaster."

Cailean moved a few steps down the boardwalk and then spun to pin Tobias with a severe stare. "And we'll renegotiate the terms of her bulk purchase of flour and sugar from you. As a married woman, she'll receive a better rate." He smiled as Tobias paled before Cailean continued on his way.

He stopped in to see the preacher, arranging for the wedding in two weeks. He considered marrying her within the week, but the preacher warned against garnering further gossip with such a hasty marriage. Cailean bowed to his guidance as he wanted no further speculation as to their rush down the aisle.

Upon exiting the preacher's rectory, dazed and fighting panic, he stopped short at the sight of Mrs. Jameson. She stood as tall as her five foot frame allowed, her body ramrod straight and corseted to within an inch of life. He nodded to her and hoped to scoot around her. However, she outmaneuvered him and blocked his path.

"Mr. MacKinnon, I was appalled at the scene I witnessed last night."

He bit back a groan. "I'm certain many other circumstances other than my discussion with Miss Evan has appalled you to a greater extent." He met her censorious glare. "Such as your husband, Vincent's, antics or the fact your son, Walter, has followed in his father's footsteps." He failed to outpace her as she stumbled, quickly righting herself and keeping him in conversation.

"I couldn't believe a man of your upstanding position in this town would carry on in such a manner with a woman of such questionable reputation. Why, I'd be concerned about business if I were you! Who would want their horses cared for by those who are so easily seduced by harlots?"

Any trace of amusement faded, and he clamped his jaw tight. His cheeks reddened with anger, and he stopped to face her. He canted toward her. "I would refrain from speaking about upstanding women in this community. Miss Evans is an honorable woman, as is our schoolteacher, Miss Leticia Browne." He glared her into silence. "I'd hate for those who offer you their meager support by purchasing your tatting to reconsider their generosity."

"Why I never! What a horrible thing to imply. I'd never contemplate damaging anyone's reputation." She looked around as though searching for a friendly ally.

"There isn't anyone in town who'd willingly buy that pile of dung from you." He nodded and maneuvered around her.

He stomped away from her, deciding at the last moment to make one more stop before returning to the livery. He squinted as he entered the darkened interior of the lawyer's office. "Hello, Warren," Cailean said. "I have need of your help." He sat in the chair across from his friend and stretched his legs out in front of him. "And of your discretion."

Warren smiled and steepled his hands over his belly. "It seems you're in a pickle. Never thought I'd see the day Cailean MacKinnon would arrive here after setting the town's jaws to jabbering. Nor did I think to see you going toe-to-toe with the likes of Mrs. Jameson." He laughed as he rose, moving to a back room a moment where he emerged with two steaming cups of coffee. "It's too early yet to think without reinforcement."

Cailean hissed as he burned his tongue on the hot beverage. After he blew on it and took another sip, he sighed. "I wish I could teach Sorcha to cook anything, even to brew coffee. She hates the kitchen."

"Seems to me her talents must lie elsewhere." Warren warmed his hands a moment before setting his cup down on the desk. "I'd try to discover those and foster them."

Cailean's gaze focused on his friend and frowned. "How can you know more about my sister than I do?"

He shrugged. "It helps not to live with her. And I'm not occupied in the livery." He smiled as he took a sip of his cooling coffee. "You know me. I spend my days sitting in my rocker as I watch the town busy itself outside my window." Cailean laughed as he knew Warren was often so run off his feet he could use three assistants. "But I know Sorcha isn't why you're here."

Cailean grimaced at his friend's inquisitive look. He fought the urge to shift in his chair like a recalcitrant student. "I'm to marry." He watched as Warren spun his head to the side and spewed his swig of coffee into the waste bin. "That's the first time I've ever taken you off guard," Cailean said as he grinned with pleasure.

Warren coughed and sputtered a moment before taking another sip of coffee. "Miss Evans must be the lucky woman."

Cailean nodded. When Warren waited for him to speak, he ran a hand through his brown hair. "I just spoke with the preacher. We'll marry in two weeks. After last night's goings-on, I have to wed her." His gaze became distant as his friend watched him with amusement.

"If the rumors are true, you won't find it a hardship." He raised an eyebrow as Cailean glared at him. "I mean, that it seems you and Miss Evans suit, at least in some regards."

Cailean sighed. "I think we do."

Warren chuckled as he settled into his chair, one leg crossed over the other knee. "I'd think that would please you." He waited a moment and then spoke when Cailean remained silent. "What can I do to help you? I wouldn't think you'd need a lawyer's aid before your marriage."

"Miss Evans has money from her father. I made her a promise I wouldn't touch it." He met his friend's gaze. "However, when I was at the preacher's, he mentioned that I was a fortunate man to marry a woman with property." He scowled. "I don't want Annabelle or anyone to believe I'm marrying her for money."

Warren raised an eyebrow, his hands crossed over his belly. "I wouldn't think it matters what the townsfolk believe. What matters is what you and Annabelle know to be true."

Cailean sighed. "We're only marrying due to gossip and her fear of the townsfolk's reactions to her actions. Plus the man renting to her advised her this morning how he doesn't want a harlot in his storefront."

Warren snorted. "Dan Stubbens was always the first to act and the last to think." He settled into his chair as he thought. "I can pressure Dan. I wrote the lease, and he has no right to threaten Miss Evans with eviction." His grin was slightly wicked. "I'd rather enjoy spouting lawyerly nonsense at him."

Cailean laughed. "I also want a contract between Miss Evans and myself."

"You want a contract written up, stating that what your wife brings into the marriage is hers and that you can't touch it?" At Cailean's nod, Warren said, "That shouldn't be difficult. It's a rather commonplace occurrence in many states out East, and there is precedent for it. I'd prefer to have a meeting with both of you so that I know the particulars of what she would like included. That way you can both agree to the wording of the contract."

Cailean nodded. "I'd prefer if you'd keep this private."

Warren rolled his eyes and waved toward the door. He smiled as he shook Cailean's hand. "I'll see you later this afternoon?"

Cailean nodded and left.

When Cailean ushered Annabelle into Warren's office that afternoon, he shared an amused smile with his friend. Annabelle sat stiffly and maintained her distance from Cailean.

"Now that you are both here, I have the papers prepared for you to sign," Warren said.

Annabelle looked from Warren to Cailean. "Would you please explain why I am here?"

Warren raised an eyebrow at Cailean who shrugged. "Mr. MacKinnon visited me this morning and explained that you are to wed. He wanted to ensure that the property, specifically the money brought to the marriage from your late father, remained under your control even after the wedding."

Annabelle gasped, and her starched-stiff posture wilted. She gaped at Cailean. "This is why you wanted me here?"

He nodded, his eyes glinting with a hidden smile at her surprise. "Aye. I realized I was asking you to trust me when I'd given you little reason to."

She shared a long look with him before focusing on Warren. "Will you please explain what you have prepared for us?"

He turned the document around so that she and Cailean could read it easily. "It's a very simple procedure. This is a codicil to the recognized legal rights bestowed to your husband upon your marriage. It states that Miss Evans's premarriage property remains hers, and I wrote out that it specifically meant the money left her by her father. Is there anything else I need to add?"

Annabelle shook her head and bit her lip.

"Now, if Mr. MacKinnon were to die, his property would become yours, as is the legal precedent set in the territory. Unless you would like that altered?" He looked to Cailean.

"No," Cailean said as he shook his head. "I'd want to ensure she was well provided for."

Warren nodded. "Fine. Then, if this is an acceptable document to you both, you both must sign it the day of your wedding or sometime afterward and have it witnessed. I'd then keep it in a secure place."

Cailean nodded and held out his hand. "Thank you, Warren."

"Thank you, Mr. Clark." Annabelle rose and stepped ahead of Cailean so that his hand hung in midair rather than on the small of her back.

She bustled down the boardwalk to her bakery and stepped inside. Cailean followed her, shutting the door behind them. After she locked the front door, she moved to the back and set her purse on the clean counter. She paced the area between the sink, icebox, and counter, while he stood on the other side of the counter, watching her erratic movements.

"What's the matter, Annabelle? I thought this would please you." His brows furrowed as she appeared more agitated at his words.

She spun around, her back to him. When he saw her shoulders quiver, he closed the distance between them and turned her to face him. A few tears leaked from her eyes.

"I never meant to make ye cry," he whispered. His fingers rose to swipe at her cheeks, his calluses evoking a shudder as they swiped along her soft skin.

She watched him with a hint of wonder, unease, and confusion. "I don't understand why you visited him. You said your word was your bond."

He smiled as his hand dropped to her waist, holding her in place in front of him. "My word *is* my bond. And I don't like it when it's questioned. But I realized you needed reassurances." He looked deeply into her eyes. "I didn't want to start our marriage with distrust."

"Thank you," she whispered. She stood on her tiptoes and kissed him softly on his lips.

He groaned, kissing her a moment before easing away. "Why were you crying?" he whispered into her ear as he kissed the side of her neck.

"No one has ever cared about my wishes before." She shuddered as he nibbled at her earlobe.

"Your wishes are quickly becoming my greatest concern." He kissed her along her jaw before kissing her mouth again. He backed her until she was pressed against the icebox, his mouth slanting over hers as though he couldn't kiss her deeply enough or long enough. Her hands tugged him closer as they stroked through his silky hair while her body arched into his. He broke the kiss to nibble at her jaw as he panted, "I want ye, Annabelle."

She traced her hand over his cheek and shook her head. "Not until we are wed. I ... can't."

He dropped his head to her shoulder and took a few deep breaths. "I never meant any disrespect." He pushed himself away, leaving her plastered to the icebox, holding its handle to maintain her balance. His gaze darkened as he beheld her, mussed with kiss-swollen lips. He spun and marched to the other side of the counter.

"I won't visit you much. Not until the wedding." He saw her shoulders stoop. "Not because I don't want to." He met her gaze as the quick flash of despair and humiliation lifted. "But because I have no desire to cause you to feel shame." His gaze darkened further. "I want you, Annabelle. And I think you want me too. But I will wait until our wedding day afore I attempt to entice you into my bed."

She smiled as she watched him, any sadness having disappeared with his words. "Do you know you sound more like your brothers, more like a Scotsman, when you feel deep emotions?" Her smile grew as he flushed. "Thank you."

He nodded at her whispered words. "I tried to forget Scotland when I arrived in this country. Part of forgetting was trying to not sound like a Scotsman." He shrugged. "Some days I succeed more than others."

"It's part of who you are. No matter how hard you try, the past is always with you, like your shadow."

His passionate gaze faded as he sobered. "Aye, that I ken too well." He took a deep breath and looked around her clean kitchen. "I hope you have a good evening, Annabelle." He spent a few moments on one last lingering look before he slipped out the back door.

After he'd walked a few doors away from hers, he paused and took a deep breath. He scrubbed at his face before returning to the livery and Alistair's inquisitive questions.

~

A few days before they were to be married, Cailean knocked on her back door. It was late afternoon, and he knew the bakery was sold out from what Alistair had reported from Leticia. He knocked again before trying the door. He frowned when he found it unlocked and eased it open. He tiptoed into the kitchen area, noting it clean and ready for another day of baking. He ignored the front room as that would only contain bare shelves.

After a few more steps, he poked his head into her private back room, stilling at the sight of her. She lay with her head on top of crossed arms on her small desk. She breathed deeply as she slept, and he studied her. He had never seen her with such an expression of peace, as she appeared to half smile while she slept. Her black hair was tied back in a long braid down her back, although loose tendrils framed her face.

He shifted, and his boot heels sounded. She jerked upright, her eyes widening in alarm. Her gaze flew to the doorway, while her hands searched for something on her desk. Only when she recognized him did she cease her frantic movements and calmed. "Cailean," she breathed. "What are you doing here?" She swiped at her mouth and shook her head as she attempted to shake away the remnants of sleep. "Why do you think you can barge in here uninvited?"

He watched her as his tender yearning faded. "I didn't barge in here. I knocked numerous times. I know it was wrong, but, when I tried the back door and it was open, I wanted to ensure you were fine."

She flushed at his concern and her cantankerousness. She yawned hugely, hiding it behind a bended elbow. "I must have forgotten to lock it after Leticia left. Why are you here?" She motioned for him to sit, blushing when she realized the only available seat was her cot.

He perched on the edge of it, his hat held between his fingers. "We are to marry in a few days. I wanted to ensure you were well." His gaze held a nearly feral intensity as it met hers. "I haven't seen you in too long."

"I'm fine. I have a dress and will meet you at the church at the appropriate time." She waved around the room. "I have little to move to your house." When he continued to stare at her, she cleared her throat. "If you'd prefer, I could continue to live here. I know my bakery hours aren't conducive to a harmonious home life."

He frowned. "You'll be very welcome in my home. And we'll adapt to your hours as needed." He saw her fidgeting, and the furrows between his eyes deepened. "What is it?"

"I've heard rumors," she stammered out. "And I need to know if they're true." His gaze became shuttered as he stared at her implacably. "Have you been threatening my business associates?"

He sputtered out a laugh and twirled his hat while he watched her. "Hell yes." At her glare his laugh turned into a chuckle before he contained it.

"I am my own woman. I am in control of my business and who I deal with. I do not appreciate you speaking with my associates without my consent or my knowledge."

He shook his head in confusion. "You are joking, aren't you? You have to know the only reason I'd speak to those so-called associates is to aid you. I spoke with Tobias to insist he understood you will renegotiate your terms with him so that he'll no longer bleed you dry for your basic necessities. I spoke with Warren to ensure you'd not be evicted."

With rising indignation, she clamped her fists together on her lap. "Those were my tasks." She thumped a hand to her chest. "I should have done them, not you!"

He shook his head at her anger. "I don't understand you. I acted as your fiancée to ensure you'd have less cost in the future and no difficulty in remaining open. I refuse to feel guilty for aiding you. They're the same actions I would take as your husband."

She shook her head as she continued to glare at him. "Spoken like a man. You spoke *for* me, not *with* me, not in support of me. You took away my ability to speak for myself. Why can't you see that I want some voice in my own business?"

He leaned forward so his elbows were braced on his knees and was now almost nose to nose with her. "And why can't you see that a man needs to feel as though he's providing some help to his woman when he's able to? When you deny him that, then you deny his reason for being."

"That's absurd, and you know it!" She glared at him and then rolled her eyes.

"Is it? Is it absurd that I was thinking you'd be pleased I'd aided you? That I took time out of my day to ensure you'd remain safe here in this bakery you've called home?" He met her irate gaze. "That I informed Tobias how you were to marry me and that you were not fair game to the miners?" He took a deep breath as he attempted to calm his anger. "I only thought of you."

She shook her head as her ire abated. "I suppose I can see your point of view. However, you must see that, to me, it's as though you didn't respect me enough to act for myself."

He shook his head with disappointment as he stared at her. "Why would you want to continue to struggle all on your own when someone is willing to share the burdens with you?"

She shrugged. "To *share* them, yes. If you'd been raised to believe you weren't capable, then each small success is a victory."

He frowned. "Aye, but a solitary victory is pathetic." He froze as the words left his lips. "I didn't mean that."

She paled and looked at her clasped hands on her lap. "Of course you'd believe that my desire to do things on my own would be pathetic. I understand how a man as strong and capable as you would believe that. However, I refuse to concede—"

"Dammit, I'm not asking you to concede! I'm asking you to realize you're no longer alone. You have me. You have my siblings. We'll struggle with you. In three days, you'll be a MacKinnon."

She shook her head sadly. "I'll still be Annabelle Evans, sister of Fidelia Evans, no matter what last name I'm given."

He rocked back to sit on his haunches as though she had hit him with a solid right hook. "One day you'll want my support. You'll have to hope I'm still willing to offer it." He rose, storming out of her room and slamming the back door behind him.

CHAPTER 7

*A*listair grabbed two glasses of punch and walked over to Annabelle who stood on the side of the room. "Here," he said, handing her one of the glasses. He watched as her wary gaze flitted from him to the glass and back to him again. He attempted a reassuring smile, and she finally accepted the glass.

"Thank you," she whispered.

"If I were a newly married woman, I'd try to act a bit more joyful. Especially if the entire town were watching," Alistair said as he leaned on the wall next to her.

She frowned at his words, before smiling at him as though he'd told her a great joke. "Next you'll tell me what to say."

"It's too late for that," he teased. "Ye already had me thinking ye werena goin' to accept my brother afore the whole town when I realized ye'd whispered yer vows." He shook his head. "Should have shouted 'em for all of us to hear."

"They were between Cailean and me," Annabelle retorted, a blush on her previously pale cheeks.

Alistair chuckled. "Seein' how the townsfolk didna believe ye'd marry him, nor he ye, it would have been more convincing had ye shouted it out." He shrugged. "But they're yer memories, not ours."

Alistair frowned as he watched his brother across the room with a few of his friends, including Warren, the lawyer.

"What I'd like to know is what ye did to anger him so." Alistair drained his small cup of punch, wincing. "Too sweet."

"He doesn't like my independence," Annabelle said with a sniff, ignoring his critique of the punch.

Alistair laughed, earning a glare across the room from Cailean. "And ye dinna enjoy his interference." When she stiffened, Alistair nodded as though having puzzled out a riddle. "I wondered what he was mutterin' about the past few days. Now I ken."

"This has nothing to do with you, Mr. MacKinnon," Annabelle said stiffly.

He laughed harder. "Of course it does. Ye're my sister now. An' I'm Alistair, not Mr. MacKinnon." He met her chagrined gaze. "Ye'll have to accustom yerself to a bit of interference in yer life now that ye're no longer alone."

"I was never alone," she snapped.

His gaze sharpened. "Aye, ye always had yer sister, but who's supported ye all these years?" When she remained mute, he nodded. "Now ye've me and Ewan and Sorcha. And Cailean." He watched as she shifted uncomfortably.

"I am my own woman," she whispered with fierce determination.

"Aye, ye are. But now ye have a chance to be more than alone. Ye have a chance for *more*, Annabelle. That's a gift most rarely receive. I'd think twice afore rejecting it." His countenance brightened when he beheld Leticia approaching with Hortence.

"Ah, there ye are," he said with a broad smile, clasping Leticia's hand before lifting Hortence into his arms and kissing her on her cheek. "How are ye, little love?" He chuckled when she whispered something in his ear.

He met Leticia's concerned stare. "She's worried there willna be enough cake." He ran a hand down her back.

"Oh," Annabelle breathed. "Don't worry, Hortence. I made one special for the MacKinnons. It's waiting for them at their home for after the party. I'm sure they'll give you a piece."

Leticia shook her head at Annabelle. "With all you had to do, you made another cake?"

Annabelle shrugged. "When I'm nervous, I bake. It calms me." She smiled. "Don't tell Cailean, but I made one for us too." She bit her lip. "Do you have any idea where we are going after we leave this reception?"

Alistair chuckled. "If I told ye, he'd kill me. He wants to surprise ye." He nodded, and she looked in that direction to see Cailean, her husband, walking toward her. Alistair and Leticia drifted away, and she stood alone, staring into his hazel eyes.

"Hello, Annabelle," he whispered. "The townsfolk are restless. Will you cut the cake with me?"

She smiled, hiding her resentment at the forced formality between them. He reached for her hand, and she clasped his, walking by his side toward the wedding cake she had baked for them. When they sliced it, she heard him sigh. "What is it?" she murmured as she smiled to those watching and applauding.

"It's a white cake," he said as he continued to cut pieces of cake and hand them to her to give to the waiting townsfolk.

She smiled to the well-wishers and bit back a giggle. "I hope they think it's delicious."

"They will," he said. When they finished handing out cake, he cleaned his hands on a napkin before wrapping an arm around her waist. "Dance with me?" He smiled as she nodded bashfully. Two men played a fiddle and a guitar in a corner, and the music transformed into a waltz.

She tripped over his feet and blushed.

"Follow my lead," he murmured in her ear. "I don't know how to dance the waltz well, as you know from the town celebration, but we can still dance." He led them around the floor, each step more fluid and graceful as she abandoned the waltz dance steps she had learned and allowed herself to move with him. She rested her head against his shoulder and breathed in his scent, a mixture of horses, straw, sandalwood aftershave—and Cailean. When the dance ended, she opened

her eyes, surprised to see the townsfolk watching them with speculation and delight.

"Are you ready to leave?" he whispered in her ear. At her nod, he
linked his fingers with hers and led her toward his siblings and Leticia. He laughed at their teasing and seemed entranced as she blushed.

She hugged Leticia and Hortence, waved at the townsfolk, and
walked beside Cailean to the waiting carriage. She smiled at him as he
helped her into it and sighed with pleasure to no longer be
surrounded by the townsfolk. She fiddled with the pin on her hat to
ensure it was secure and waved again at the well-wishers as Cailean
eased the team into motion with a soft *click*ing sound and a gentle
flick of the reins.

"Where are we going?" Annabelle asked as they rolled out of town.

"A friend of mine has a small cabin outside of town. He didn't
think it right we spent our first night together at the house with all
my siblings." He smiled at her as she blushed. "He'll be fine as he's up
at the mines for the next week or two."

"That was very thoughtful of him." Annabelle gripped the seat as it
hit a pothole, and the wagon rattled down the road. She took a deep
breath and focused on the passing scenery, unable to have a conversation while in the rattling wagon.

As they left town, the valley became broader, and the grassland
spread out before them. The rangeland was turning a pale yellow after
the spring rains dried up and the heat of summer came, although a
hint of green remained. Cottonwood trees and small shrubs lined a
small stream on her right. Red-winged blackbirds called and flitted
around, the red on their wings a surprising splash of color. After miles
of admiring the scenery, she tilted her head to marvel at the wide-
open sky that looked as though it never ended.

The road split, and they made a turn, leaving the grassland behind
them as they headed toward the mountains. The air cooled slightly as
they rose out of the valley floor. Distant homesteads dotted the landscape. The road rounded a bend, affording a view over the valley. She
marveled at the large herds of cattle grazing freely. They seemed to be
corralled by streams or trees as no fences dotted the landscape.

Cailean noted her interest and pointed to a large white clapboard house in the distance. "The Tompkins's grandson lives there. Manages a huge herd of cattle." Annabelle nodded as she recalled hearing about their reclusive grandson.

As they approached the cabin, tall plants swayed in the breeze with their green stalks and a puffed-out cloudlike top in a creamy lacelike pattern. "What are those?" Annabelle asked.

"That's bear grass," Cailean said with a chuckle. "Some years there's a lot of it, others just a few stalks. This year there's more than usual."

They arrived at the cabin, and Cailean jumped from the wagon and held his arms up to help her down. She paused by the wagon, closing her eyes, raising her head, and breathing deeply of the fresh pine smell mingled with the scent of freshly cut hay. Her expression relaxed further with each deep breath, and, after a few minutes, she opened her eyes to smile at Cailean, watching her. "Isn't it beautiful here?"

He nodded, his eyes lit with a bright intensity. "Aye. More beautiful every moment." She ducked her head. He placed a few fingers under her chin to raise her gaze to meet his appreciative one. "There's no embarrassment in me finding my wife lovely." Her flush intensified, but she maintained eye contact.

He cleared his throat after a moment and led her into the cabin. He brought in a few boxes she'd insisted on bringing from the bakery and a bag with clothes. "I'll tend the horses," he said with a quick kiss to her cheek.

Annabelle stood in the small wooden cabin. Most of the boards were well chinked, although she could still see through a few of them to the outside. Along the front were two windows on either side of the door. A small area with a table and a counter with a wash bin comprised the kitchen space, while the potbelly stove acted as the main source of heat and cooktop. There was no oven. Behind the table, a sheet covered the wall. On the other side of the cabin was a comfortable-looking bed. A table by the bed held a lamp and a thick book, and a lamp hung from a hook in the middle of the ceiling.

Cailean entered the cabin and set his hat on a hook by the door. He watched out of the corner of his eye as she set a small basket of food on the table. "Would you like help?" he asked as she stood, staring around the sparsely decorated room. He pulled back the sheet to reveal a shelf of plates, pots, and plans. He handed her plates and found silverware, and she set the table.

"I wasn't sure where we were going," she whispered, as she blushed and pulled out a plate of sandwiches. "If I'd known we wouldn't be at your house, I would have made more food."

He rubbed his stomach and smiled. "These will be delicious." He motioned for her to sit and pushed in her chair for her. After taking a chicken sandwich, he passed the plate to her. He gobbled down his sandwich, frowning to note that she nibbled at hers. "Aren't you hungry?"

She smiled and took a large bite of her sandwich. After he'd eaten three and she barely one, he rapped his fingers on the table.

"I baked us a cake," she blurted out. She pointed to the basket on the floor. At his delighted smile, she rose and pulled out a small two-layer cake covered in white frosting.

"How smart I was to marry the town's baker," he teased. When she cut it, he stared at it with delight. "It's chocolate?"

At his whispered question, she nodded. "I asked Alistair what your favorite was, and he said anything chocolate." She shrugged, although a smile teased her lips.

He reached forward, his fingers tracing the smile on her lips. "Thank you." She shrugged as though it were of no consequence, but he shook his head. "Thank you for your thoughtfulness."

"I wanted to give you something on our wedding day. I wasn't sure what you needed, and so I decided to bake you a cake."

He stilled. "I don't have a gift for you."

She took a deep breath and met his worried gaze. "You gave me your name," she whispered. "I know I acted as though I wouldn't appreciate that gift a few days ago, and I want to apologize. I hope we are able to find harmony in our marriage."

He traced his thumb over her cheek. "I want harmony too." He

smiled as she gave him a large piece of the cake and sighed with pleasure. "I could eat the whole cake now."

She laughed. "It's yours. You can do as you like."

He watched her, his expression softening as she laughed. "We
should save it as a treat." He leaned forward and kissed her softly.
"Thank you." After he helped her clear the plates, he studied the tiny
living space, with the bed in the corner of the large space. He saw her
shudder even though it was far from cold.

"Dance with me," he cajoled, holding his hand out to her. She
stepped into his embrace, and they swayed in place. He hummed a
soft tune for them as he moved them in slow circles.

"You sing better than you dance," she murmured, tucking her face
into his shoulder.

"That's faint praise," he teased. He ran his hands over her back,
easing her closer as they moved. "There's no need to be afraid of me,"
he whispered as he felt her relax with each turn, and he slowly held
her against him. After many minutes, they stood swaying together,
barely moving. He looked down at her, resting her head against his
shoulder with a peaceful expression. He traced a finger down the side
of her jaw and coaxed her to meet his gaze.

Awareness flared an instant before he lowered his head and kissed
her. The kiss began softly, hesitant, as though relearning her after a
long absence. In a few short minutes, he wanted more and gripped her
head, kissing her deeply. He growled his satisfaction as she met his
passion with her own.

He turned them toward the bed, pausing when she bumped up
against the edge of it. "I love this dress, but it must go," he rasped, as
he kissed the side of her neck. His fingers worked on the demure
white gown with buttons down the back, freeing her from it as he
pushed it down over her hips. His mouth dipped, kissing her collarbone, before he backed up a step.

He raised a hand, tracing her kiss-swollen lips with his fingers and
met her passion-filled gaze. "I want you. I want us to make love," he
whispered around panting breaths. His breath hitched when she
kissed his fingers.

"So do I," she whispered. She pulled at his waistcoat and jerked on the buttons, inadvertently tearing one off. She dropped her hands. "Forgive me."

He laughed, kissing her on her chin, neck, and then lips. "Never apologize for showing me what you feel. What you want." He unbuttoned his waistcoat and shirt, flinging them aside.

She raised her hands and then lowered them again, uncertainty and embarrassment flickering in her expression. He grasped one of her hands and spread it on his chest, palm open. "It's acceptable for you to touch me. For you to want to touch me. We are married." He worked on the front ties to her corset, releasing her from the confining garment.

As the corset landed on the floor, she fell backward onto the bed, her breath coming to her in a loud gasp. She lay on her elbows as her eyes fluttered close, and she took a deep breath.

"Annabelle! Are you all right?" He ran a hand over her shoulders, and he leaned over her, tracing her cheek with his fingers.

"I tied my corset too tight," she whispered. "When it's released, sometimes I faint with all the air that comes rushing back in." She took another deep breath and opened her eyes again.

"I'm goin' to burn the *bluidy* thing," Cailean said, his accent as strong as his indignation. "Here. Let me hold you." He lay next to her and pulled her close against his shoulder.

She continued to take deep breaths, while her fingers played with the hair on his chest. After many moments, she kissed his shoulder. He stiffened with her gentle touch, and she ran a hand down his chest to his abdomen and back up again.

He pushed her to her back and stared at her, his eyes gleaming with passion as he saw her embarrassment. "Why touch me like that when it makes you embarrassed?"

She met his gaze bravely. "Because you enjoy it. And I know enough that we don't continue with our clothes on." She gasped when he swooped forward to kiss her. His busy hands freed her of her petticoats, urging her to lift up so he could toss those aside to join his clothes on the floor.

"I should take more care with your clothes, but I can't at this moment." He ran a hand down her leg and grinned at the garter holding up her stockings. He tickled her as he teased a finger underneath it and eased it off. He repeated the process on her other leg, and she squirmed.

"You please me, Belle," he whispered into her ear. "So much." He rose to shuck off his pants. He paused when he saw her ease replaced with panic. "It's all right, Belle."

She bit her lip. "No one's ever called me Belle. I've always been Anna." She blinked away tears.

"You're Belle to me," he whispered, kissing her eyes and forestalling the shedding of any tears. "You're beautiful to me."

She pushed on his shoulders, rising on her elbows. "I don't think I can do this. It'll make me no better than my sister." Her panicked gaze collided with his confused one.

"You are my wife. I am your husband. There is nothing wicked in us loving each other this way," he whispered. He kissed her and felt her resistance fade. When he looked into her eyes again, he frowned. "You're still uncertain." His large callused palm cupped her cheek.

"I ... I'm afraid," she admitted, her voice breaking.

He eased away from her enough to give her space but kept his hand against her cheek. "Of me?"

She nodded, then shook her head. "Of the pain. Of what it means. Of what I've given up." She closed her eyes in defeat. "I'm not making any sense." She flopped onto her back with her arms spread wide. "Just do it then," she ordered with a quivering voice. When he chuckled, she raised her head and glared at him.

He ran his fingertips from her cheek, down to her jaw, over her neck to her collarbone. Then he bent forward and kissed one shoulder and the next. "I refuse to rush this. To make you feel as though this is a perfunctory duty for me. I want you to feel joy in our touch and as little pain as possible." He kissed his way to her breasts, earning a gasp and her arching into his touch.

"Let me teach you pleasure," he whispered as he continued to kiss her.

~

A nnabelle woke the first morning as a married woman, nearly falling out of the bed. Cailean lay along her backside, twitching as though in the midst of a dream and snoring softly. She toppled out of the bed and found his half-buttoned shirt on the floor. She tugged it over her head as she tiptoed to the front door. When she got outside, dawn was breaking, and she was able to discern the outhouse in the distance. After stubbing her toes a few times, she made it there and back. When she shut the door softly behind her, she tripped on a shoe and muttered a curse.

She blushed when she faced the bed to find Cailean watching her with fond amusement in his gaze. She waved outside as explanation, tugging his shirt collar tight around her. He smiled and held open the covers for her. She climbed into bed, bumping her head into his chest and settled on her side, facing him.

"For a moment, I thought you'd abandoned me," he teased. He traced a hand over her fingers clutching the shirt closed. She shook her head as she watched him with wide eyes. "I hadn't thought you prone to silence, Belle."

She batted at his hands and soon their fingers were entangled. His smile dimmed when he saw her bite her trembling lip and felt her heave out a deep breath. "What is it?" he whispered, dipping his head to meet her downcast gaze.

"I never thought it would be like this," she whispered.

He frowned when she fell silent again. He groaned in frustration as he felt her wet cheeks when he cupped one with the palm of his hand. "Why are you crying? I'm sorry about last night."

At his whispered words of regret, she shook her head vehemently. "No! I don't want you to apologize." She raised her eyes to meet his worried gaze as tears slowly leaked out. "I ... I'm ashamed."

He sucked in a deep breath and dropped his hand. "Of what we shared?" At her silence, he rolled away to the edge of the bed and sat up as though he would rise. He ran a shaking hand through his hair and sat with slumped shoulders.

She rolled after him and grabbed onto his arm, preventing him from standing. "No! That's not what I meant." She patted his cheek he kept turned firmly away from her. "Please, talk to me."

At the pleading in her voice, he turned.

"I know this was only a marriage of convenience," she whispered.

He stared at her with her long black hair tumbling over her shoulders and light brown eyes lit with worry. "All we seem to do is misunderstand each other."

"Please, listen to me." When he gave a slight nod, she grasped his hand and tugged him so that he followed her and lay next to her on the bed. "I'm not ashamed of what we shared. It was wondrous and strange." She flushed. "But mostly wondrous." Her worry eased when she saw his pleasure at her words.

"Then what did you mean?" He ran a hand through her hair, holding her closer so that they shared the same breath.

"I'm ashamed for judging my sister," she whispered. She met his startled gaze. "Not for what has happened to her now, although I fear she had little choice." She closed her eyes as tears leaked down her cheeks. "I'm ashamed I failed to support her five years ago when my father threw her out of the house."

"Why would he do such a thing to his daughter?" Cailean asked, rubbing away Annabelle's tears.

"He believed our value came from our purity and our skills and taught us that, without either, we had little worth. I was never attractive, like Fidelia, so I focused on baking."

"Why are you ashamed?" Cailean whispered when she fell silent.

"She fell in love. And our father threw her out because she acted on that love. And I judged her. I called her unworthy. A harlot. And turned my back on her pleas for help."

Cailean studied her as she attempted to compose herself as she told the story in an emotionless voice. "How would you have been able to aid your sister?"

"I had a little money saved from my bakery earnings in Maine. I was supposed to give everything I earned to my father when I first opened my bakery, but I always held some back. It wasn't much as I was just twenty. I should have given it to her." She closed her eyes and turned her head into the pillow.

"*Shhh*, love," Cailean murmured. "We all make mistakes when we are young. When those we trust teach us incorrectly. If we are lucky, we are given the opportunity to repair any damage we did."

She sniffled as she curled into his arms. "If I'd given her the money, maybe she would have been able to choose another path."

He held her, stroking a hand down her back. "And maybe she wouldn't have. You'll never know, Belle." He continued to hold her, caressing her head and back as she calmed in his embrace. "I'm sorry I hurt you last night."

She kissed his chest at his whispered comment. "I know." She rested her cheek against his chest. "I could never feel ashamed of what we shared. It was more than I ever thought could happen between a man and a woman." She raised luminous eyes to meet his. "I finally understand why Fidelia was willing to risk our father's wrath."

He swallowed and let out a stuttering breath as he stared at her. He ran his hands through her long hair until they became entangled in a knot. "You're wrong, you know." He leaned forward and kissed her softly. "You're more beautiful than your sister. And there's so much more we can share." He laughed as she reddened at his words. "Someday you won't blush when I say such things."

He eased her against his chest and murmured gentle words in her ear as though singing her a lullaby. She closed her eyes and succumbed to sleep in his arms.

A few hours later, Annabelle woke with Cailean's arm wrapped around her middle and his leg hitched over hers as though anchoring her in place. She arched into him, then stilled when she felt the evidence of his desire. His arm around her tightened and she gasped at his firm grip on her. She squirmed a little, and he woke, groaning.

"I can't breathe," she whispered. When his arm around her relaxed, she took a deep breath, although he didn't release her from his grasp. She smiled as he kissed the back of her neck.

"Will you forgive me if I don't let you go?" he whispered into her ear. "I find I enjoy holding you."

She giggled and then sighed with contentment as his hands slowly stroked over her. "I find I enjoy being held." At his groan of approval, she arched into him. "Will you think me shameless if I ask you to love me again?"

He moved so that she lay on her back, and he leaned over her, running a hand from her forehead to cheek. "Never. Although I worry it's too soon." He grinned as she blushed red.

She pulled him to her, kissing his bottom lip. "I promise it's not." He groaned again, gratefully forfeiting the argument.

A nnabelle laid in his arms, her back to his front, shivering with delight as his callused fingers played over her shoulders and back. "Is it always like this?" she whispered.

"What do you mean?" he asked, his breath tickling her ear. He felt her stiffen, and then he groaned as he eased away from her so she could scoot and face him. He traced a finger over the wrinkles between her brows before kissing them away.

"What is it like for my sister?"

He froze in his movements, pulling back to meet her embarrassed gaze. "Not like this." He cupped her cheek. "I …" He swore softly. "I think you'd have to ask her."

"Did you ever visit the Boudoir?"

He nodded, his shoulders tensing as he answered her. "Aye. A few times." He waited as he saw her attempt and fail to ask a question. "I was never with your sister, Belle." He felt her relax incrementally in his arms. "I never felt like I do with you."

"What do you mean?"

He pushed away, flopping onto his back. He stared at the ceiling and shook his head. "Never, not once in my life, did I imagine having such a conversation with you." He looked at her with fond exaspera-tion. "I should have known better."

She bent her head. He tugged her to lean her head on his shoulder and played with the ends of her tangled black hair. "I went to the

Boudoir on nights I felt I was drowning in loneliness. When I thought I'd never know happiness again. And, for a moment, I didn't feel alone."

"So it helped," she whispered.

He closed his eyes. "When it was over, I always felt guilty and lonelier than when I arrived. It's why my visits were infrequent." He moved so he lay on his side and faced her. "With you, Belle"—he paused as his eyes glowed—"the loneliness doesn't return."

She smiled as she leaned forward and kissed him. "Thank you for answering my questions. I never thought to be able to speak to my husband like this." A rosy flush covered her exposed skin.

He laughed and leaned on an elbow. "What were your parents like? Did your father treat your mother well?"

Annabelle froze a moment before letting out a stuttering breath. "My father was strict. Liked to have his home and life organized. If something was out of place, we were punished."

"Punished?" He traced a finger over her shoulder.

"Slapped knuckles, no supper. Or he would forbid us from reading." She closed her eyes. "That was the worst. I loved to read and to escape to another place." She shrugged. "He thought it led to dangerous ideas and that I should be content with what I have. 'Dreams only lead to disaster.'" She shared a chagrined smile with her husband. "That was his favorite phrase."

"How sad." He kissed her softly. "An' your mother?"

"Did everything in her power to please him. Kept a tidy home. Had dinner on the table at six o'clock sharp every night. Never said a word against any of his decrees." Annabelle's unfocused gaze met her husband's worried one. "And then she died. Caught a fever."

He watched her with a fierce intensity. "And you lost your buffer from the bully." At her nod, he sighed. "What did he do?"

"If he caught me speaking with a young man, I was locked in my room for a week so that I had time to reflect on my impure thoughts. When I scorched his favorite linen shirt while ironing, he took away my clothing budget for a year. If I burned supper, I had to forego meals with him and my sister for a month." She smiled. "He thought that was a hardship. It was a reprieve."

"I would have burned every *bluidy* dinner afterward," Cailean muttered, earning a startled laugh from her. "Did he ever hit you?"

She shook her head, and she felt him relax. "He swung at me a few times when he was deep into a bottle, but his aim was terrible, and he tended to do himself more harm." She took a long inhale and met her husband's worried gaze. "I hate drink."

He nodded. "I can understand why. I can't promise I'll never have another drink again. I like my odd whiskey here and there. But I can promise you that I'll never drink to excess or threaten you."

She nodded and snuggled into his embrace. His large hands held her close against his chest, and he thought about what she had told him as she slipped back into sleep.

～

T he following morning, his head shot up, and he strode toward her at her gasp of surprise upon opening the front door. "Belle?" he asked as he grabbed her shoulders to pull her into the safety of their small cabin. He peered over her and smiled. On the doorstep sat a basket. He hefted it up and set it on the kitchen table as Annabelle shut the door.

After lifting the checkered cloth covering the basket, he grinned at his wife. "Seems Alistair was concerned we wouldn't have enough provisions and would have to come back to town earlier than we wanted." He extracted a jug of milk, a wedge of cheese, two loaves of bread, fruit, and a plate of sliced ham. "This should keep us going through tomorrow."

"If we economize!" she said with a laugh. "I've never seen someone eat like you."

He pulled her close and kissed her. "You haven't been around Ewan yet. He's worse than I am." He kissed her again, cutting short her giggle. "Come back to bed," he coaxed, tugging her in that direction.

"We were to go on a walk," she protested, arching into his touch. "I can't return to town only able to describe the inside of the cabin!"

He kissed down her neck, his hands roving over her corset-free front. "I'd think that would be a testament to a well-spent honeymoon." He groaned as she gripped his hands and held them out to their sides.

"No, Cailean. I want a walk. We can consider the rest later." He seemed mollified at her promise of *later*. She spun, grabbed her hat and walked outside. She smiled as she heard his laughter following her.

He grabbed her hand, and they walked, fingers entwined, along a small path. The air smelled of last night's rain, crisp and clean. She took a deep breath and relaxed further. "I never knew a place could be so beautiful." When her husband remained quiet, she looked at him to see his gaze distant. "What was Scotland like?"

"Wild, rough, unpopulated. A bit like here." He paused as they looked over a field thick with grassland, birds swooping and calling to each other overhead. A meadowlark sang, its song changing slightly as it continued to warble. "I'm from Skye, aye?" He didn't wait for her to acknowledge her answer. "It's an island in the Highlands and cut off from most of the world. You come to feel as though it's the only place on earth.

"My father had a croft. A small piece of land he tilled for potatoes. We raised a few animals, chickens mainly and a goat for milk." He sighed. "Wasn't much of a life but seemed like heaven to a young lad. There were hills to explore, lochs to swim in, and fish to be caught. The threat of fairies hiding in the streams, waiting to trick you into joining them in their world." He caught her staring at him with rapt attention.

"Why did you ever leave?"

"I never thought to. But the croft was small, and Father had four children." He shrugged. "I had no reason to stay."

She frowned as he began to walk again. "I've seen you with your siblings. You adore them. You had every reason to stay." Her protests silenced suddenly when she remembered what Leticia had told her. "You lost your wife."

His gaze jerked to her. "Aye. I lost my wife. I had no reason to stay."

Annabelle nodded, the spring in her step absent, and her joy in the summer day diminished. "I'm sorry she died."

He squeezed her hand. "As am I. It was twelve years ago, Belle. I'm trying to move on." He stopped underneath a large cottonwood tree. A brook trickled nearby, and the air was cooler and more humid in the shade. He cupped her face with his hands. "I know neither of us chose this marriage. It was foisted on us. I'd like to think you could be happy. With me." He leaned forward and kissed her. He smiled at her automatic response.

"We are at day two of our marriage. So far, you have succeeded."

He laughed at her impertinence and kissed her again.

CHAPTER 8

hree days after they were married, they returned to town. Annabelle sat with perfect posture as the wagon rolled to a stop in front of Cailean's house. He helped her down and ran a soothing hand over her back. "It will be fine. I promise."

"Your sister hates me," she whispered.

"But my brothers like you," he countered with a smile. "Come." He held out his hand and led her up the steps into the house.

She exhaled with relief to find it empty. After he showed her the parlor, covered in only a thin layer of dust, they peeked into the kitchen to see the rising bread on the windowsill and the stove banked. "Sorcha must be nearby if she's baking bread."

"She's probably pestering Al at the livery." He tugged at Annabelle's hand and led her upstairs. He pointed to the doors of his siblings' rooms before entering their room. "This is ours." Inside, a large window let in the summer light. White wallpaper with fragile blue flowers running through it covered the walls. A bureau sat along the wall by the door while a chest for blankets sat at the foot of the bed. Two chairs faced each other next to the window with a small table between them, a bouquet of wildflowers atop it.

"This is lovely," Annabelle breathed.

Cailean shrugged as he looked around. "The chairs are new. We can remove them if you think the room is too crowded."

She shook her head. "No, they're perfect. I like having a space that is ours." She moved into the room, her finger tracing over the wood of the hope chest before she sat in one of the chairs. "There is no privacy screen."

"I never needed one." He looked around the cramped room. "If you want one, we'll have to remove something."

She met his worried gaze. "You've seen all there is to see. I shouldn't need one." She relaxed as he sat on the chair facing her.

He reached out, his hand clasping hers. "I want you to feel at home, Belle. I want this to be *your* home. *Our* home." He leaned closer, and she canted forward to meet him.

She squealed as he picked her up and tossed her onto the bed. He levered himself over her, keeping most of his weight off her by propping himself on his elbows. He deepened the kiss, sighing with pleasure as she clasped him to her. She rucked her hands under his tucked-in shirt, tracing her fingers along his muscled back.

The door opened after a soft knock, and Cailean raised his head to see Sorcha stock-still, her light-blue eyes widened in dismay. "I beg yer pardon!"

Annabelle giggled, and Cailean smiled as he pushed himself off his wife. "Sorcha! Don't go." He leaped off the bed and grabbed his sister's arm as she spun away and out of the room. He tugged her back inside. "Thank you for making this room so comfortable for Annabelle and me."

Sorcha nodded, her gaze downcast, and cheeks reddened. "Forgive me for interrupting."

Cailean failed to fully bite back a laugh. "Next time, knock and then wait for an answer." He chucked her under her chin until she met his gaze. "No need to be embarrassed, Sorch."

"Thank you for the flowers. I couldn't feel more welcome," Annabelle said as she stood, running a hand over her skirt as she attempted to ease the wrinkles from her dress. "Cailean showed me the main areas of the house. Perhaps we could spend this afternoon together, and you could help me settle in?"

Sorcha nodded.

Annabelle smiled at her. "I saw you were baking bread. We could make a surprise treat for your brothers for tonight." She ran a hand down Cailean's arm as she slipped past him and followed Sorcha out of their room. They walked downstairs to the kitchen, and Annabelle paused as she glanced around.

Sorcha walked to the loaves of bread covered in cloth and peered underneath them, her shoulders stooping afterward. Annabelle joined her and smiled.

"You have them in the windowsill, and a cool breeze blows today. Let's set them by the stove and see if the warmth encourages the yeast to rise." They transferred the loaves to a shelf above the stove.

"I hate the kitchen," Sorcha blurted out. "No matter how long I spend in it, I will always hate it."

Annabelle chuckled. "You should be admired for your honesty." She looked at the fine embroidery on the cuff of Sorcha's dress. "I imagine you dislike the kitchen as much as I dislike needlework."

Sorcha watched her with confusion. "But everyone does needlework!"

"Yes, and every woman is *supposed* to cook." She shrugged. "Just because we are supposed to do it doesn't mean we have to like it. In fact, I'd rather barter with you—my mending of Cailean's shirts and buttons for cooking dinner."

Sorcha's light-blue eyes widened with delight. "Are ye serious?"

"Terribly so. I dread every minute of needlework. I stick myself, bleed all over the cloth, and then barely sew the button on tight enough to prevent it from falling off. It's a travesty I'm allowed near a needle." She smiled as Sorcha laughed. "I might need you to go to the store or the butcher's for me as I'll be busy most days at the bakery until four."

Sorcha sighed with happiness. "That shouldna be a problem."

Annabelle moved around the kitchen and examined the rather rudimentary cooking implements. She paused and pushed a strand of hair behind her ear before facing Sorcha. "I never meant to trap your brother into marriage." She blushed. "I know you don't have any great regard for me or for my sister, but I'm not the type of woman who would plot to embrace a man and be caught by the town's largest gossip."

Sorcha bit her lip. "I'm sorry."

Annabelle's expression remained guarded. "For what?"

"I've been horrible to ye. Said mean things about ye." She paused. "I had no right."

She nodded as Sorcha dipped her head as though in shame. "We all do and say things we aren't proud of, Sorcha. And I know I wasn't who you hoped for in a sister, who you wanted for your brother." Her gentle smile seemed to soothe Sorcha.

"I'm sorry for the mean things I've said about yer sister."

Annabelle paled. "Thank you for saying so. But I know you aren't the first, and you won't be the last." She cleared her throat. "She has chosen a difficult path, but I refuse to abandon her." She met Sorcha's startled gaze. "Just as I would think none of your brothers would abandon you or you they." She saw understanding and respect glint in Sorcha's gaze. "Come. Let's have a cup of tea while we determine what you have on hand that I can use to concoct as a surprise for tonight."

The following morning, Annabelle poked her head into the back door of the café's kitchen. She sniffed appreciatively and smiled at Irene. "I have today's bread." She held up a basket.

Irene smiled and picked up a cloth to wipe her hands. "What are you doing back so soon?" she asked as she accepted the basket. "My patrons will be mighty glad to not have to eat my feeble attempts at rolls. They each weigh as much as a brick compared to yours."

Harold walked in and shook his head at the sight of Annabelle in their kitchen. "Thought that husband of yours could keep you occupied for longer than a few days." He chortled as Annabelle flushed crimson. "You'll have to adjust to some teasing in town. Folks still can't believe you corralled the eldest MacKinnon. Nor that he looked so darned happy at his wedding."

"The dance you shared at your wedding feast has been the most discussed event the past few days in the café," Irene said with a shake of her head. "Seems folks can't believe the man chose to wed the baker."

Annabelle sighed and sat on her customary perch by the kitchen table. "You mean, they can't reconcile themselves with the fact he married a woman whose sister works at the Boudoir."

Harold nodded. "That too. Although there were plenty of grumbles by the men in here. Many thought they should have challenged Cailean for that dance with you at the Founders' Celebration, and then they would have had a chance to marry you instead of him."

Irene shot her a knowing glance. "If any of them had sense, they'd have seen the attraction between the two of you from the day you arrived." She frowned as Annabelle bent her head and studied her hands. "Are you all right, Miss Annabelle?"

"Of course. I just wish the townsfolk would let us be so we could find our way without their meddling." She frowned as Harold snorted. "I know that will never happen."

Harold sobered. "As long as he treats you well, Miss Annabelle"—he relaxed when she smiled and nodded—"then that's as it should be. Although I don't know why you continue to work at the bakery."

Irene threw her towel at her husband. "She enjoys it. And, if he has any sense, he'll be thankful for the extra income. Besides, the townsfolk wouldn't know what to do without her delicious treats."

Annabelle rose. "I must return to the bakery. I have to open soon, and I don't want the bread in the oven to burn. I'll see you later this afternoon!" She smiled as she slipped out the door.

Annabelle carried a basket laden with bread, cookies, and sweet rolls. She smiled to those she passed as she made her way to the back door of the Boudoir while Leticia worked the storefront at the bakery. It was early afternoon, and the cases were nearly sold out as customers had lined up after her absence. However, the women at the Boudoir preferred to breakfast after noon, so Annabelle had begun to deliver their basket of goods after the morning rush and when the baking was done for the day. The back door opened with alacrity at her approach, and she smiled at the Madam.

"You have some nerve depriving your customers of your services for four days," she snapped as Annabelle moved past her into the kitchen. Dilapidated cupboards with chipped white paint clung to the walls, while rickety benches sat along a battered oak trestle table.

Annabelle set the basket on the table and smiled again at the Madam. "You knew I was to be away for my wedding day and the few days of my honeymoon. Although I'm pleased my customers appreciate my pastries and breads." She met the Madam's stare evenly.

The Madam looked her up and down, her eyes squinting as though seeing hidden aspects of Annabelle. "Seems that man knows his way around a woman from the look of pleasure in your eyes."

"I'd thank you to refrain from speaking about my husband in such a manner." She stiffened at the Madam's cackling laughter, her hands gripped in the folds of her skirt.

"What else should we do except gossip about men and their inabilities?" She failed in her attempt to hide her envy. "Few have the prowess they believe."

Annabelle blushed and glared at the Madam.

"If you have difficulties with your husband, you would still be welcomed here. I wouldn't earn as great a price the first time a man bid on you and won the right to you, but it would still be quite a profitable evening."

"You shouldn't speak to my sister in such a way," Fidelia said from the doorway. She wore a casual day dress that covered her bosom and legs. She wore no makeup, and her hair was loosely tied back with a light green ribbon. "She is a married woman with a profession and deserves your respect."

The Madam spun on Fidelia and glared at her. "I am a woman with a profession, and I imagine I do quite a bit better than your sister." She took a deep breath, her natural blush overpowering her already rouged cheeks. "I believe she understands I meant no disrespect and only suggested the need for options."

The Madam moved toward the basket, but Annabelle grabbed the handle and tugged it next to her on the table. She shook her head. "As you are such a successful businesswoman, I'd prefer payment on delivery from now on, rather than weekly as we had negotiated last month. Supplies are becoming increasingly expensive."

The Madam glared at Annabelle before she nodded and stormed from the room.

Fidelia heaved out a sigh as she eased into the kitchen area. "You're smart to get payment now. She's being hounded about unpaid liquor bills." Fidelia grabbed a sweet bun and bit into it. "Heaven."

Annabelle smiled at her sister's whispered word. "Can you walk with me a few moments? I know you aren't on duty again until the evening." She clamped her mouth shut as the Madam stormed in, her glare intensifying when she saw Fidelia already eating a bun.

As Annabelle accepted the money, she said, "I want to ensure you understand that I expect payment with each delivery every day, except for Sundays when the bakery is closed."

"My girls work seven days a week. I fail to understand why you need a day off." The Madam glared at her.

Annabelle shrugged. "I run a different business, and I take one day a week for myself and my family." She tucked the money into a pocket of her apron. She tilted her head toward the door, and her sister blinked her agreement.

When they were outside, away from the Boudoir and walking in the opposite direction of town and her bakery, Annabelle took a deep breath of the pine forest air. "How are you, Dee?" The childhood nickname slipped out.

"No different than how I was before you married." She glared at a man who walked past them, staring at the two sisters with a lascivious glint in his eyes. "The Madam will be angry that I failed to encourage him."

"The Madam is a nasty woman." Annabelle shuddered. "I wouldn't sell her any goods except it would deprive you of them." She met her sister's stare. "I'd sell out most days without bringing her a basket of goods. And probably make a little more than I do from selling to her."

"Don't do me any favors."

Annabelle stiffened at the harsh tone of her sister's voice. "Dee, can't you see I want us to be sisters again? I dream of a time when you're free of this profession. When you come to dinner at my home, and I go to yours."

Her sister stared at her with indulgent condescension. "I am what I am, Anna. A whore." She chortled as Annabelle bristled at the word. "Get used to it. I have."

Annabelle gripped her sister's arm as she turned to march away. "I refuse to believe that. I know you. I know who you were. You wanted more from life than this."

Fidelia's gaze filled with anguish, regret, and then loathing. "This is life, Anna. Grow up. This is what comes of daring to dream too big. Just as Father said."

"I'm sorry," Annabelle whispered. "I'm sorry I didn't support you all those years ago. I should have given you the money I had saved."

"Nothing you could have given me could have prevented what happened. Except your support. If I'd known I had a place to return to … that I would have been welcomed by you …" She bit her lip and shook her head before she freed her arm, marching back to return to the Boudoir.

Cailean buried his nose in his wife's nape, her hair spilling over his face as he inhaled her scent. One arm was slung over her belly, and he tugged her back tighter against his chest. He mumbled his pleasure as he emerged from a restful slumber. "I love Sundays," he whispered, his voice gravelly from sleep. He kissed her skin and sighed as he fought tumbling back into sleep.

He felt her relax in his arms at his touch and kissed her nape again.

"What's the matter, Belle? You've been upset since yesterday, but, by the time I came to bed last night, you were asleep."

She shivered in his arms, and he pushed himself up on his elbow, easing her backward so he could see her face. He frowned when he saw tears coursing down her cheeks. "Have I upset you?" He traced away her tears with soft swipes of his fingers.

"No." She pushed him so he lay on his back and rested her head on his shoulder, her erratic breaths calming as he stroked a hand down her back. "I didn't want to ruin our morning together. We only have the one morning a week where I wake up in your arms."

He chuckled. "You wake every morning in my arms. I'm the one dead to the world when you sneak out to start baking your breads." He played with her hair as he waited for her to speak.

"I had another run-in with my sister yesterday." She rubbed her face against his chest before twisting to prop herself on an elbow to meet his curious gaze. "First I saw the Madam, and she was as insulting as ever."

Cailean's gaze darkened, but he held his tongue.

She smiled as she traced fingers over his pursed lips. "Thank you for not demanding I cease bringing my baked goods to the Boudoir." Her smile lit her eyes, and he grinned at her as he cupped her cheek.

"I promise that I'll try not to be an overbearing husband, Belle. There will be times when I will speak out. Especially when I feel a need to protect you." His gaze softened as she leaned into his touch. "I imagine you bring goods to the Boudoir solely for your sister?"

Annabelle nodded. "And she defended me again yesterday against the vile things the Madam said. The Madam seems to derive great pleasure in taunting me with having to work someday at the Boudoir."

She shivered in disgust as Cailean nodded his head in encouragement for her to share her concerns. He spoke gently. "You know you'll never work there. You're one of us now, Belle. If something were to happen to me, my brothers would care for you." He frowned as she flushed. "Why do her words affect you so?"

Annabelle spoke, her words emerging haltingly. "Before, when she'd taunt me, I was affronted on principle. I didn't truly know what she meant." She turned her head into his palm as she scrubbed away an errant tear. "Now, now after you ..." She looked into his eyes shining with dedication and warmth. "Now I can't imagine how Fidelia allows any man she doesn't care for to touch her like this."

"She's done what she must to survive, Belle."

She nodded. "I'm proud of her ability to survive. She had no one. But there won't be a day of my life that I'm not ashamed I didn't do something to aid her." She closed her eyes. "That she didn't feel she could ask her own sister for help after Aaron died."

She let out a long, stuttering breath. "After I left the Boudoir yesterday, Fidelia and I went on a walk. I wanted to explain to her again how sorry I was. That I'd been an innocent fool, trapped by societal conventions and expectations. That I regret every day not supporting her. That I understand now why she'd run away, why the lure of Aaron's love was so strong."

Cailean's touch gentled even further as he saw the despair in his wife's eyes. "Some hurts are too deep to be soothed by a mere apology."

"What else can I do?" She swiped at her eyes. "I've tried for the past month to make amends, and it's done more harm than good."

"Continue to show her that you accept her as your sister, regardless of her ... profession. That you want to support her now however you can." He sighed. "She needs more than words from you, Belle. When she visits you, she slinks in and out of your back door. When you go on walks, you walk out of town, rather than boldly down the boardwalk." He raised her hand and kissed her palm. "Your actions don't match your words, for they say you're ashamed."

She sat as though struck dumb. "I never meant ... I thought ..." She shook her head. "All I seem to do is make things worse." She scooted away from him as though to rise from bed, and he grabbed her shoulder and eased her to her back, keeping a firm grip on her arms as he leaned over her.

"No. Ignoring her, never seeking her out would have been much worse. You're doing the best you can, Belle. Let me help you. You're not alone anymore." He kissed her tenderly on her brow, cheek, and then finally lips. He eased away and met her worried gaze before she stared at a place over his shoulder as though considering how to remedy her relationship with her sister.

"Have her to dinner here with us."

Her gaze shot to his and shook her head. "You don't want her near Sorcha."

"I want you happy." He leaned forward and kissed her before a teasing smile flirted with his lips. "A wise woman once told me that it's not a catching disease. And I know you'd like your sister by your side some Sunday dinner. I'd want my family with me if they weren't already here."

"Thank you, husband," she whispered. She turned her face to kiss his shoulder. "Thank you for wanting to share my burdens."

"Always, my Belle," he murmured as he leaned forward, kissing her jaw and neck as his hips pressed into hers. "And to share the pleasure as well."

She nodded as she blushed, arched up, and kissed him. He groaned, releasing her arms so she could snake them around his neck. "Ignore the livery for a little while longer. Make love with me," she gasped as he eased her nightgown up and tossed it to the floor.

"Alistair will understand," he rasped as he peppered her neck with kisses. "I'll make it up to him when he weds Leticia."

She giggled and forgot about her sister, Alistair, and the outside world.

Sorcha slammed a cast-iron pot onto the stove. When that failed to alleviate her frustration, she kicked the stove and then grunted as she stubbed her toe. She hopped a few times in an attempt to relieve the pain.

"Serves ye right," Ewan said with a chuckle as he leaned against the doorjamb that led into the kitchen and dining area.

"Don't ye dare laugh at me!" Sorcha swirled to face him, brandishing a wooden spoon and waving it in his direction.

"I don't know why ye're so upset. We're having Sunday dinner like we always do, and Annabelle's sister is coming this time." He shrugged.

"Even ye can't be that nonchalant about having one of the Boudoir's finest present at our table." She glared at her youngest brother as he shrugged again.

He sidled into the room, staying on the far side of the dining room table so as to remain out of her reach and the spoon's thwacking distance.

"I never expected the likes of her would be in our house."

"Ye've made yer peace with Annabelle now that ye no longer have to bake bread and she cooks most nights—even after all that time on her feet baking at her shop." He studied his sister as he hitched a hip onto a windowsill. "It seems to me ye've taken to her company better than to almost any woman ye've ever known."

Sorcha glared at him as she turned toward the stove and stirred the pot of stew. "Annabelle has been patient as I've adjusted to her living here. And I like not having to cook."

Ewan nodded. "Then I'd think ye could repay her kindness by treating her sister civilly. It's what Mother would have wanted ye to do."

Sorcha's shoulders tightened again at the mention of their mother. "Don't speak to me of what she would or wouldna like." She tapped the wooden spoon and took a deep breath. "It's because of how Mother was that I'm determined to treat Annabelle's sister well."

Ewan froze as he studied his sister, but the moment was lost as Alistair, Leticia, and Hortence burst into the room. Alistair entertained Hortence while Leticia cut up a loaf of bread on the oak sideboard. Ewan filled a pitcher of water and then filled glasses at the round table set for eight.

A bright gingham tablecloth covered the table with a vase of wildflowers in the center. He watched as Sorcha faded to the back of the family gathering as Annabelle, Cailean, and Fidelia entered. Annabelle had looped her arm through her sister's, and Cailean stood behind the two women, preventing an easy escape by Fidelia.

"Welcome," Ewan boomed as the room quieted at their arrival. He moved forward and shook Fidelia's hand. "It's wonderful to meet ye at last." His ears were tinged a bright red as everyone ignored the fact he had already met her numerous times at the Boudoir.

"A pleasure, I'm sure," she murmured, her blue eyes gleaming with irony. Fidelia wore her most demure dress with a shawl covering her shoulders and bosom. Her face was freshly scrubbed, and she wore no scent. Without the trappings of her profession, she appeared years younger, and her eyes had lost the cynical squint she had perfected.

Alistair chuckled and reached out his hand. "I'm Alistair. And this is my Leticia and her daughter, Hortence. We're to marry next summer."

"God willing," Fidelia whispered. "Lovely to meet you."

"I'm Sorcha." She stood by the stove, the wooden spoon gripped in her hands. She finally nodded her welcome to Annabelle's sister.

"Thank you for welcoming me," Fidelia said, her gaze on Sorcha. "What you have prepared smells delicious."

"Well, Anna—" Sorcha began but was cut off by her sister-in-law.

"Sorcha has become a wonderful cook in the past few months. Although I believe her real talent lies in embroidery." Annabelle squeezed her sister's arm in encouragement and smiled at Sorcha as Annabelle coaxed her sister toward the table set for Sunday dinner.

After they were settled, and the food had been served, the discussion turned to the potential for statehood for Montana.

"I hope it occurs soon. Montana needs to have a voice in Congress and to be seen as something other than a backwater place filled with vigilantes, cowboys, and Indians," Leticia said.

"I agree. We are a diverse group, and it would be good to see our needs represented," Cailean said.

"However, as long as Congress remains split between the Democrats in the House and the Republicans in the Senate, I doubt they will agree for us to become a state. They don't want any states to enter that might alter the balance of control," Alistair said.

"It's shortsighted," Ewan argued. "No state remains affiliated with one party forever. Besides, we need to have the opportunity to represent ourselves in Congress. And raise our own taxes. We should be able to tax the railroad, but we can't as a territory."

"And vote for our own judges, rather than wait for Congress to send us a man who knows nothing about us," Leticia said.

"Well, we'll have to hope Congress will grant us statehood if the voters agree in November to the state constitution drafted in January. But I see no reason for it to change anytime soon." Cailean sighed as he stretched out his legs and played with Annabelle's hand.

"What do you think, Fidelia?" Alistair asked.

She sat, picking at her food as the family talked around her. "I don't have an opinion. Why should I?"

Leticia laughed. "The question is, why shouldn't you? You live here. You … work here. You have as great a right to be interested in what will happen and how it will affect you."

"Few would care about those who live in the shadows," Fidelia whispered.

After a moment of uncomfortable silence, Ewan smirked at Cailean. "Ye were smart to avoid Mrs. Jameson at the Fourth of July party a few weeks ago, Cail. She's angrier than a beehive that ye married Anna and are happy with her."

Cailean rolled his eyes. "That woman was too busy searching for another man for her daughter to notice us." He looked at Ewan. "I'd be careful."

Ewan laughed. "Why do ye think I spend all the time at the Boudoir? I dinna want the mothers in the town to get notions I'm the marryin' kind." He laughed harder when Fidelia snorted in disgust.

Everyone at the table became silent a moment before the conversation moved to the latest gossip about Tommy Twothumbs nearly blowing himself up with a stick of dynamite in the Obsidian mining camp up in the mountains. "I can't believe he didna use a longer fuse," Ewan marveled. "Almost destroyed his nickname."

"I think he lived up to it. *Bluidy* idiot coulda killed himself and five others with his incompetence," Alistair said with a shake of his head.

"I'm sure it's not because of his clumsiness this time. It's because he's as miserly as he is all thumbs." Annabelle smiled as they groaned at her poor pun. "The man's always going on about costs. I hear him complaining when I'm talking with Tobias." She rolled her eyes.

"That must be unpleasant," Fidelia murmured. "Most things to do with that man are."

The adults around the table laughed.

"If you mean Tobias," Annabelle said, "I agree. I'm thankful Cailean negotiated a better price for my supplies. Tobias wasn't pleased, but it's a perk of being a married woman." Annabelle shared a smile with her husband.

"The only good thing to come out of the explosion is the daft man managed to discover a new vein of silver. Used twice as much dynamite as he needed and blew the area to smithereens." Alistair sighed as he pushed away his plate. "Now his main problem, other than losing the tip of one of his fingers, is keeping ahold of his claim."

They laughed again.

"I can just see the man. Coming into town in a new suit with his chest puffed out." Leticia sighed. "Some men will never learn." She shook her head as Alistair took her hand and gave it a gentle squeeze.

After dinner, the men moved to the porch to chat and sip on coffee while the women cleaned up. "I'm trying to convince them that, on Sundays, they should clean as we cooked, but I'm havin' no success," Sorcha grumbled.

Annabelle laughed, her arms elbow deep in sudsy water. "It's faster with all of us working together."

Leticia handed a plate to Fidelia to stack on the table to be put away. "How did you end up in Bear Grass Springs?"

Fidelia stared at her, dumbstruck a moment, and then accepted another plate from her. "The Madam moved from our previous town when the customers began to leave as the mine played out. She heard about this place and moved us here."

Sorcha frowned as she studied Annabelle's sister. "Why do what ye do? Ye're smart and pretty." She saw a flash of anger and disappointment in Fidelia's eyes that were quickly masked by indifference.

"What else is a fallen woman to do? I had no man, no family to protect me or to offer aid. I lacked the references to become a schoolteacher." She squinted as she saw Leticia flush. "I thank you for dinner. I must return to the Boudoir to prepare for this evening." She shared a long look with Annabelle before she slipped outside through the front door, avoiding the men outside at the back door.

"I'm sorry, Anna. I never meant to make her go," Sorcha whispered. She wrung a dish towel in her agitation. "I wanted to understand."

Annabelle gave a small pat to her sister-in-law's shoulder and attempted a smile. "I never thought she'd remain with us for as long as she did today, so I am thankful for the time I had with her. And she told you more in a few moments of questions than I'd learned after months in town."

Cailean entered the kitchen and frowned. "Where's Fidelia?" When the women gave a collective shrug, he sighed. "Perhaps she'll remain long enough next time to eat your delicious dessert." He kissed Annabelle on the forehead and squeezed Sorcha's shoulder. "Thank you for welcoming her."

Sorcha fought tears and repeated, "I never meant to make her go." At Cailean's confused stare, she whispered, "I asked her why she does what she does when she's smart and pretty."

Cailean sighed and pinched the bridge of his nose. "Never judge a person and their decisions, Sorch. Hunger, desperation, and the desire for perceived safety are powerful motivators. I imagine she preferred the protection a place like the Boudoir could provide, rather than attempting to live alone."

Annabelle took a shaky breath and nodded. "I believe Sorcha was curious. But my sister is sensitive and sees judgment where there was none. Don't worry, Sorcha. She'll come back, and she'll realize our curiosity is merely a way to know her better." She leaned into Cailean's side a moment before she extracted the huckleberry pie she had made to celebrate her sister's visit.

"I fear she's missed the best part of the meal," Ewan said as he handed out small slices of the pie.

Annabelle smiled and deftly changed the topic. "I have so many huckleberries in my icebox that I barely have room for milk and butter. I fear you will be sick of huckleberries by the time I'm finished using them in my baked goods."

Cailean took a bite of the pie and closed his eyes. "Not possible. This is even better than chocolate." He smiled at Annabelle as she beamed with pleasure.

Alistair and Ewan laughed while Sorcha giggled. Cailean winked at Annabelle and gobbled down his pie.

CHAPTER 9

A few weeks later in early August, Ewan sat on a large wood stump, a piece of straw between his teeth as he watched Alistair work. He smiled as his brother shot a glare in his direction.

"Ye could help. Cail is detained again with his bride." Alistair grunted as he pushed Ewan off the stump and picked up hay to spread over the floor of the stall. Ewan leaned against the wall before laughing and helping his brother muck out and clean the stall.

"Seems Cail is taken with Annabelle," Ewan said as he moved to the next stall.

"If he were any more taken, they'd be a pair of those twins that move around together." He nodded when Ewan's confused expression cleared.

"The twin brothers from Siam, Chang and Eng, who were born joined together?" Ewan asked.

"Aye."

When Cailean burst into the barn, Ewan leaned on the edge of his shovel. Cail hefted a wheelbarrow to push outside and smiled appreciatively at Ewan .

"Seems Sundays do ye good," Ewan teased.

Cailean met the amused stares of his brothers. "Don't start. I've already told Annabelle that I'll have to make up this time after Alistair marries."

Alistair puffed out his chest and nodded. "Aye, that ye will. I've waited long enough for my bride."

Ewan laughed. "An' Anna will have Hortence for company?"

Alistair groaned. "With my luck, I'll still be to work on time." He heaved his pitchfork into a pile of hay and sat down.

"Is Fidelia coming for dinner today?" Ewan asked as he swiped at the sweat on his brow. He loaded up the now-empty wheelbarrow.

Cailean shook his head and leaned against a post. "She wrote Belle a note yesterday, saying she felt under the weather." He frowned. "Belle's worried it means someone mistreated her, and Fidelia doesn't want us to see the bruises."

Ewan frowned. "I'll go to the Boudoir tonight to ensure she's all right." Cailean nodded his thanks.

Alistair rose and crooned to one of the horses as he moved it into the mucked-out stall Ewan had just readied. Alistair ran a hand down its nose and earned a whinny of approval.

They worked in harmonious silence for a while before taking a break. "You seem distracted, Cail." His eldest brother's attempt at relaxed geniality was forced.

Ewan perked up at Alistair's comment and nodded. "What's the matter, Cail? I thought your lovely bride soothed all your restless worries."

He growled and heaved his shovel against a far wall, earning a nicker of disapproval from the horses. "I ran into that busybody yesterday. Mrs. Jameson."

Ewan and Alistair groaned. "I hope ye stayed downwind. Now that it's summer an' she doesna believe in washin' herself, never mind her clothes ..." Ewan sniffed as though attempting to clear his sinuses of the smell.

Cailean chortled out a laugh. "I fear many think I stink worse than she does due to working in the livery."

"Ye bathe daily," Alistair grumbled. "There's no comparison." He watched his brother and waited, setting aside a bridle he'd intended to repair and pulled out another large piece of wood to sit on so that he sat across from Cailean. Ewan plopped down next to him.

"The old chatterbox said she couldna wait for the bairn to be born." He cleared his throat. "Assumed it would be afore our nine-month anniversary. It's only early August now! We've not even been married two months yet."

"The miserly biddy musta placed a bet on it," Ewan said, earning a snicker from Alistair.

Alistair raised an eyebrow as he watched his somber eldest brother. "There are worse things than having the town believe ye anticipated yer vows."

"Aye," Cailean whispered. "Like Belle pregnant with our child." He shook his head and ran a shaking hand through his brown hair.

"Ye've told her how ye feel?" Alistair asked. When Cailean shrugged, Alistair groaned and fell backward to lean against a stall's wall. "Ye canna carry on as ye have with a woman—never mind yer wife—and not let her ken how ye feel."

"She knows I can't care for her. Not as she might expect."

Ewan opened and closed his mouth a few times and then shook his head. "Are ye as daft as a donkey?" He kicked his brother in the leg. "Ye have a fine woman. A woman who's forgiven yer sister for her meanness and spite, who appears to care for ye deeply, and who brings ye joy," he sputtered into silence.

"Why do ye cling to the past when it will never bring ye happiness?" Alistair rose and clapped a hand on Cailean's shoulder. "Ye need to consider that. Find an answer for that. And put Maggie and yer bairn to rest at last."

"How do you put ghosts to rest?" Cailean whispered.

"By not courting their company," Ewan snapped in a rare show of temper. "For years, ye've lived as a ghost yerself. Ye've lived no life at all. Finally ye have a chance again, Cail. Don't be a fool. For now, ye hurt more than yerself. Ye hurt yer wife. An' she donna deserve such treatment." He stormed off into a stall, and his grunts of discontent as he mucked out a stall resounded throughout the barn.

"Don't be Father," Alistair whispered. He squeezed Cailean's shoulder and moved to the tack room, leaving Cailean lost in thought.

~

A nnabelle sat on a stool in her kitchen, attempting to plan the week's specials. She doodled on the paper in front of her, rather than focusing on her bakery's offerings. After a moment, she sighed and dropped her head onto her crossed arms.

"Penny for your thoughts, Annabelle," Leticia said as she entered the back door. She met her friend's dispirited gaze with a frown. "What happened?"

"Ewan found out that my sister is being abused. It's why she won't come to Sunday dinner." She scrubbed at her forehead. "I don't know how to help her."

Leticia sat with a sigh. "All you can do is continue to show her that you accept her. That you love her. And hopefully that will be enough someday."

Annabelle nodded as she drew more shapes on the paper in front of her. "That doesn't seem enough somehow." She paused for a moment. "I don't know what happened with Cailean." She flushed at her statement. "Just saying those words makes me feel like a failure as a wife. We've only been married a few months!"

"I'm sure it's nothing. Alistair told me how he's never seen Cailean this happy." She frowned as her words failed to lift Annabelle's spirit.

"When did he tell you that? A few weeks ago?" At Leticia's nod, Annabelle dropped her head down again. "That's just it. He *was* happy a few weeks ago. Now it's as though everything changed." She shook her head. "I'm sorry. I shouldn't speak with you like this."

Leticia grumbled as she settled in for a chat on the stool across from her friend. "Who else would you speak with? You can't talk with Sorcha for any number of reasons. I'm your friend. I've been married. Nothing you say could shock me." When Annabelle remained silent, Leticia asked, "What changed?"

"I don't know why, but he no longer wants to touch me. And, when he does, it's as though he's battling against himself and angry that he did touch me afterward." She drew in a deep breath and exhaled slowly. "It's not like before. Not like we were first married when he seemed to take such joy in our time together."

Leticia smiled as she gripped her friend's arm. "Have you ever considered that your marriage is a great shock to him too?"

"I hate that he can shut me out so easily. I miss him, even when I'm in the same room with him. The Cailean I married isn't the man I'm living with." She scrubbed at her cheeks and pushed herself up. She glared at the page filled with doodles, rather than a list of items to bake during the week. "I hate that I have no ability to focus on anything else."

Leticia laughed. "It's a common occurrence when you are involved with a man. You'll adapt." She met Annabelle's worried gaze. "And he'll come around. His siblings know how fortunate he was to marry you. If there is a problem, they'll be on your side."

∼

The following week, Cailean stood with his arms slung atop a wooden pole of his paddock, staring at the distant mountains. His gaze was unfocused, and he barely registered the arrival of Annabelle. She handed him a cup of black coffee and waited with unexpected patience for some acknowledgment from him.

"These hills are so different from Scotland. There's a promise in these hills and mountains. And the people here are naive enough to believe in it." He took a sip of his coffee. "And yet they are similar. There's a roughness. A barrenness to the lochs and moors and hills of Skye. When the sun glints off the Cuillin Hills, they seem to shimmer as they rise into the sky, their granite peaks covered in snow, melting into the clouds, looking as though they're one with the heavens." He closed his eyes and inhaled deeply. "The scent of the sea is never far away, mingled with heather and the smell of loam."

He opened his eyes again and shook his head as though to clear it of memories of Scotland. "Thanks for the coffee." He took a deep sip before handing the cup back to her.

"I had hoped you'd stay with me in bed a little while this morning. It's our one morning together during the week."

He shook his head, never looking at her. "No. I need to help Alistair more. 'Tis unfair to expect him to do all the work."

She gripped his arm as he began to move away, dropping the coffee mug onto a soft patch of hay. "What have I done to upset you?"

He met her worried gaze with a flat stare and shook his head. "Nothing. You've done nothing, and everything is fine. 'Tis a busy season, and 'tis unfair to neglect my family and my duties."

She let go of his arm, and he slung his long frame under one of the planks in the paddock and entered, *click*ing to one of the horses inside. After the brindled horse approached him, and he had calmed him with a rub to his forelock, he turned to see his wife watching him. He met her inquisitive gaze with an implacable one, turning to again focus on his work. With another gentle *click*, he led the horse into the barn and a stall.

"Come, lad. Let's get you ready for your owner," he murmured. He entered the barn to curry the brindled horse and to find his brother Alistair. "I've a horse needin' care," he said to his brother.

Alistair studied him a long moment. "Seems he's not the only one in need." He murmured to the horse, earning a snuffle and whinny. "Ye're unfairly treating yer wife. Ye'd best confront yer demons, Cail."

Cailean snarled at his brother and turned to muck out a stall. "There's no need to."

Alistair *click*ed and made sounds to the horse that also disavowed his brother's claims. "It's been long enough."

Cailean grunted as he wheelbarrowed out a load of muck before repeating the process. Only after he'd laid down a fresh bed of hay in the stall did he pause. "I refuse to care for another."

His brother made a dismissive noise to the horse. "Right. Then tell me again why ye invited her sister to dinner? Because ye care so little about yer wife?" He looked over the horse's back as he ran a brush down its side, murmuring soft words as he worked.

"Yer croonin' would drive anyone mad," Cailean hissed.

Alistair half smiled as he continued his work but kept one eye on his restless brother. "Leticia likes my croonin' just fine." He smiled at Cailean before frowning. "Cease yer pacin'. Yer unsettlin' the horses."

Cailean swore and sat. "I can't care for her, Al."

"Whether ye can or canna doesna matter. It's whether ye allow yerself to."

"I canna lose another." He closed his eyes at his whispered words. "I canna live through it again."

Alistair gave the horse a pat and moved to sit next to his brother. "I was with ye. From the beginnin'. Travelin' around, leaving Skye. Understandin' I'd never see home again. Never see the hills turn purple from heather or the loch glint in welcome as we rambled home. I kent what it meant when we left."

Alistair sighed and looked around the barn filled with shadows. "I never hated ye for leavin'. But I wanted more than aimless wanderin'." He turned to look at his brother. "I thought ye'd be dead by now. Ye tempted fate enough. The bar brawls. The drunken nights. The reckless adventures." He sighed again as he let the memories go. "But we're here now, an' our family's together again. Ye have a chance for somethin' more."

Cailean's brow furrowed. "More?"

"Aye. More." He slapped his brother on his back and rose. "I'd think ye were smart enough to know its value."

Annabelle stood behind the counter in her bakery. She smiled as her last patron left and moved to flip the sign to Closed. She sighed as her shoulders stooped, and she tugged the curtains closed over the front windows. When she returned to the kitchen, serving trays and a few bowls remained to be washed up, but she threw her apron on the counter and moved to her small office—her former living quarters. After a moment's hesitation, she collapsed onto the cot and fell asleep within a few breaths.

She awoke with the sense of being watched. Lurching upright, she rubbed at her eyes and squinted at the figure sitting in the chair at her desk. "What are you doing here?" she asked around a huge yawn. "I thought you didn't want to spend time with me anymore."

Fidelia sat stooped over in the chair, her face pale under a thick coating of rouge. Her fingers idly played with the frayed edges of her plain cream-colored shawl. "Why are you sleeping here and not at home?"

Annabelle stretched and yawned. "I'm more tired than usual. I wanted to rest a few minutes before cleaning up and prepping for tomorrow." She glanced out the window and sighed as she saw long shadows, heralding late afternoon. "I never meant to sleep over an hour."

"Do you have anything left over?"

She shook her head regretfully. "I sold out." She rose and walked into the kitchen. "Although I have a few cookie pieces. Ones that fell apart as I took them off the tray." She scooted the bowl across the countertop to her sister, who sat on a stool across from her. "What happened to you?"

Fidelia curled into herself even further. "Nothing I didn't deserve."

Annabelle snorted. "No woman deserves a beating. I don't care what anyone believes."

Her sister raised confused eyes to meet Annabelle's righteous gaze. "But I'm a whore. I'm not worthy of such consideration."

Annabelle reached forward and clasped her sister's hand. "You're my sister. But that shouldn't matter. You're a woman. A person. And deserving of respect."

"I live in the shadows, Anna. Few care about what happens in the shadows."

Her sister squeezed her hand gently. "I have a feeling how we act in the shadows reveals our true character." Annabelle softened her voice. "What did he do to you?"

Fidelia closed her eyes in defeat. "I thought he was going to kill me this time. I've asked the Madam to refuse him access to me, but he pays her well, and she's a slave to money." Fidelia breathed deeply and winced, her breath exhaling on a stutter. "He slapped me, but that's nothing new. Then he kicked me, bruised a few ribs. I barely managed to scream loud enough for one of the new girls to hear. When she arrived, he was choking me." Fidelia fingered her neck, covered by a high-collared dress.

"Who?"

Fidelia met Annabelle's appalled gaze with deadened eyes at her sister's whispered question. "It doesn't matter. All men are the same, at some level."

Annabelle recoiled from her assertion. "I can't believe that's true." She frowned as her sister shrugged. "Why would only a new girl come to your rescue? Why wouldn't that Ezekial, who follows the Madam around like a wraith, aid you?"

"The others know never to interrupt a customer." Fidelia shrugged one shoulder. "And Zeke will only do what she tells him to do. If she were to let me die at a customer's hands, he wouldn't stop it."

"I thought such men were there to protect the women as much as the Madam," Annabelle muttered, earning a snort of surprise from her sister.

"Generally they are. And he does a lot to discourage the men's rowdiness downstairs. When we are in our cribs, we must fend for ourselves." Fidelia shuddered. "However, I think the Madam has come to see the danger in this man. She finally agreed I shouldn't have to see him anymore."

"Isn't he barred from her establishment?"

Fidelia's mouth quirked with an amused smile. "Only you would call a brothel an *establishment*. Only you would invite a whore to Sunday dinner with a respectable family." She swiped at her cheek. "No, he'll never be barred. His money is too important." She shared a grim smile with her sister. "And I know he'll be my customer again. The Madam's word isn't worth much."

Annabelle frowned as she watched her sister. "Don't go back there, Dee."

"I have nowhere else to go. I have nothing else to do." She met her sister's protestation with an angry glare. "And Ezekial would ensure I returned." She met Annabelle's horrified stare. "I don't have strong men around me, willing to defend me."

Annabelle bit her lip, uncertainty filling her if she could vow that her MacKinnon relatives would defend Fidelia.

Fidelia nodded her head as though understanding Annabelle's hesitation.

"You know I have the money set aside from Father for you," Annabelle said.

She snarled at the mention of his money. "I want nothing from him. He threw me out. Called me vile names when my only sin was to love a man." Fidelia flushed red. "My only consolation is that he is finally dead and can no longer torment you."

"Dee, use the money to free yourself."

"One day you will come to understand I will never be free. I am a whore, Anna. You will accept that, as I have. As the townsfolk have. As every man who looks at me has." She shook her head as Annabelle began to argue with her, ignoring her sister's plaintive gaze. "I'm no longer a seamstress with an impeccable reputation, even though I still sew a straight line and embroider beautiful work." She focused on her sister, and her expression sharpened. "I'll embroider something beautiful for your baby."

Annabelle froze. "My baby? What are you talking about?"

Fidelia raised a finger and traced Annabelle's cheeks. "Your skin is darker. Your hair thicker. You're napping in the afternoon. How long since your last courses?"

She flushed at her sister's frank question before furrowing her brow. "I haven't had one since before the wedding in late June, and it's early September now." She paled as she stood and inspected her image in the mirror in her office and returned immediately. "I can't be."

Her sister smiled as she shrugged. "I'd think you've done plenty to provoke this state." She laughed as her sister turned a brighter red. "From how he doted on you when I came to dinner, he'll be a good father. Treat you well. It seems you found a decent man, Anna." She watched her sister as envy flickered in her gaze. "The opposite of Father."

Annabelle nodded. "Cailean is a good man. But he's been very distant of late. Doesn't want much to do with me. Not like when we were first married." She took a deep breath and met her sister's gaze. "How do you keep a man's interest?"

Fidelia shook her head. "I know you think I have oodles of knowledge, but I'm a jaded prostitute. I'd say keep him in bed, but, if he's avoiding your bed for some reason, you need to discover why."

Anna nodded. "I think he no longer wants me."

Her sister shrugged. "Men can be fickle. But he didn't strike me as that sort of man. In all his time here in town, he only came to the Boudoir twice. The Madam despairs of him." She snorted. "Despairs of all the brothers."

Annabelle tilted her head to the side with curiosity. "I thought Alistair visited before Leticia and that Ewan still frequented." She blushed a beet red. "Forgive me. Such questions are unseemly."

"What the brothers do or don't do is not your business. I do know the youngest spends little, flirts outrageously, and leaves broken hearts with each departure." She sighed. "The Madam is considering banning him because he brings such discord among the girls."

Annabelle laughed. "How strange. He seems to turn things right in the family when the siblings are on the verge of coming to blows."

"Well, they aren't jealous women after an attractive man." Fidelia traced crumbs on her plate. "The new ones still believe a man would want to wed her, even with her chosen profession. I haven't had the heart to tell them that this is where they will be until they die."

"I refuse to believe that. For you. For women who want to leave that work." She met her sister's jaded gaze. "I know you believe me naive, but I refuse to stop dreaming for you, Fidelia, even though you've lost the ability to dream for yourself. The money is there for you when you finally dare to dream of a new life."

Her sister's eyes filled, and she rose in haste, knocking over the stool. "I must go. Take care, Anna." Before Annabelle could reply, Fidelia had vanished out the back door.

~

Cailean tapped on his sister's door and, rather than wait for her to answer, poked his head in. He stopped short when he saw the large spinning wheel in front of her and her expert movements.

While she worked, she hummed to herself—of loss and love and the beauty of Scotland—her hands moving fluidly as she eased the rough wool onto the wheel as her foot slowly pumped.

"'Tis the first time since you arrived I've seen you relaxed," he murmured. His voice broke her rhythm, and she jerked at his interruption.

She glared at him as her pace faltered, and a thicker piece of yarn formed. "What do ye want, Cailean?" She resumed her pace and refocused on her work.

"Is this what you'd rather spend your time on? Rather than cooking and cleaning for us?" He fingered the skeins of yarn filling the shelves in her room rather than books. At her silence, he sighed. "I can understand you'd like this more than looking after your brothers."

He sat on her bed and watched her graceful movements. "You learned that song from Mother. Just as you learned this skill," he said with a hint of nostalgia. "I had forgotten both."

"Mother was an exacting teacher," Sorcha said, the wheel coming to a halt. She moved away from it and picked up the basket of wool.

"Was she hard on you after I left?"

Sorcha stilled, her gaze on the rough fibers. "Not until Father died. Then she became stricter. Said I had to earn my place. That nothing was guaranteed." She raised a bitter gaze to Cailean and then frowned at his stoic expression. "Ye knew. All this time, ye've known."

He nodded at her whispered accusation. "Of course I knew. Their arguments were legendary." He shook his head with remorse. "I simply hoped you had been spared Mother's bitterness."

"She never wanted me," Sorcha whispered through tears. "I was never more than a drudge to her, to do her bidding."

Cailean made a noise deep in his throat, impossible to know if it was one of agreement or not. "She cared for ye as she could, Sorcha." His voice thickened as he saw his sister's anguish.

"But she wasna my mother." At Cailean's subtle nod of agreement, a tear tracked down her cheek. "I always wondered, since I was old enough to understand a parent's affection, why she never cared for me. I tried, as hard as is possible for a daughter to try, to earn her love."

"How did you discover the truth?" Cailean stoked a hand over his tensed thighs.

Sorcha set aside the basket and swiped at her cheeks. "When Mother died, a man came by the croft. Claimed to be my uncle, but I didna ken him. He wasna a MacKinnon nor one of Mother's people." She took a deep breath. "He was one of my real mother's brothers. Said he'd kept his distance all those years out of respect for Mother."

"Why did you believe him?" Cailean asked.

"Nothing in my life made sense until that moment. Why my own mother could barely tolerate the sight of me. Why my father cherished me. Why sorrow seemed to cling to Father. Why I didna look like my own brothers." She met his gaze. "Why did ye no' tell me?"

"You were a wee lass when I left. I would never have burdened you with it then." He clasped his hands together. "And then, when Father died, I'd been away too long. Was too far away." He closed his eyes a moment. "I'd always hoped Mother had come to care for you."

Cailean paused as an uncomfortable silence descended in the room. "I should have spoken with you when I suspected you had realized the truth. You should never have had to carry that burden yourself."

"Why do ye even care?" she whispered, her eyes tear-brightened. "I'm yer bastard sister."

He growled and gripped her hand. "No! You are my sister. In every way that matters. You were Father's daughter, and he loved you." Cailean's brown eyes lit with a fiery intensity, and he maintained her gaze. "I will not allow you to continue to distance yourself from us. You are one of us, Sorcha. You are a MacKinnon."

She shook her head as tears fell. "I'm no better than the women I disparage. Than your wife's sister," she whispered. "My own mother was a whore." Her voice broke on the word.

Cailean came off the bed to crouch in front of his sister. "No, she wasn't. She was a woman who fell in love with a man who should never have acted on his desire for her." He took a deep breath. "I asked Father about her, and he admitted he loved her. She lived in Portree, far away from us. Far from Mother and our croft." He cleared his throat. "She was a weaver. Mairi MacQueen," he whispered.

"Did ye know her?"

He closed his eyes and nodded. "Sometimes I traveled with Father. I remember him meeting your mother. She had hair that shone like fire in the sun, clear blue eyes, and a smile that would light up a room. Her brother ran the pub Father liked in Portree, and she sold her weavings there." He shrugged. "I never realized he had formed an attachment with her, but, soon after we met her, I ceased traveling with Father. He gave me more responsibilities on the croft."

Sorcha crumpled forward and fell against her brother's strong shoulders as she cried.

"It's all right, Sorcha. *Shh. Shh* ..." He patted her back and let her cry.

"Why did she no' want me? Her brother only said it was best I lived with Father and his wife," she whispered. "Her brother refused to have me meet the other family who lived on Skye. Said he shouldn't acknowledge me."

"She died. Took a fever after your birth," Cailean murmured. "Her family threw her out when they realized she was pregnant out of wedlock and refused to take you. When Father realized you were destined for the orphanage, he went for you. And lived with Mother's wrath every day for the rest of his life."

He stroked a hand over the back of her head. "You have to understand your uncle was acting against his family's wishes to see you. To meet you." Cailean waited until she nodded her head in agreement.

"How do you know all this?"

He stroked a hand down her back, murmuring soothing words as she cried. "I was with Father when he went for you. I saw his fear when he thought you lost to him and then his joy when he found you." He kissed her head. "Father loved you, Sorcha."

She clung to Cailean as her sobs eased. "I'm angry and bitter and sad," she whispered.

He tilted her head up so her gaze could meet his. "I know you are. But don't allow the injustices you perceived were done against you to turn you against those who would help you." He met her mutinous stare. "Against those who would befriend you." He brushed away her tears with his thumbs. "Against those who love you."

"I want to hate yer wife." She pulled out a handkerchief and swiped at her nose. "She didna become bitter and angry, even though her father tore apart her family. How can she remain optimistic amid all she's faced?"

Cailean squeezed his sister's shoulders. "That's no reason to dislike her. That's a reason to admire her. And to try to emulate her." He paused. "I'm sorry you had to bear the brunt of Mother's years of disappointment." His gaze sobered further as he watched his sister. "She allowed her bitterness at injustices against her to taint her future. Don't be like her. Be like Father. Like your mother. Grasp the joys. Live a full life. It's what Mairi would have wanted for you." He pulled her close as she shuddered out another sob.

Annabelle leaned against the side of the settee in the parlor, half asleep as she awaited her husband's arrival. One window was cracked open, and she could hear mothers calling for their children to come in for dinner, while the scent of woodsmoke and crisp fall air seeped into the room. She shivered and tugged a blanket over her while her mind replayed the scene with her sister and then her appointment with the town doctor after she left her bakery.

She turned her face into her husband's soft touch and then curled into his arms when he sat next to her on the sofa. "Cailean," she whispered.

"My Belle," he murmured, kissing her on her forehead. "I think you need to consider working less hours or hiring more help. You're too tired."

She pushed against him as she struggled awake. She sat with her elbows perched on his chest and her face leaning toward his. "Why are you worried about me now, when you've avoided me for weeks?"

He smiled as he stroked a finger down her cheek. "I've missed you. I've been a fool." He kissed her softly, and she leaned into him.

She met his smile. "I've missed you too."

His gaze sharpened. "You seem inordinately pleased with yourself, Belle. Did you outsmart Tobias today?"

She laughed as she gripped Cailean's hand. "No. I'm not tired due to work. I'm tired because I'm to have our child." She smiled at him as a wondrous joy filled her. "I saw the doctor today, and he confirmed my suspicions."

She frowned as he froze beneath her before pushing her off him. "Cailean?" She turned to watch his erratic movements as he rose and paced around the parlor. "I know we never talked about children. But, with what we've been doing, I assumed you wanted children as much as I do."

"Idiot!" He tugged at the hair at the back of his scalp. "Imbecile!" He kicked at a chair leg. At her whispering his name again, he spun to face her. "Do you know why I never spoke to you of children?" His panting breaths and wild gaze killed her wondrous joy. "'Tis because I never wanted a child. Never wanted to go through that hell again."

"*Again?*" She swiped at her cheeks as he stared at her with dawning horror.

"Ye'll die just like her." He shook his head and gazed out the front window, ignoring her.

"I'm nothing like her! I'm my own person. I'm strong. We'll have a strong baby." She leaped forward, tugging at his arm to turn him to face her. "Please, Cailean."

"I dinna want this," he said, shaking his head. "Not again."

"I don't understand why you can't try," Annabelle whispered, her voice breaking on the word *try*. She swiped at her cheeks and bravely met Cailean's stony gaze. "I … I love you."

"I've never wanted nor sought yer love. An' I certainly dinna love ye." His words were thickened by his Scottish brogue. "Dinna blame me for no' returnin' unwanted sentiments."

"Cailean," Annabelle breathed. She held a hand to her heart and shuddered. "Please."

"I swore … I swore I'd never love again. I keep my vows." His cold gaze raked over her. "How could ye ever think ye could compare to my Maggie?"

Annabelle jerked back as though he'd struck her, the faint hope in her eyes extinguished by his words. "I … of course. How foolish of me." She spun away and ran upstairs to the room they shared.

His boots *thunk*ed with his heavy steps into the kitchen area, and he glared at his siblings. "I'd thank ye not to spread gossip about what ye overheard."

"Ye're a damn fool, Cail," Alistair snapped. "How could ye treat yer wife like that?"

"When I want yer advice, I'll ask for it." He slammed the back door shut behind him and stood on the rear porch, shrugging his shoulders as he tried to loosen the tension from them. He took deep breaths and attempted to focus on the early evening sounds of birds chirping as they settled for the night. Instead, all he heard were Maggie's tortured screams. Her cries for him to help her. Her whimpers to let her die. He gripped the porch railing as he faltered, barely remaining on his feet.

At the soft touch to his back, he growled as he spun to face his sister.

"No amount of groveling can take away the words ye just spoke to yer wife," Sorcha whispered. "Why were ye mean?" She met his wild, trapped gaze. "Ye know ye love her. Ye know ye'll love yer bairn."

"I can't. I won't," he rasped, as though the words were torn from his chest. He stared at the nearby trees, softly swaying in a gentle evening breeze. "Not when they'll die too."

"Maggie was like an aunt to me," Sorcha continued in her soft voice. "I never thought another could take her place. Never wanted to give another the chance." She gripped her brother's arm and tugged him to face her. "Yer Annabelle's special. Ye know that. Ye must accept it."

"I refuse to lose her too," he choked out as he bent forward and dropped his head into the crook of his sister's shoulder.

She stroked his back, holding him close as he shuddered. "Ye daft man. Don't ye realize? Ye just did."

CHAPTER 10

*A*nnabelle slipped into her bakery and moved to the back rooms. Although her living space had become more of an office for her since her marriage, the area retained the small cot for the times she had a chance to take a catnap between baking and opening. She sank onto it and fought tears. Her husband's voice rang in her ears, and she hugged her belly. "What am I to do?" she whispered to herself. She collapsed to her side, as she lost her battle, and sobs burst forth.

After his shattering comments, she had packed enough items to escape his house. "*His* house, never *ours*," she whispered to herself. She lay on her side, her head pillowed on one of her arms, and contemplated her future. When her thoughts only became more muddled as she replayed what had occurred, she closed her eyes and prayed for sleep. But this evening's conversation with her husband kept her up most of the night.

She woke with a start a few hours later. She stretched with a loud groan, lit an oil lamp, and checked the time on her small watch. She arched her back again to wake herself up as it was almost time to start preparing her breads for the morning rush. She washed and readied for the day, changing into a simple sky-blue dress. After pulling her hair in a tight bun, she emerged from the back room and began the process of measuring her ingredients.

She relished the monotony of the work that required just enough concentration that her mind couldn't wander but not so much that she had to fear harming herself or others if she stood staring into space a moment or two. After one such instance, she shook herself and commanded herself to focus on her work at hand, not the devastating words from the previous night.

As the bread rose, she worked on her special of the day, snickerdoodle cookies.

When her first customer of the day arrived, she was busy stocking the shelves. She froze a moment as she watched Sorcha stroll into the bakery before Annabelle forced herself to continue with her activity. "Please let me know if there is anything you'd wish to purchase."

"I don't want to purchase anything. Let me help," Sorcha said. "Ye've need of help now that Leticia has returned to teaching."

"Cailean won't like you being here, Sorcha." Annabelle continued stocking the shelves as her sister-in-law shucked her coat and moved to the back room. She frowned when Sorcha returned, having found an apron to cover her dress.

"Teach me the prices so I don't beggar ye or bleed yer customers dry." She waited for Annabelle to speak, Sorcha's eyes glimmering with triumph when Annabelle named each item and its price.

"Are there any special prices? Like buy two, get one half off? Or buy twelve cookies, get another free?"

"The business has been brisk. I haven't needed to resort to such tactics yet. I may as winter approaches." She rose and had Sorcha repeat back the names and prices. "Thank you, Sorcha. It's been a struggle without Leticia."

Sorcha watched her intently. "Ye aren't alone, Annabelle. Ye're a MacKinnon now. An' we take care of our own." She frowned as Annabelle snorted and then fought a sob. "He'll come around," Sorcha soothed.

Annabelle shook her head and sniffled. "I must see to the rest of the orders and baking for the day. If you need me ..." She waved to the back.

Sorcha looked to the front and smiled broadly at the first customer as Annabelle slipped away.

Three hours later, Sorcha poked her head in the back. "Do ye have more of everything? We're about out."

Annabelle frowned. "It's only just past noon. We can't have sold out already."

Sorcha smiled. "I sweet-talked most into buying extra." She winked at Annabelle. "There is little but one cookie left."

Annabelle looked at what she had in the back and shook her head. "What I have here is for the café, restaurant, and Boudoir."

"I thought ye already brought food to the café and hotel," Sorcha said.

"I bring them by breakfast and lunch rolls before I open. These are for dinner." She sighed as she looked around. "If you are to continue to help me, I'll need another baker!"

Sorcha pushed Annabelle onto a stool. "Sit down afore ye fall down. I've never seen ye look so tired before."

Annabelle shrugged.

"Let me make these deliveries. Tell me how much they should pay ye, and I'll collect what they owe ye." She memorized what Annabelle said and lifted two baskets: one for the hotel and the other for the café. "I'll come back for the one for the Boudoir."

"You can't go there!" Annabelle gasped. "Cailean would never forgive me for allowing you to be exposed to the Madam."

Sorcha scoffed. "He didna mind yer sister coming around, and I agree with him. An' he doesna forbid Ewan from going there." She shrugged. "It's midday. I'm working with ye, and I have goods that need delivery. He has no right to complain."

Annabelle groaned. "He will. Make no mistake."

Sorcha smiled. "Good. As long as ye rest. Ye look awful, Anna."

Annabelle nodded. "I feel awful. And I hate every woman who said that pregnancy was a breeze." She smiled at Sorcha as her sister-in-law carried the two baskets and made her way out the back door.

Annabelle barely made it to her cot before she collapsed and fell into a fitful sleep, overcome by exhaustion.

~

Cailean stood stock-still in his bedroom and closed his eyes. He breathed deeply, the hint of almond in the air. His gaze roved the room, intent to discover something missing. He ripped open dresser drawers and then the closet, unable to discern if they were emptier than last week. He strode downstairs and into the parlor. "Sorcha, have you seen Annabelle?"

Sorcha raised an eyebrow as she looked at her brother. "Aye. Every day at her bakery. She's lookin' about as poor as ye, although ye have the misfortune of that beard." She focused on her needlework and ignored her brother's growl of frustration.

"Was she here in this house?" he demanded.

His sister raised an eyebrow at him. "I don't know why ye'd care. But, aye, she was. Earlier this afternoon, when she knew ye'd be busy at the livery. She came by for a few more of her things."

"If she refuses to live here, she is not to enter our room," Cailean snapped.

"Ye're bein' unreasonable." Sorcha's eyes flared with anger. "She has every right to come for a few of her clothes, an' I refuse to bar her entrance when she comes here." She glared at her brother as he silently dared her to defy him. "Fine. But you canna stop me from bringing clothes to her."

"This is between Belle and me," Cailean hissed.

"No, it is no'. Ye married her and wanted us to treat her like a sister. Just like Maggie. Then when ye decide ye canna bear to care for her—or yer own bairn—ye're upset when we continue to love her. Aye, Cailean. *Love.*"

He breathed deeply as he glared at his sister. "I don't want ye going to her bakery anymore."

"Ye canna stop me. I want to help her. I need to help her. If I didn't, she'd have to close." She paled as she glared at her brother. "That's what ye want!" She rose and hit him on his shoulder. "Ye want to force her to close so she has to crawl back to ye." She shook her head in anger. "I fear she's stronger than ye realize and little would cause her to come back to ye."

He glared at his sister, the tic in his jaw continuing even though he remained silent. However, he stood as though rooted in place. "How is she?" The question emerged as though ripped from him.

"What's the matter with ye? It's as though ye can't stand the thought of her, and yet ye want to ken how she is?" Sorcha shook her head. "If ye really want to know, ye can visit her. I refuse to be yer spy." She watched him with a mixture of frustration and disappointment. "I thought ye better than this, Cail. Ye tell me to live a full life and grasp at joy, but ye're a hypocrite."

He gripped her arm as she moved to march past him. "Don't. Don't take sides. Don't judge. Ye have no idea …" His eyes glimmered as he met her shocked gaze.

"Nor do ye. For, if ye did, ye'd be holdin' her in yer arms right now, givin' thanks for second chances." She wrenched her arm free, her footsteps sounding on the stairs.

Cailean entered the back door of the bakery, frowning as he saw Sorcha walking in the opposite direction with a basket looped over her arm. He paused at the doorway, wary as he saw Annabelle freeze with the door's opening. "It's me, Belle." He frowned as she became more withdrawn with his presence.

"Why are you here, Cailean?" She swiped at the countertop.

He fought an amused smile as her counter was already polished clean. "I wanted to see my wife. When I realized you were avoiding the house and coming to steal away clothes when I wasn't present, I thought I should visit you."

"I'm not stealing anything. I retrieved articles I already owned before our marriage." She glared at him. "In the future, I'd prefer if you entered through the front door, like my customers."

"But I'm not your customer, am I, Belle?" In an instant he stood across from her, leaning over the counter so close to her that they shared the same breath. "I'm your husband."

"Why does that matter? You haven't acted like one for weeks. You don't want the child I'm carrying. You don't want the family we'll have." She raised her eyebrows as though daring him to contradict her and also preventing herself from crying. "Or have you suddenly changed your opinion on fatherhood?"

He watched her with shuttered eyes before he backed away and sat on the stool across from her. "I saw Sorcha leave. She looked like she was making a delivery."

Annabelle swiped at her cheeks. "She helps me when she is able to."

"The café and hotel are in the opposite direction," he whispered to himself. He rose, knocking the stool to the floor. "You're allowing my sister to deliver your sweets to the Boudoir? You're exposing her to that … that …"

She lifted her shoulders as though in helpless surrender. "I couldn't have stopped her had I tried." She met his incredulous glare. "And I did try. She thinks I'm working too hard as it is with the amount of baking I'm doing."

A mirthless laugh burst forth, and he shook his head as he stared at her. "And here I was, concerned about her exposure to your sister when I married you. That wasn't good enough, was it? You had to expose her to the whole horde of whores." His head shot to the side as she slapped him.

She raised her hand, covering her mouth, as her eyes rounded in shock, dismay, and a miniscule amount of pleasure at what she had done. "Don't speak of my sister like that. Don't disparage your own sister by believing the delivery of a few sweets will in any way corrupt her."

"You have no right! Her reputation will be tarnished, and she'll be seen as no better than a …"

She took a step back from his roar, her cheeks flushed with agitation. "I think you should leave, Cailean."

"I thought I had made myself clear when we married that I wanted no interference with Sorcha."

"No, you didn't. You were delighted when I befriended her. When I helped teach her to cook, and she attempted to teach me how to improve my needlework. You're not truly upset about her going to the back door at the Boudoir to deliver a basket of goodies. You're angry because I'm not bending to your will." She glared at him as she vibrated with anger. "I am not returning to your home to stem the gossip swirling around town. I refuse to live in a home where you tolerate my presence at best and at worst resent my very existence. My child will be raised knowing it is cherished and loved. As that is impossible in your home, we will be fine here."

"Belle," Cailean whispered, his voice thickened.

"Get out." Her raspy voice matched her authoritative stance. She shook her head with disappointment as he nodded and rose. She swiped her face free of tears again and met his confused gaze. "You won't even fight for us. I hate you for marrying me when you will only ever love her."

His eyes shone with anguish before he spun on his heel and stormed out the back door.

On a Sunday in mid-October, Alistair stood beside Ewan and knocked on the back door of the bakery. When it inched open, Alistair smiled in an attempt to reassure Annabelle. "May we come in, Anna?"

She backed away and watched them warily as they entered. She shivered as the cold fall air followed them inside. "I'm sorry it's cold in here. I spend my free day in my room, where there is a small stove."

Alistair waved away her concern. "'Tis warmer here than in the livery." He motioned for her to sit, and he and Ewan settled on stools facing her on the other side of the butcher block counter. "How are ye, Anna?"

Her hand immediately dropped to her belly. "I'm fine."

Ewan frowned as he looked her over. "Ye dinna look fine. Ye look wrung out." His frown deepened at the purple smudges under her eyes. "Is there anythin' ye need?"

Annabelle bit back a mirthless laugh as she blinked to hold in her tears. "Except a husband who desires our child?" She sniffed and shook her head. "I'm fine."

"No matter how many times ye say it, it willna make it true," Alistair said. "I ken Cailean's actin' like an idiot, but I hope ye will be able to forgive him." He frowned as his reassuring smile failed to soothe her. "When he sees ye healthy, with a bairn in yer arms, he'll overcome his fears."

She shook her head, then whispered fervently, "I need him now."

Ewan sighed and rubbed at his head. "Aye, we ken that." He shared a look with Alistair. "We want ye to know ye are a MacKinnon. We will always care for ye, look after ye, as much as ye will let us."

Annabelle lost her battle with tears, and they streaked down her cheeks. "That's lovely of you to say now, but I know you will side with Cailean if ever you had to choose."

Alistair gripped her hand. "I wouldna be too sure about that." He squeezed her hand gently as she swallowed a sob. "If ever ye need anythin', Anna, all ye have to do is ask."

She nodded. "Thank you," she whispered.

A few weeks later, Alistair sat on his customary wooden stump set against the side of the barn, sipping water from a metal cup. He watched the light change over the mountains, transforming from a dusky purple to a light pink to a near crimson before the sun burst over the top. Birds chirped, and the sounds of the town awakening carried on the early morning breeze.

"Cail, come sit," he coaxed as his eldest brother moved with forced purpose, as though on leading strings. "Ye've barely slept in weeks."

Cailean slumped onto the other piece of wood, scooting so that his back rested against the wall of the barn. "I'm fine." He closed his eyes, turning his face up to the warm breeze blowing over them on this early November day.

"Ye almost pitchforked yer own foot yesterday," Alistair said with a snort. "Imagine tryin' to explain that to the doctor." He picked at a piece of hay and twirled it between his fingers. "Yer Annabelle is stronger than ye think. She'll not come crawling back to ye."

Cailean snorted, and Alistair hit him in his arm in case he'd drifted off to sleep. Cailean opened an eye and glared at his brother. "Sorcha told me the same thing a month ago. I know of Belle's strength."

Alistair snorted again. "I doubt ye do. For, if ye did, the thought of her having yer child wouldna have had ye turn into a weak-kneed lad."

Cailean opened both eyes as he met his brother's challenging stare. "What do you want, Alistair? For me to be infallible?" He shook his head in disappointment. "I hardly think someone who's known no disappointment in life has the right to judge me."

Alistair sat a moment and nodded. "Yer greatest fear is lovin' her and losin' her." At Cailean's *humph* of agreement, Alistair cleared his throat in disgust. "Well, I congratulate ye, brother, for it seems ye've been successful."

Cailean glared at his brother as he rose and disappeared into the back room of the livery to do paperwork.

Alistair kept busy as he curried horses and reshod the doctor's horse when he saw the horseshoes were worn. He was just finishing when the doctor arrived. "Not a moment too soon, Doc. This lovely lady needed a new pair of shoes." He rose and stroked a hand down her nose, earning a soft whinny.

After the doctor gave him absentminded thanks, Alistair watched him closely as the doctor fidgeted with his horse. "Is there anythin' else, Doc?" Alistair scratched the horse behind one of its ears, earning a half-closed eye roll of ecstasy and a shift in his direction, away from his owner.

The doctor chuckled. "I can see you'd charm my own horse away from me," he said as he plucked a carrot from his pocket, rubbing his horse's muzzle after it chomped the carrot in a few quick bites. "I can't speak with you about what worries me. It would be unethical and go against my training. However, I would advise that your brother visit his wife."

Alistair stiffened, his hand patting the side of the horse absently as he focused on the doctor. "Why?"

"Can't say. Hopefully she will." He *click*ed to his horse and led her out of the barn. "Thanks again, Alistair."

"Of course," he muttered, his gaze distant. He stormed into the small office space Cailean had sequestered himself into with the excuse of working on the books. Instead of tallying a row of figures, he slept with his head against the wall.

He bolted awake when the door slammed shut. "Alistair," he grumbled, biting off a snore. He stretched and yawned.

"I wondered how ye'd have so much paperwork. Ye come in here every day to sleep!" Alistair shouted, his boot heels thundering on the floorboards. At Cailean's impassive silence, his ire mounted. "I just saw the doc. He wouldna say much, other than that ye should visit yer wife."

Cailean ran a hand through his hair and picked up a quill. He glared at his brother when it was ripped from his hands.

"She's yer wife," Alistair bellowed, his brows furrowed as he watched his brother, perplexed. "How can ye no' go to her when ye ken she's been ill?"

Cailean rubbed a hand over his face and shook off the remnants of sleep. "I'm sure 'tis nothing more than an exaggeration."

Alistair kicked at the desk. "Have ye no' wondered why Sorcha's bakin' bread again? 'Tis because yer wife has been too ill to open her bakery for days." When Cailean watched him with concern lighting his eyes, Alistair nodded. "It's no' because Sorcha has a new penchant for baking."

Cailean dropped his head into his hands. "How can I go to her? I've been an ass."

"How can ye no'? No' when ye ken she's ill. She needs ye. Go to her, Cailean." Alistair watched his brother with a pleading, desperate intensity. He sighed when Cailean pushed himself upright.

"If I find this was a hoax, I will never forgive you."

Alistair frowned at his brother. "Ye should ken I'd never do that to ye, Cail. Ye're out of yer mind with worry for her. Go." He pushed on his brother's back, causing him to stumble as he was propelled from the small office. Alistair stood with his hands on his hips as he watched his eldest brother make slow progress toward his wife.

CHAPTER 11

Cailean knocked on the back door to his wife's bakery. He nodded to Mr. Finlay, the banker, as he walked past, attempting a smile before he pounded on the door again. When no answer came, he reached into his pocket and used the spare key Annabelle had given him after they were first married. He slipped inside and frowned at the stale air and faint scent of illness.

He poked his head into the front room, absently noting the drawn curtains over the windows and the empty shelves. After taking a deep breath, he firmed his shoulders and poked his head into his wife's office. He stood stock-still a moment before rushing to her bedside. "Belle!" He ran a hand over her clammy forehead.

He frowned as a shiver racked her body, and she moaned from the movement it wrought. She curled tighter under the blankets as her shuddering intensified. He looked around the room, blanching when he saw a bucket filled with bloody towels and sheets. After a moment's indecision, he scooped her up and marched from her sickroom and out the front door. He walked the short distance to his house next to the livery, shouting for Sorcha and Alistair when he arrived.

After carefully placing her on their bed, he pulled away her blankets and ran a hand over her. He elicited a cry of distress when he touched her lower belly. When he heard Alistair's heavy footfalls, Cailean bellowed, "Get the doctor. Now!"

Sorcha entered the room with a basin filled with lukewarm water and cloths. She pushed Cailean to the other side of the bed, where he sat, holding Annabelle's hand. Sorcha swiped at her sister-in-law's face, crooning to her softly. "'Tis a bad fever, Cailean."

He flinched at her whispered words. "She can't die."

Sorcha touched him softly on his shoulder. "I'd make yer peace with her now. While ye can."

He motioned for Sorcha to leave him alone with his wife. When the door closed behind her, he lowered his head to rest beside Annabelle's, tears coursing down his cheeks. "Oh, Belle, don't die. Please don't die," he whispered. "I've been a fool. Ye've every right to despise me. I despise me." He swiped at her cheek. "Give me a chance to show ye how much I love ye." He looked at her as though hoping for some reaction to his words, his accent thickening with his deep emotion. "I understan' ye dinna want to forgive me too quickly. But I'll never stop makin' it up to ye."

When her shudders seemed to intensify rather than lessen, he pulled her so she was in his lap, enveloped in his embrace. His throat was thickened to the point he was unable to speak, so he rocked her as he held her.

He jolted from a half-dreaming state when Alistair hit him on the shoulder. "Cail, the doctor is here."

Cailean settled Annabelle on the bed and scooted away. He rose and shook the doctor's hand. "I wish you'd advised me how ill she was earlier."

The doctor shook his head as his gaze roved over Annabelle. "She wasn't this ill when I visited her yesterday. She's taken a turn for the worse in the night." He pinned a disapproving stare on Cailean. "The severity of her illness might have been prevented had she been under her family's watchful eye."

Cailean flushed at the doctor's admonishment and nodded. "She's here now," he rasped. "And I'm no' leaving for yer exam. I need to be here."

After examining her, the doctor scrubbed his hands clean in the basin of water Sorcha had left at the bedside. "There's little to do. I'm afraid a piece of tissue has become lodged inside and is festering. It will continue to fester until she dies."

Cailean shook his head blankly. "I don't understand."

The doctor's gaze held a weary compassion. "She lost the child, but not all the tissue came out when she bled. What remains will slowly kill her."

Cailean shook his head as he glanced from Annabelle shuddering on the bed to the doctor giving him another death sentence. He swayed, held upright only by the quick actions of the doctor grabbing onto his arm. "You could be mistaken."

"I've seen this more times than I care to recall," the doctor whispered mournfully. He patted Cailean on the shoulder and moved from the room.

Cailean collapsed onto a hard chair in the corner as he watched Annabelle. Tears streamed down his face, wetting his shirt, and he shook his head. "Sorcha!"

At his wounded cry, his sister came running. "I'm so sorry, Cailean," she whispered.

"Find the midwife. The one the doctor says is incompetent. I want her opinion. I … I can't give up on Belle." He swiped at his face as he moved to Annabelle and pulled her into his arms again. He held her, crooning sweet nothings as she shivered and shook and cried out every once in a while in pain. He ignored Alistair as he poked his head in, Cailean's entire focus on Annabelle.

The midwife arrived and shooed him from the room. He motioned for Sorcha to remain, and he left to pace the small hallway. Alistair awaited him, leaning against the wall, his concerned gaze focused on him. "I'm fine."

"Like hell ye are," Alistair snapped. "Ye look as bad as Annabelle in there."

Cailean collapsed down the wall until he sat, leaning against it.

"She lost the babe. She lost our bairn," he whispered. His unfocused gaze sharpened at Annabelle's scream. Alistair's hand to his shoulder kept him in place. "I wasn't with her when she suffered so."

Alistair sank to his haunches, facing his eldest brother. "Ye weren't to know, Cail. Ye went to her today. Focus on that. Ye're doin' all ye can for her now."

Cailean raised haunted, wounded eyes to his brother. "I can't lose her too. I can't, Al."

Alistair squeezed his brother's shoulder, and then he began to pace, his head canting toward the door every once in a while to listen in on the midwife's words. "Seems to have quite a bit to say about our doc," Alistair mused. "None of it complimentary."

"I don't give a damn about their feud. I just want her to save Belle." Cailean rested his head on his bended knees, his lips moving as though in a silent prayer.

After over an hour, Sorcha emerged with the midwife. Cailean rushed past them into the room to find Annabelle resting on clean sheets. Although still feverish, she no longer shook, and she appeared restful. He lay down next to her, wrapping an arm around her as he pulled her close.

"Cail," Sorcha whispered, "we must continue to give her willow bark tea, and the midwife will come back tonight to change the poultice."

"What did she do, Sorch?" he whispered. "How did she help her when the doctor couldn't?"

Sorcha watched him with wide eyes. "I'll not describe to you what she did, but she used herbs and believes she has a chance of saving Annabelle."

Cailean closed his eyes. "Thank you, Sorcha. I'll remain here with her for now."

～

A nnabelle cracked open her eyes and groaned as she attempted to move. Every muscle ached, and she did not have the strength to move her arms. Her finger twitched, tracing a hand held in hers. She gave it a gentle squeeze and gasped as the bed shifted with another's movement.

"You're awake!" Cailean rasped, sitting up and jostling her with his movement.

She attempted to croak out an answer but licked her dry lips. She sighed appreciatively as he held a cup to her lips, and she took a few sips of cold water. "Thank you."

After he set down the cup, he continued to stare at her with wonder. "I can't believe you're awake. That you've come back to me." He raised her hand and kissed it.

"How long was I asleep?" she whispered, tugging on her hand until he released it.

"Four days." He ran a finger over her temple. "I feared I'd lost ye."

She leaned against the pillow, shying away from his touch. She closed her eyes, and her breathing deepened.

"Rest, Belle." He kissed her on her forehead before rising.

When the door closed behind him, she opened her eyes and curled onto her side, the motion slow and painful. She held a hand over her lower abdomen, grimacing at a lingering cramp. When it ceased, she hugged a pillow to her and stared out the window. Children's voices, joyous and laughing as they shrieked while they played, rose to taunt her. She pulled the pillow closer to her but didn't have the energy to rise and close the window.

She remained with her back to the door when it creaked open. She sniffed, stiffening at the heavy perfume. "Fidelia?" she whispered.

"Oh, Annabelle," her sister choked out. "I was terrified when Ewan brought the news that you were ill and might die." Her sister pulled a chair over to sit facing her. She wore her most demure outfit, a light-blue dress with puffy sleeves, covered bodice, and barely visible pantaloons. She wore minimal rouge, and her hair was pulled back in a loose knot.

"Did Cailean see you come in?" Annabelle whispered, reaching for her sister but unable to lift her hand off the bed. Instead, she slid it across the quilt and clasped her sister's hand when her sister grabbed hers.

"Of course. He sent Ewan to inform me. He welcomed me here from the start." She blinked away tears. "I've been here every day since he found you at your bakery." She swiped at her tears with her free hand. "I don't know what I would have done had I lost you too."

"I hope you were treated well here," Annabelle said.

Fidelia chuckled. "Your husband's family treated me like royalty. Made me tea, fed me, and never once acted as though I were below them." She blinked away tears. "Only at your bakery and in this house have I been seen as more than a prostitute."

"You're my sister. I've been trying to tell you that." She closed her eyes with fatigue. "What happened? Why am I so tired?"

Fidelia ran a hand over Annabelle's matted, sweaty crown. "You had a terrible fever. The doctor said you would die." Her eyes overflowed, and her grip tightened on her sister's hand. "Your husband refused to accept that decree and ordered the midwife here. She saved your life."

Annabelle closed her eyes, her words mumbled from her fatigue. "I don't know why he'd care. He hasn't been concerned about me for months."

Her sister snorted. "If there's one thing I understand, it's men. That man of yours was desperate for you to improve. He loves you, sister." She sighed as Annabelle had drifted to sleep. "You may not want to acknowledge it, but he does." She kissed her sister on her cool forehead and rose.

Two days later when Sorcha entered Annabelle's room, as she did often daily to check on her sister-in-law's progress, she frowned. She marched to the curtains and flung them open, earning a groan from Annabelle as she pulled the covers over her and covered her face. "Ye can't keep hidin' in here forever. Ye have to face him sometime," Sorcha snapped. When Annabelle remained curled on her side, Sorcha sighed and clapped her hands together. "Come, Annabelle. This isna who ye are."

Annabelle peeked her head out from under the bed linen. "Would you help me return to my store? I'd be most comfortable there."

Sorcha glared at her. "I would no'. Do ye expect me to run over there, bringin' ye yer meals three times a day? Haulin' yer wash from there to here an' back?" She shook her head in consternation. "Ye need to face him an' have it out."

Annabelle remained curled on her side but refused to look at her sister-in-law. "There's little for us to discuss."

Sorcha sat next to her and gripped her shoulder, forcing Annabelle to meet her irate gaze. "Except for the fact he fought for ye. Wouldna let ye die. Begged and pleaded and bargained with the devil himself to ensure ye lived."

Annabelle closed her eyes in exhaustion and defeat. "He was too late in his concern."

Sorcha shook Annabelle by the shoulder. "Are ye tellin' me ye've never done a thing ye regret? Never acted out o' fear an' then learned ye'd been a fool?"

Annabelle looked at Sorcha and shook her head. "I don't have it in me to forgive him, Sorcha." Her gaze filled with a dulled grief, she pulled away from Sorcha's grasp. "Thank you for caring for me while I was ill."

"'Twasn't me, ye daft woman! 'Twas Cailean. He never left yer side." Sorcha's chest heaved as she breathed heavily.

Annabelle tugged her knees toward her chest, pulling the blankets over her head and blocking Sorcha out.

Sorcha gave a grunt of disapproval and stormed from the room. She marched down the stairs and outside to the livery.

Cailean worked beside Alistair, pausing as he saw his sister's approach. "Sorcha? Is it Belle?"

She came to an abrupt halt in front of him, kicking up a bit of dirt and horse dung. "'Tis. She's drowning in despair, and ye're out here muckin' a stall." She hit him on his chest. "Why aren't ye with her?"

Cailean shook his head. "She's asleep every time I'm in the room with her. I've no desire to interrupt her recovery."

"She's feignin' sleep, Cail. She wants to return to her bakery. Escape from ye. Escape from feelin' anythin' ever again. Ye must make her realize the truth."

Cailean froze at his sister's words. "She's not returning to the bakery. She can't. She's not strong enough." He thrust the handle of his pitchfork at his sister and took off at a run toward the house, leaving his siblings to stare after him.

~

Cailean rushed through his bedroom door, frowning when he saw Annabelle attempting to dress on her own. "What are you doing?" He watched her in confusion as she turned away from him and sat with a thud on the edge of the bed, her dress beside her. She wore a chemise but no corset.

"I would have thought it obvious. I'm dressing." She swiped at her brow, sweating from the exertion.

"You're nowhere healthy enough to be up and about on your own. Every time I've looked in on you, you've been asleep." He sat in the chair opposite her. "Why are you intent on leaving now?"

"There's no reason for me to stay," she whispered. "I need to learn to be independent again." She jerked away her head when he reached to stroke her face. "Don't touch me!"

He dropped his hand as though avoiding a viper's bite and stared at her. "Annabelle, you must let me explain."

She shook her head, pulling her dress to cover herself. "There's nothing to talk about. You were afraid. Cowardly in the face of your fears." She raised her disdainful gaze to meet his. "I should have known better than to marry a complete stranger."

"We can be happy, Belle." His whispered entreaty evoked a shiver.

"How? When will I do something that reminds you of her and

causes you to shut me out again? I can't live life like that." She swiped at her face as a few tears fell. "I know divorce is not common, but I refuse to live with a man controlled by his past."

"Annabelle, I love you."

She slapped him, a half-screech erupting from her. "How dare you! How dare you say such words to me now?" Her expression became livid. "It's acceptable for you to speak of love now, but not for me the night I told you that I was expecting our child? I will never forget your disdain of my feelings when compared to how you felt for her. What makes you think I'd believe anything you'd say ever again?"

He took a deep breath, but no words emerged as he stuttered around a choked sound. Finally he whispered, "I'm here now, facing my fears."

"Where were you when I was desperate to share the joy of our baby?" She slapped at his hand as he reached toward her. "Where were you when I lay on my cot bleeding to death from the loss of our child? Where were you when the fever struck? Where were you when I needed someone to hold me when I thought I would die?" She took a deep, stuttering breath. "You were here, moping about your first wife and reliving your agony. You weren't thinking about me."

"Belle, forgive me." His shattered gaze met her irate one, and they stared at each other for long moments.

"I don't know if I can. I want more from life than a man who's unable to see the good fortune he's been given until it's too late."

"You don't want me?" He held himself stiffly away from her as he waited for her to speak.

"No, not any longer. Not now." She let out a deep breath as her anger abated, and her muscles relaxed.

A tear tracked down his cheek. "You're not strong enough to leave today, Belle."

"I refuse to spend another day in your company."

He gripped his thigh and nodded. "Please remain here until you're fully healed. I promise I won't bother you further." After a searching gaze, he rose and left, silently shutting the door behind him.

～

S orcha set down a bowl of boiled potatoes on the table with a loud *thunk*. Alistair glared from the bowl to her and frowned as he saw his despair echoed in her eyes. "No need to take out yer frustrations on the potatoes." He yelped as she *thwack*ed him on his shoulder with a wooden spoon. "Hit me with that again, and I'll break it in half."

She huffed and moved to the stove, extracting a roasted chicken. After it was carved and set at the table, she sat. "I'm sorry."

He reached over and patted her hand. "Aye. Me too."

Ewan wandered in, rubbing his stomach. "Where's Cail?" He sighed when he met his siblings' bleak stares. "Still out in the barn?"

At Alistair's nod, Ewan plopped into his chair. "He'll have to learn he canna survive on whiskey."

"I'm afraid that, by the time he wants to learn that lesson, 'twill be too late," Sorcha whispered. "What if it kills him?"

Alistair gripped her hand. "He'll improve once she's out of the house."

Ewan snorted. "Just because she's in her bakery doesna mean he'll no longer want her." He rubbed at his forehead. "Damn fool. Realizing too late he loved her."

Their food untouched, they stared morosely at it.

"What did ye mean, Alistair?" Sorcha asked.

He watched her curiously.

"I snuck out to the barn yesterday," she said, "and I heard ye yell at Cail to quit acting like Father."

Alistair shot a quick glance at Ewan and then looked at Sorcha again. He raised an eyebrow, and she nodded. "Father had the opportunity to be happy. He had loved another, aye."

At this Ewan jerked in his chair and stared from Alistair to Sorcha and back.

Alistair continued. "Father could have made amends with Mother. He could have ensured ye were treated better, Sorcha. Instead, he licked his wounds."

"Making everything worse," Sorcha whispered.

"Aye," Alistair said. "For everyone."

Ewan held up a hand, his gaze flitting between his siblings. "Are ye telling me that Father was unfaithful?" At Alistair's nod, Ewan asked, "An' we have another sibling?"

"Aye," Alistair said.

"We have to find him! He has to know he's one of us." Ewan watched them with excited, confused eyes as his siblings met his gaze with calm acceptance.

"She's right here." Alistair nodded at their sister. "Sorcha." Alistair watched as shock, disbelief, and then understanding came over Ewan's features.

"I always thought ye'd suspected," Sorcha said.

Ewan shook his head. "I never understood why Mother treated ye so poorly."

"Father clung to his sorrow and disappointment with as much fervency as Cailean. It seems to be a family trait," Alistair muttered. "An' not one to be admired." He took a scoop of potatoes, plopping it on Sorcha's plate before repeating that for his and Ewan's plates. He then served up the chicken and nodded to their full plates, silently ordering them to eat.

As they stuffed forkfuls of food they barely tasted into their mouths, their expressions were distant. "What can we do for him?" Sorcha whispered, her fork falling to her plate. "Even after Maggie, he wasn't this low."

Alistair snorted. "Aye, he was. Ye just didna see it." He shrugged at Ewan's and Sorcha's confused stares. "We left soon after the funeral. I could tell he was filled with a need to escape. So I joined him as he fled." He sighed. "I helped pull him back from the brink that time too."

"What did ye do?" Ewan asked.

Alistair's gaze became distant. "Followed him when he went out at night, intent on mischief. He relished a good fight. An' in New York City, someone was always willing to fight a stupid young Scotsman." He sighed. "I bandaged his ribs, patched his wounds, and filled the whiskey bottles half full of water."

Sorcha gripped his arm. "Ye must do that again!"

He half smiled as Ewan laughed. "Ye already have, have ye no'?" Ewan asked.

"Will he no' ken the difference?" Sorcha asked.

"Cailean's never been one to drink. He'll know something's wrong with the whiskey but blame it on being in Montana." Alistair shrugged, his brown eyes momentarily lit with mischief. "He has for the past few days every morning in the livery."

Sorcha pushed around the uneaten potatoes and chicken on her plate. "Do ye think she'll ever forgive him?" Her anxious gaze moved from one brother to the other.

"I half understand Cail. Annabelle's still a mystery." Alistair sighed. "We must hope she is able to forgive what she believes is unforgiveable."

CHAPTER 12

$\mathcal{A}$nnabelle moved around her bakery, her pace slower than usual. She'd returned to her store two days ago and had spent the time restocking inventory and cleaning. Now she stood in her kitchen area and prepared dough for the first day of business. She inhaled the scent of yeast and relished the feel of her fingers digging into it. She patted the dough, covered it, and left it to rise as she moved on to a batch of cookie dough. She had two hours until opening, and she hoped the locals would return after her monthlong absence.

She glanced toward the back door at a gentle tap on the wood. She washed her hands clean and cracked it open, unable to hide a smile as she flung it open. "Leticia," she breathed, pulling her friend in for a hug. "It's wonderful to see you."

Leticia smiled and looked around the bakery. "I can't believe you're already back to work."

"I needed something to do. Besides, I'd been away long enough, and I didn't want anyone else to get the idea of starting a bakery in my absence."

Leticia moved into the store, and Annabelle glanced behind her, frowning. "Where's Hortence?"

187

"She's with Alistair before school. He didn't mind. She wanted to see the horses, and I wanted time with you."

"He seems taken with your daughter," Annabelle murmured. "You're very fortunate."

Leticia smiled at Annabelle before focusing on her friend. She frowned upon noticing that the smile failed to give her a gentle glow and that an air of despair clung to her. "I still don't believe you are well enough to be here, working again."

Annabelle spun away and returned to her cookie dough. "I have to do something. If I don't, I fear I'll go mad." She plucked out small portions of dough with a spoon before placing them on a baking sheet. "Besides, Christmas is approaching, and I hope to have a successful holiday season."

Leticia frowned. "Many do their own baking for the holidays."

Annabelle smiled. "I know. But there are enough who won't want to. Or who will want to supplement what they bake with a few of my goodies." She smiled at her friend. "Either way, I'll have my regulars looking for breakfast rolls and loaves of bread." She eased onto a stool as she worked.

Leticia's gaze sobered even further as Annabelle rarely stood still when working, never mind sat.

"How are things between you and Alistair?"

Leticia was unable to fight a smile. "Good. He's proclaiming this his favorite Christmas yet as it's the last Christmas before we wed in June."

Annabelle raised an eyebrow. "Have you set the date?"

"I've only promised no later than next summer, and he insists we wed in June." She bit her lip. "I think that will be all right."

Annabelle frowned. "Why wouldn't it be? You have a man who's eager to wed you, who has a stable career, and who adores your daughter. I'd think you'd wed him next week if you could."

Leticia forced a laugh. "Life is never that simple, Annabelle."

After a few moments of silence, Annabelle said, "How is the school year?"

"Oh, it's fine. There are forty-four children. It's a challenge to meet all their needs." She shrugged. "I do my best."

Annabelle smiled as she attempted to reassure her. "I'm sure you do a wonderful job." She grunted as she hefted the tray into the oven. "I didn't realize how weak I'd be."

"Cailean would be disappointed to see you working already."

Annabelle pinched her mouth shut and shook her head. "He lost his right to be concerned about me months ago."

Leticia wrung her hands as Annabelle placed a hot cookie tray on the cooling rack and then sat once more. Leticia pulled out a stool across from Annabelle. "I can imagine how you feel, Annabelle. When I lost my husband …" She shrugged. "Loss of any kind is terrible. It makes you examine your life. The life you thought you would live is gone, and you have to create a new life." She gripped her friend's hand. "It doesn't mean it is a worse life. Just different."

"You don't understand. Your husband died. Now you have found Alistair." She swiped at a tear. "Mine is alive but doesn't want me."

"I fear he wants you, very much."

Annabelle glared at Leticia. "He didn't when I needed him the most." Her mouth firmed as she fought tears and an overwhelming anger. "He will force me to live with the infamy of divorce." She pounded her fist on the countertop. "He promised he was saving me from gossip and the notoriety my sister lives with. Instead, I'll suffer as much as she does."

"Only if you are foolish enough to push for a divorce. He doesn't want one. He wants you back."

Annabelle crumpled on her stool. "I remember my frustration with my sister. That no matter how many times I apologized, a part of her never forgave me." Annabelle shook her head. "Now I understand perfectly. I fear I don't know how to forgive. Not for the things that truly need forgiveness."

Leticia gripped her hand. "Your pain is fresh. Give yourself time to heal. Don't act rashly now when you don't know what you'll want or feel when the grief passes." She shared a bittersweet smile with Annabelle. "Grief makes everyone irrational."

~

Annabelle sat in the kitchen at the back of the Sunflower Café, hidden from view of other patrons. She watched as Irene and Harold worked in silent harmony as they prepared meals and served them. When there was a lull, they joined Annabelle in the kitchen for a moment.

"I couldn't have been more surprised to see you arrive with your basket of breads this morning," Irene said.

Harold grunted with disapproval. "You should be at home, resting. You are in no condition to work."

Annabelle attempted a weak smile. "I'm much improved, and I needed something to do. I reopened the bakery a few days ago but didn't have the energy to make all the breads and treats for the café and hotel until today."

"I should think not," Harold growled. "What can your husband be thinking to allow you to return to work?" He frowned as Annabelle stiffened at his comment. "It's right and proper for a husband to concern himself with his wife's care."

Irene studied Annabelle. "Unless you've been foolish and are unwilling to allow him to aid you through this difficult time." She met Annabelle's despair-filled glare with an implacable stare. "Being angry with your husband won't change what happened." She shook her head in disgust and left the kitchen with a hand-held pot of coffee.

Harold remained with Annabelle in the kitchen, sitting in silence next to her as they listened to Irene laugh and chat with customers in the café dining room. "I fear you've made a mess of things, Miss Annabelle."

She sighed, rubbing at her head. "I fail to see how this is my fault, Mr. Tompkins."

"Running away rather than facing your problems ain't going to solve them. Just delays the whole process." He sighed. "Irene isn't really mad at you. Just reminds her of times she'd rather forget."

Annabelle watched him, the despair in her gaze dimmed by concern for her friend. "What do you mean?"

He crossed his legs and tapped one finger on his bent knee. "You've heard us talk about our grandson, Frederick. Couldn't be more proud of him. Or of his brothers." His voice faded away for a moment. "His father was our pride and joy." He shared a chagrined smile with Annabelle. "Now I'm sure all parents will tell you that about their children, but, when I saw him, I knew my life had been worth living because I had such a son."

After a few moments of silence, Annabelle whispered, "What made him so special?"

"Oh, he was ornery and stubborn and couldn't be bothered by fools. Hated the café 'cause he had to make small talk, and he never saw the point on wastin' breath talkin' to folk you'd never see again or would rather avoid in town." His lips curved into a small smile. "But he was loyal and hardworking and smart. He never let his mother or me down, not when we really needed him.

"Raised fine sons, against all odds." His eyes clouded but waved away her question. "And then he died. From a damn lung infection." He cleared his throat and blinked a few times. "A man isn't supposed to bury his son."

"I'm sorry, Mr. Tompkins." She sniffled as she swiped at her cheek.

"That woman"—he nodded into the café, in Irene's direction —"wouldn't let me wallow in my grief. No matter how much I would rather've spent my days alone on horseback, watchin' cattle chew their cud, she forced me to face life. To face being alive."

He raised grief-stricken, passionate eyes to meet Annabelle's gaze dulled by grief. "You can't allow yourself to become lost to the sadness, Miss Annabelle. And you can't come through this alone. You need your husband."

Annabelle shook her head. "The only similarity in our situations is that we lost someone precious to us."

He gripped her hand, preventing her from rising and marching out of the café. "I lost my son. You lost the dream of your child. Don't lose your marriage too." He clamped his jaw shut for a moment and then spoke again with a graveled voice as though fighting deep emotions.

"Unlike me, you have the hope of another baby. Junior was the only child we ever had."

Tears coursed down Annabelle's cheeks. "I'm so sorry for your loss, Mr. Tompkins." He nodded as she pulled out a handkerchief and scrubbed at her face.

"Charming the ladies again, Harold?" Irene asked as she entered the kitchen. She moved to the large silver pot half filled with coffee to fill up her portable carafe. Then she set it down and slung an arm around Annabelle, pulling her into a hug. "Oh, my dear, I'm so terribly sorry about what happened." She smiled her thanks as Harold rose and returned to the main room of the café, leaving her behind with Annabelle.

Annabelle watched Irene. "Mr. Tompkins just told me about how devastating your son's death was." She covered her eyes. "I feel heartless because I didn't consider how you had suffered when you mentioned he had died."

Irene cupped Annabelle's cheeks. "Sometimes, until we've experience the same agony, we can't fully understand the words. Hearing someone say, 'My son died,' will never resonate in the same way until you can understand what that kind of pain is." She swiped at Annabelle's cheeks. "In a way, it's refreshing you didn't look at us as people to be pitied, as many in this town do. They know we run the café in an attempt to keep busy."

"You are the last people on earth I would ever pity," Annabelle stuttered out. "Forgive me. I can't seem to stop crying these days."

Irene nodded. "I understand. You feel as though you lost your child as well as your husband. I hope with time you come to realize your husband and his love were never as lost to you as you feared."

A week later, Sorcha sat in Annabelle's kitchen, her hands wrapped around a warm cup of coffee. She blew on it before taking a sip. "Ah, this tastes delicious. Someday ye'll have to teach me the trick of brewing a good pot." She watched as Annabelle appeared to only half listen. "I know my brothers sneak out to the café for a cup most days."

She frowned as Annabelle fought a smile. "There's no harm in admitting ye enjoy hearing about him." After she took another sip, she traced a pattern alongside the cup. "Is that why ye won't go into the café anymore? Because ye don't want to run into Cailean?"

Annabelle sat across from her and took a sip of water. "I spend time with Irene and Harold. Just not in the dining room of their café." She picked up a cloth and wiped her counters clean.

Sorcha made a disapproving sound in her throat. "'Tis as Alistair said. Yer hidin' away from the world. The only time I see ye, outside of the kitchen, are the few times ye sweep the boardwalk." Her gaze narrowed. "Ye're watchin' the livery for any sign of Cailean. Why won't ye admit you want to see him?"

Annabelle tossed down the cloth before slamming her open palm onto the counter. "I yearn for a glimpse of him. And yet I have no desire to speak with him. To hear his excuses." She bowed her head before releasing a deep breath. "I know I married him, and the only recourse is a divorce, but I have no energy for that right now."

Sorcha gripped her hand. "I hope ye never have the energy for it." She tugged until Annabelle sat on a stool next to her. "He's miserable, worse than one of those bears in the woods they tell stories about here." She saw a flicker of curiosity in Annabelle's gaze and barreled on. "He won't tell stories, won't give us advice, won't act like our elder brother." Her jaw firmed. "He works, eats, and then disappears."

"Where does he go?" Annabelle whispered.

Sorcha shrugged. "I dinna ken. At first it was to the livery, but now he leaves out the back door and disappears. I've tried to stay awake until he returns, but he's in the kitchen when I wake on the sofa." Sorcha gripped Annabelle's hand. "Ye have to forgive him, Annabelle. Please."

Annabelle shook her head as a tear leaked out. "I don't know if I can. I never knew I could hurt like this." She swiped at her cheeks. "I don't know if I can give someone, even my husband, the ability to cause such pain again."

"What's the point of livin' if ye don't risk pain?"

Annabelle huffed out an incredulous laugh. "I'll ask you that after you've lived through what I have."

"Ye have the love of a good man. Don't toss it away."

Annabelle closed her eyes. "He doesn't love me, Sorcha. He will only ever love his Maggie and the baby they lost." She swiped at her cheek. "I should have heeded his warning that he'd never love me when he proposed."

"He was frightened, Annabelle. Don't make him suffer for his fear."

She watched her sister-in-law with confusion. "You're worried about his suffering? Have you ever thought of mine? Have you ever considered what it did to me to know my husband wanted nothing to do with me once I became with child? I know that one of you badgered him into visiting me, and that is the only reason he found me as I lay ill in my room at the bakery. Otherwise, I would have died. He had no concern for me."

Sorcha's eyes lit with loyal passion. "Ye're wrong. But ye'll have to discover that for yerself." She rose and nodded at Annabelle. "I hope ye have a fine evenin'." She marched out the back door, slamming it behind her.

～

Annabelle entered the General Store and bit back a sigh when she saw it was empty of other patrons. She squared her shoulders and approached Tobias, her smile friendly but impersonal. "Hello, Mr. Sutton. I've come to inquire after the delivery of the flour and sugar to my bakery. It didn't arrive this morning as expected."

He looked her up and down, his smile more jeering than friendly. "Seems to me that we should renegotiate our terms now that you're no longer with that MacKinnon."

She stiffened and met his gaze. "We are married. He would be most distressed to learn you've changed in your treatment toward me." She bristled at his snort. "I am his wife."

"In name only, missus." His smile widened when he saw her indignation. "I've watched him come and go from the Boudoir every night for the past two weeks. I'd hardly call him a dedicated husband." He looked her over. "Or you a desirable wife."

She clamped her jaw shut a moment before she spoke. Her voice emerged raspy and pain laced. "I'd thank you not to speak of my marriage."

"Does it bother you that your husband prefers your sister to you?" He laughed. "Never fear, Mrs. MacKinnon," he said in a loud voice as the bell chimed and other customers entered, "your shipment was delayed due to a train derailment because of the weather. Should be in tomorrow in time for your Christmas baking." He nodded at her as though in a deferential manner although his eyes were lit with malevolence as she backed away.

She bumped into the customers, mumbling an apology before she escaped onto the boardwalk. Her gaze immediately sought out her husband's livery, and she forced herself to return to her bakery rather than march across the street to confront him.

That evening she stood on the back porch of her husband's home, listening to bits and pieces of the stilted conversations that emerged through the kitchen door. She heard Sorcha's soft voice and Alistair's deep baritone. A cold wind blew, and she silently cursed herself as a jealous fool for standing outside on a mid-December evening. When the back door burst open, she emerged from the shadows.

"Cailean," she whispered.

He spun to face her, his face lit by the light from the kitchen window. She shuddered as the temperature had plummeted during the evening. "Belle! What are you doing here, standing in the cold? Why didn't you come inside for supper with us?" He reached a hand out as though to stroke some warmth into her but then thought better of it and dropped his hand.

"I must speak with you," she said.

He nodded and gripped her elbow, dragging her into the warmth of the house. She barely acknowledged the gaping, shocked hellos from Alistair and Sorcha with a nod. Ewan watched them with an amused twinkle in his eyes. Cailean pulled her into the front sitting room and slammed the door behind them. "'Tis warm in here." He pushed her onto the sofa and threw a blanket over her. "I don't want you catching a chill."

Her confused gaze clashed with his worried one. "Why do you care?"

He froze at her blunt question, then bent over her as he tucked the blanket around her.

"I know you visit the ladies at the Boudoir every night, so I don't know why you'd presume to show concern for me now."

He moved from her and sat in a chair away from her, too far for him to touch her. "I see. You're only here because you're jealous?"

She flushed at his incredulous tone. "Don't be indignant with me. I have acted with honor since we separated. I'd hoped you'd act the same."

His eyes lit with disappointment as he beheld her. "This is what you think of me? You listen to one man's evil gossip and jump to believe the worst conclusion?" Cailean rose and strode to the window, staring outside.

"Your sister also remarked that you leave the house every night, for destinations unknown, and return at ungodly hours." Annabelle shrugged as she watched him tense with her words. "What was I to think?"

"You love your sister," he whispered.

She frowned. "Yes, I do. I hate the life she's been forced to lead." She swallowed as he remained silent. "I was advised today that you find her company more entertaining than you ever found mine."

He turned to face her, leaning against the deep window frame, his emotions masked. "I visit her most nights. I give her time away from the miners to just be." He bowed his head. "The only thing I ask of her is that she tell me stories of when you were young."

"You mean you don't … ?"

"I want you, Belle. If I can't have you, I'll find a way to survive." He let out a humorless chuckle. "Although spending time with your sister has brought more torment than comfort." His desolate gaze met hers. "It's only made me miss ye more."

"It must have cost you a fortune," she whispered.

He shrugged. "It was worth it. I've money saved. My wife costs me no upkeep. She won't even accept an allowance for clothes."

She bowed her head, her shivers intensifying.

"Should I call the doctor?" he asked, moving toward her. His erratic movements stilled when she raised her eyes to his, and he saw tears leaking out.

"No, I'm not ill." She sniffled. "Well, I am heartsick." She accepted his handkerchief and swiped at her face and nose. "I miss you."

He canted toward her at her whispered admission. "I miss you too, Belle. Desperately."

She shook her head as her shaking intensified. "I don't know if I can trust you again. If I can allow myself to love you again."

He sat next to her on the sofa and pulled her onto his lap, cuddling her.

Her shivers and shaking continued as she lost her battle and sobbed.

"Do you know what my greatest fear was?" He paused for a moment as though awaiting a response before he continued his one-sided conversation. "I promised myself, with that vow to Maggie, never to marry, never to love. It was never about Maggie and the bairn. It was always about me."

He kissed Annabelle's temple as her sobs continued. "'Twas always about what I feared suffering again. I was a coward, and I failed myself. I failed you."

"You hurt me," she whispered, "and your worst fear almost came true."

He shuddered at her words. "Give me a chance, Belle."

She met his entreating gaze and shook her head in confusion.

"Let me court you as I should have upon first seeing you. Let me show you how much I treasure you."

"I'm not moving back in," she whispered.

He nodded, holding her close. "Not yet." He sat, rocking her on his lap, as he felt the first moment of peace since he had learned of her pregnancy.

~

F idelia knocked at the rear door to the bakery with her shoulders thrown back as she met the glares of the women and the leers of the men who passed by. She wore a modest dress with nary a ruffle or petticoat visible, and her woolen shawl covered her immodest cut to the bodice of the dress. She relaxed as the door opened.

"Fidelia!" Annabelle opened her arms to her sister and pulled her into a hug before tugging her into the warmth of the bakery. She pushed her sister onto a stool before extracting a jug of milk from the icebox. As she slipped off the lid to a tin of cookies she'd set aside, she studied her sister. "Are you all right?"

Fidelia hunched into herself on the chair. "I'm fine. Just had a bit of trouble last night with one of my customers."

The tin rattled on the countertop as Annabelle gripped her sister's chin to better study her face. Her frown intensified as she discerned the bruises makeup couldn't fully hide. "Who did this?"

Fidelia rolled her eyes as she reached for a cookie. She nibbled on it and muttered her thanks as Annabelle poured her a glass of milk. "It doesn't matter. If it wasn't the man last night, it would be another." She shrugged her shoulders. "Some men like to rough up women."

"How can you accept such treatment? You deserve better." She recoiled at the look of disdain and hopelessness in her sister's gaze.

"I'm a whore, Anna. It's best you come to accept it. Your husband has. Your new family has. They treat me fine, which is more than I expected. I thought they'd make you sever all ties with me, which is only what I deserve." She took a sip of the milk, licking at her upper lip. "I'm especially thankful they were more forgiving than most."

"I know you've spent time with Cailean." When Fidelia began to protest, Annabelle motioned for her to remain quiet. "He explained to me that he paid for your time to give you a break and to learn more about me. I trust what he told me was true."

Fidelia paused with the cookie halfway to her lips. "How can you? Trust a man?" She took a deep breath. "After Father and all he did?"

Annabelle scooted a stool over to sit across from Fidelia. "I'm sorry, Dee." Her hand shot out to still Fidelia's instinctive motion to rise and flee. "I'm sorry I didn't listen to you when he threw you out. I should have known better."

Fidelia firmed her jaw and remained silent for a long moment. "Don't expect me to forgive you, Anna. Or to ever forgive Father."

Annabelle released her sister's arm and sighed with relief when she remained seated across from her. "I understand."

Fidelia shook her head. "I don't believe you do." She glanced at the upside-down watch pinned to Annabelle's dress. "I need to go soon. Before I do, I want to know how you knew you could trust what your husband told you was the truth—about the time he spent with me."

Annabelle shrugged. "I don't know how to explain it. He's a good man. A decent man. And I trusted him."

"But he hurt you." Fidelia's eyes shone with outrage.

"Yes, although I imagine I hurt him too." She rubbed at her temple. "I've come to realize that the makings of a good relationship do not come from the ability to always be happy. They come from the ability to acknowledge our mistakes and to apologize."

"So you will forgive him?" Fidelia asked.

"I'm not sure. Maybe." She attempted a smile for her sister. "I felt at peace with him last night. The first time I've felt any peace since I lost the baby." She ran a hand over her stomach before she met her sister's silent, inquisitive gaze. "I fear I'm not brave enough to forgive him. To love him again."

Her sister scoffed at Annabelle's whispered confession. "You're the bravest person I know. You regularly defied Father. You traveled here alone to find me. You stand up to the Madam." Her sister's smile was tinged with pride. "If you want to forgive him, you will."

Annabelle sighed. "How will I know?"

Fidelia shook her head. "You're asking the wrong person. I've spent my life feeding my resentments. I don't know what I would do if I had to give them up." She squeezed her sister's hand and rose. "Good luck, Anna."

Annabelle watched as her sister slipped out the back door, and she rested her head on her arms. Her mind was awhirl with possibilities, and she fell asleep before determining what she wanted to do.

~

Cailean whistled while he worked the following morning. He had already hauled in the water for the troughs and started mucking out stalls. Soon he'd work on repairing tack. He paused, swiping at sweat on his brow. "Why are you staring at me?"

Alistair shrugged. "Ye seem different the past few days. I hope 'tis a sign of things to come."

Cailean leaned against the handle of his shovel, extending his break. "I've realized I haven't lost Annabelle."

Alistair's eyebrows shot up. "I thought she'd never forgive the visits to the Boudoir."

Cailean shook his head and smiled. "She believed me. I think she'll check what I said with her sister, but she'll soon know I told her the truth." He watched his brother with hope in his eyes. "Do you know what she said to me?" At Alistair's shake of his head, he took a deep breath. "She said I'd almost lost her."

Alistair watched him in confusion. "I dinna ken the importance of that. Ye *did* almost lose her."

Cailean beamed. "It means she doesn't consider herself lost to me. I still have a chance to win her back." He frowned. "The only problem is, I have to learn how to woo my own wife."

Alistair chuckled. "Ye've never had to woo a woman afore. Should be interestin' to watch ye now."

Cailean thrust the shovel against one of the stalls and kicked at a mound of dung. "What would you do?"

Alistair shook his head as he fought laughter. "I ken what I'd do to win my Leticia. But each woman's different. Ye have to know what they like. Leticia loves books, long walks, and time spent with her daughter. What does yer Annabelle like?"

Cailean rubbed at his head. "Baking. Caring for others. I don't know what to do *for* her."

Alistair scratched his chin. "Women like flowers. 'Tis a pity winter came early this year." He watched his brother. "Do little things, every day, that show her that ye care."

Cailean nodded and rose. He stretched a moment before he moved to the office to work on the books. He also wanted time alone to plot ways to woo his recalcitrant wife.

CHAPTER 13

*J*anuary turned into February, and Annabelle prepared for Valentine's Day. She had ordered a half-dozen heart-shaped cake tins from a catalog and had been completely booked for the cakes on the first day she had advertised the special in her shop. To compensate for those who missed the cake special, she planned to make heart-shaped cookies.

Each morning, she woke to find her wood box at the back door freshly stocked and a fresh pail of water waiting on the step. When it snowed heavily, it was cleared away before she could shovel it aside. Tobias's threat to raise his prices for the purchase of flour, sugar, and her other sundries vanished. She smiled as she envisioned Cailean speaking with Tobias.

Her smile faded as she thought about her husband. She sat at her desk on a Sunday morning, refusing to think about the few perfect Sunday mornings she had spent with Cailean before everything had gone so wrong. He had to be the one aiding her. She shied away from imagining she had another admirer. "What am I to do?" she whispered to herself.

Christmas had been a stilted, formal affair where she had joined them for dinner. She had sat between Sorcha and Ewan and evaded

Cailean's intense stare. His gifts of a cookbook, a baking tin, and a book filled with poems by Robert Burns had embarrassed her. She had baked a cake for the family and had not brought a gift for him. After dinner, he had attempted to coax her into the parlor for quiet conversation, but she had remained in the kitchen with Sorcha before sneaking out the back door while he was in a deep discussion with Ewan.

She covered her face with her hands before dropping her head into her crossed arms. "I don't know what to do," she muttered. She had belatedly read the poems, only then finding he had written notes for her after his favorite verses. Words of hope, praise, and love, meant for her eyes only. She swiped at her cheeks as she raised her head and attempted to focus on her list of things she needed to do before the February 14 rush later in the week.

∽

Cailean kicked at a bucket in the livery, grunting when the water within remained frozen in place yet the wood shattered from his abuse. "*Bluidy* hell," he groaned as he hopped on one foot.

"Serves ye right for destroyin' a perfectly good bucket," Alistair said with a raised eyebrow. "What's got ye so fashed?"

Cailean plopped onto a stool and attempted to massage his toes through his boots. "Nothing matters, Al." At his brother's confused stare, he said, "It doesn't matter what I do. Annabelle will never forgive me."

Alistair set the pitchfork into the dirt and leaned against it. "Seems to me ye've shown her yer constancy. Ye're there every day with water and wood. But have ye told her that ye loved her? Other than when ye thought her dying?"

Cailean frowned. "I don't know. I think so, but I can't be certain." He glared at his brother. "But I've damn well shown her every day how I feel."

Alistair shrugged. "Ye hurt her, Cail. More than ye'll ever understand. Some hurts take a lot longer to heal than others." He watched his brother intently. "She might not believe ye are sincere until she's with babe and ye don't act like a madman."

Cailean glared at him. "How am I to ever get her with babe if she won't even talk with me on Christmas? I haven't held her since we spoke before Christmas when she cried in my arms." He set an elbow on his thigh and leaned his head on his hand. "I can't go on like this, Al. If she wants a divorce, I can't deny her one."

Alistair grunted. "No. Although, from what I hear, she's no' interested in anyone else. She has a more limited life than when she arrived here." He frowned. "An' that's saying something. Irene and Harold gave me an earful last week when they saw me walkin' down the boardwalk. Thought we had ruined her spirit and were preventin' her from coming in for her customary chats."

Cailean's shoulders stooped. "I hate that she's this sad. That I caused her such despair."

Alistair watched his brother. "Ye've always had a knack for believing you were more responsible than ye are for the woes of those around ye." He sighed and sat on a stool near his brother. The pair of stools were Christmas gifts from Sorcha. "Ye caused a part of her sadness, Cail. The loss of the bairn would have always caused a tremendous sorrow."

Cailean nodded. "But I didn't make it any better."

Alistair raised both hands. "No, ye didn't. But ye have to ken she'd have sorrow, no matter how ye acted. She would have had less had ye been less of an ass, but she would have needed to mourn, no matter how ye were."

Cailean nodded. "It doesn't help me with how to woo her back home." He and Alistair shared a long look, and Cailean's smile was ironic as he said, "I don't know how I'll give up the hope of her."

Two days before Valentine's Day, Annabelle woke with a start. She stilled as she attempted to slow her stuttering heartbeat. A pounding on her front door propelled her into action. She lit a lamp and moved to the front of her shop. "Yes?" she called out.

"Miss Evans? Mrs. MacKinnon?" a nervous voice called out. A woman's voice.

"Yes?" Annabelle peered around the curtain. She frowned at the woman covered in a cloak. When she raised the lamp, the woman's face was covered in rouge. Annabelle flipped the lock and opened the door. "What happened?"

"Charity. She's hurt." The woman glanced over her shoulder. "I wasn't to leave. Wasn't to tell you. Ezekial will be fierce angry. But you must come."

Annabelle nodded. "I'll be there directly. Go before the Madam misses you." She shut the door and raced to her back room where she donned warm clothes and her boots. When she approached her front door, she froze. After a moment's hesitation, she rushed outside, locked it, and then raced to Cailean's house.

She pounded on the front door, shivering in the cold evening air. After many minutes, the door flew open to an irate Cailean. His expression altered from irritation to concern the moment he saw her. "Belle?" he whispered, his hand rising to stroke her cheek.

"I need you, Cailean. I need your help." At his nod, she whispered, "One of the girls from the Boudoir just woke me. She said Fidelia's been hurt. I don't want to go there alone."

He pulled her into a tight embrace for a moment. "Nor should ye." He kissed her on her head before he eased away. "Give me a minute." He tugged her inside before he disappeared upstairs. She heard *thunks* as he moved around, and then he rejoined her a few minutes later. He threw on a heavy coat, hat, and scarf. He pulled out another scarf and wrapped that around her neck.

As he ushered her outside, he looped her arm through his. They clambered over a snowbank, making their way to the mostly clear boardwalk. The snow spit, and the wind howled, and he kept a tight hold of her arm. The boardwalk was deserted this time of night due to the cold. Singing and loud chatter emerged from the Stumble-Out's closed doors, its windows steamed over and providing a rare sense of mystique to the seedy saloon. When they arrived at the Boudoir, rather than enter the front, she led him to the back entrance where she slipped inside in front of him.

The Madam stood in the kitchen with the doctor. They turned to look at Annabelle and Cailean as they entered. "How dare you come here?" the Madam screeched. She wore a black dress with red accents, and her makeup was demurely done, accenting her intelligent eyes. Unlike her girls, who looked tawdry and cheap when seeing customers, she looked regal and refined.

"I want my sister," Annabelle demanded. "I know she's hurt." At the doctor's nod, she stiffened her shoulders.

"It's nothing she hasn't suffered before. She'll recover and continue to be a good asset." She glared at Annabelle. "You should not have been summoned, and you should have known better than to come here."

"I believe it's for Miss Fidelia to decide if she wishes to remain here," Cailean said, as he squeezed Annabelle's shoulder in support.

"Are you hoping she'll leave with you tonight so you can have wife and whore at home?" the Madam taunted, her smile widening as Annabelle flinched. "I've always known men were depraved, but most men attempt to shield their wives from their baser instincts."

The tic in his jaw was clearly visible as he looked at the Madam. "I'd be careful what you say."

"You aren't taking her from me! She's my highest earner. You'll have to pay me to get her!"

"Are you saying you own her?" Annabelle asked. "I'd hate to believe you'd hold someone here against her will."

The Madam flushed in agitation but clamped her jaw shut as she realized that Annabelle and Cailean were a unified front.

Cailean looked at the doctor. "If you would show us to Fidelia?" He glared the Madam into silence and propelled Annabelle into following the doctor. They walked upstairs to find Ezekial standing guard outside her miniscule room barely large enough for a cot.

"Fat lot of good you are!" Annabelle snapped at the large man. "If you had any sense, you would have ensured Fidelia's safety long before now." She met the man's blazing glare with her own before allowing Cailean to lead her into the room.

Fidelia lay motionless on her back, her face battered, neck bruised, and breathing labored and shallow. "What happened to her?" Annabelle asked as she knelt beside her sister and took her hand.

"The man who has become obsessed with her attacked her again. Even though the Madam insists she wrung a promise out of him that he wouldn't harm her." The doctor sighed. "She has at least two broken ribs."

"Does she have any other injuries?" Cailean asked.

"I'm hopeful she has no internal injuries, but it's too early to know. And she hasn't regained consciousness since his attack. I fear she may have head trauma."

"Will she die?" Annabelle asked as she fought tears.

"I can't say." He cleared his throat. "If you will excuse me? I have other patients who require my expertise." He left them alone with her.

"Belle, we can't get her back to the house between us without hurting her."

She turned to look at him. "What do you mean?"

"We can't leave her here." His gaze softened as he saw gratitude flicker through hers. "We need to get her home, but I don't want to leave you here to contend with the Madam."

She shivered. "I don't relish walking through town alone at night." She leaned into him as he sat behind her. "There is no good solution."

Just then Ewan poked his head into the small crib. "What are you two doing here?" His eyes narrowed as he saw a motionless Fidelia lying on her cot. He met Cailean's grim gaze. "Want me to get the sleigh?"

Cailean nodded and Ewan disappeared. "Who would have thought I'd be thankful my brother visited the Boudoir?" He sighed as Annabelle sniffled around a chuckle. "She'll recover, Belle. She's strong, resilient, and stubborn, like you."

"I don't want her to return to work here," she whispered.

"Why don't you worry about that another day?" Cailean

murmured, leaning forward to breathe in her almond scent and kiss her behind one ear. "I've missed you."

She shook her head as she first leaned away from him before sagging into his embrace. "I'm not rational tonight, Cailean."

"I know, and it's unfair of me." He nuzzled her nape. "Thank you for coming to me to help you. Thank you for not coming here alone."

"All I could think of was that I needed help, and I knew you would help me. I never doubted, not for a moment, that you would."

His chest expanded with relief at her words. "Thank you."

After a moment, where she held her sister's hand but was cocooned in his embrace, she whispered, "I don't know what this means for us."

He shushed her. "I know it's a step forward, rather than the long slide backward I've been experiencing." His arm around her waist tightened for a moment. "And I refuse to ask why or doubt it."

They were interrupted by the arrival of Ewan and Alistair. "I woke him up. Thought the more help, the better."

Annabelle rose and slipped from the room. She flinched as Fidelia moaned from being moved and followed as Cailean carried her outside. A two-seater sleigh awaited them. Alistair helped Annabelle in, and she slid all the way to the far side of it. Cailean hefted Fidelia in with Alistair's assistance so that her head rested on Annabelle's shoulder, and her bottom was on the seat.

He clambered in the back seat and lifted Fidelia's legs so they stretched over his lap, and he smiled at Annabelle. "I hope she's comfortable like this."

Ewan and Alistair sat on the front seat of the sleigh, and Alistair eased them into motion for the short ride home. Fidelia moaned again as the sleigh rocked.

"I'm surprised ye couldna have carried her to the house," Alistair teased.

"She's heavier than she looks," Ewan said, with a wink over his shoulder to his brother and sister-in-law. "I should think Cail wouldna have wanted to drop her."

"Hush, ye two jabberin' idiots," Cailean groused. He stilled when he heard Annabelle giggle. "Does their bantering amuse you?"

She shook her head. "No. It's how easy they can rile you. I've missed it." She met his gaze filled with longing for a moment, until Fidelia moaned again. Then her focus returned to her injured sister. When they arrived at the house, Alistair moved to help ease Fidelia into Cailean's arms, and Ewan flung the front door open after tying the horse to the hitching post.

Sorcha stood in the entry to the kitchen, and she paled as she saw the bruises already forming on Fidelia's face. "I have warm water and cloths ready. I don't ken what else ye might need."

Annabelle gripped her hand. "I don't either, except your support. Thank you." She followed Cailean upstairs, where he placed Fidelia in Alistair's freshly made bed. Sorcha entered with a pan of water and cloths over her arm. Annabelle turned to her. "Can you help me undress her so we can better see her injuries?"

Cailean squeezed Annabelle's shoulder before leaving. He muttered something to Alistair that she didn't hear, and she began the torturous task of attempting to remove her sister's clothes without causing her undue pain. She resorted to cutting away her gown, corset, and petticoats. Sorcha swiped away dried blood and cleaned her as best she could.

"Oh my," Sorcha breathed as she beheld the bruising along her left ribs. "Who would do such a thing? And why?" She raised tormented eyes to Annabelle.

"A horrible man." Annabelle's mouth firmed as she swiped a hand over her sister's ribs, eliciting a yowl of pain. "The doctor suspected she had two broken ribs," Annabelle murmured. "Although how he ascertained anything through all these layers of clothing is beyond me." As they finally stripped Fidelia of her Boudoir outfit, a knock sounded on the door.

Sorcha pulled the sheet over Fidelia as Annabelle answered the door, opening it only a crack. "Yes?" she asked. She frowned as a short, stocky woman stood in front of her. "Who are you?"

"I'm a midwife, but I also have experience with other healing needs." She pushed Annabelle aside and barged into the room. "I wouldn't look doubtful, miss. I'm the reason you're alive."

Annabelle bit back a protest when Sorcha nodded her agreement. "Who sent for you?"

"Your husband. Seems he has quite a bit of sense." She grumbled as she looked at Fidelia. "Quite a bit more than this poor woman."

"My sister," Annabelle said.

"So the rumors are true. However, I'd recommend she give up her trade if she cares to see thirty." She opened up her bag, extracting herbs and lotions. "I need you to steep these in water, like a tisane, for five minutes. Then she must drink it. It will help with her swelling and pain."

Sorcha snatched the packet of herbs and left for the kitchen.

Annabelle remained and aided the woman to massage soothing oils and lotions into her sister's arms, legs, and neck. The midwife bound Fidelia's ribs and gently probed for other injuries. Annabelle heaved a sigh of relief as the woman shook her head.

"I believe she was fortunate and was spared anything more than broken ribs and bruising. However, she will feel tremendous pain for many days to come." The midwife swiped at her hands with one of the clean cloths.

Sorcha returned with the tisane, and they eased Fidelia up where she could swallow and not choke. Fidelia struggled for a moment but eventually drank it down when she realized she would be left in peace when it was gone.

The midwife rose, turned to her bag, and extracted more satchels, placing them on a table. "I will leave these with you. Give her a tisane four times a day. Watch for fever. And if she has trouble breathing, call for me immediately. Otherwise I will be here tomorrow evening to ensure she is improving. That is, unless I have a baby to deliver." She disappeared from the room as quickly as she had appeared.

"What a remarkable woman," Annabelle breathed as the door closed after her.

"'Tis one way of describing her," Sorcha said around a chuckle. "Come. Ye need some sleep."

Annabelle nodded, fatigue suddenly overwhelming her, and she moved to the room she had shared with Cailean. She crawled under the quilt, fully dressed. Her last thought before she fell into a dreamless sleep was that she would finally sleep in his arms again.

∼

C ailean woke the next morning, stretched his arms out, and groaned with a feeling of regret to find the space next to him empty. He had never expected to find Annabelle asleep in their bed last night, and he had curled around her as she slumbered, cherishing each moment she spent in his arms.

He rose, scrubbed at his face, and dressed. When he walked into the kitchen, he poured himself a cup of coffee before returning upstairs. He poked his head into Alistair's room to check on their patient, finding Sorcha sitting beside the bed, reading a book. She motioned for him to remain quiet.

"Where's Belle?" he whispered.

"At the bakery. She has much to do to prepare for tomorrow."

"Tomorrow?" he asked.

She rolled her eyes. "Valentine's Day."

"Damn," he muttered. He nodded toward Fidelia. "Thanks." After backing out of the room, he returned downstairs where he took two large sips of the tepid coffee before donning his winter outerwear.

He trudged through the snow to the back door of the bakery and let himself in. He frowned when he saw the dark smudges under his wife's eyes as he stepped inside the warm sweet-smelling haven.

"Cailean, I can't right now," she said, her arms elbow deep in dough. The front door jingled, and she groaned.

He motioned for her to remain where she was, and he met her customer. After ascertaining the prices, cajoling them to purchase more, and sharing bits of gossip, he returned to her. "You can't run this place on your own." He shook his head in apology as he sounded grumpier than he intended.

"I know. I wanted to wait until Leticia is done with teaching so she could work with me full-time after she marries Alistair, and Sorcha has been helping, but today …" She shrugged her shoulders. "Nothing has gone right." She sighed. "Except you walking in the door and seeing to my customers."

He smiled at her olive branch and attended to the suddenly steady stream of customers who arrived. He had little time to talk with his wife until the shelves were nearly empty. "That didn't take long."

She smiled. "It took you thirty minutes longer than Sorcha," she teased.

"You'll have to dock my pay."

She flushed at his words, his deep voice rolling over her. "Why are you here?" she asked as she poured batter into heart-shaped cake tins.

He shook his head, fascinated as he watched her work. "What are you doing?"

"I advertised a special for Valentine's Day. I thought if I set the limit at fifteen cakes, I'd never have to make so many. I'm the fool as I had presold all of them the first day."

"You have to make fifteen of those heart-shaped cakes today?"

"Yes, and decorate them. I won't get much sleep tonight." She frowned. "And it means I won't have any time with Fidelia tonight."

He settled on a stool beside her. "You know we'll take care of her. She'll want for nothing, except your company." He watched as she washed bowls and prepared to make more dough. "What can I do?"

She smiled. "You've done plenty by manning the front. I'm hours ahead of where I thought I'd be because you came by." She paused and poured herself a glass of water before she swiped at her brow. "Why are you here, Cailean?"

He shrugged before meeting her gaze. His intense hazel eyes bore into her light brown ones. "I missed you. I woke with instant regret, somehow knowing you were no longer in my arms." He watched as she broke her gaze from his. "I miss you, Belle. I want you back."

She closed her eyes and leaned her hands on the counter. She bowed her head forward as though in prayer.

"What do I have to do, Belle, to prove to you that I'm sorry? To show that I love you?"

Her head jerked up, and her eyes shone with intense emotion.

"Because I do," he rasped. "I love you, and I don't know what else to do."

She shook her head. "There isn't anything else you can do, Cailean." She swiped at her cheeks and looked at the mess around her. "I can't discuss this right now."

His eyes became bleaker than when she remembered him speaking about his beloved Maggie. "I understand. I'll try to be out of the house when you visit your sister."

"Cailean ..." she whispered and then sighed as he slammed the back door behind him. She took a deep breath, battling her own regret and the urge to race after him before focusing on her baking. "Tomorrow," she whispered to herself. "Tomorrow."

That evening Annabelle groaned at the tapping on her back door. She set aside the bowl of frosting she was mixing together for the cakes and absently licked a finger as she moved to the door. "Yes?" she asked as she inched it open. She smiled, opening it farther and motioning for Harold to enter. "How lovely to see you."

He laughed and moved into the room with alacrity as though he feared she would change her mind and shoo him from the room. "I always love visiting. Smells like paradise in here."

"Well, it should smell better than usual with all the cakes I'm baking for tomorrow."

He smiled. "It's why I've come. Irene wants to know if you can make two more." At her groan, he shrugged. "Seems word got out you'd be supplying us with a few cakes, and many are clamoring for a piece."

Annabelle sighed, and her shoulders stooped. "I'll do what I can."

"Which is considerable." He settled onto a stool and motioned for her to continue working. He smiled as she stirred the frosting and then watched with fascination as she decorated a cake. "You make it look easy. Irene grumbles the entire time she's doing such work."

Annabelle laughed. "I doubt she'd want you spreading such tales."

He grinned. "Seems you had a visitor today." At Annabelle's confused expression, he said, "Heard that husband of yours came by and helped you run the bakery today."

"Oh. Yes, he did. I don't know what I would have done without his help." She stilled her movements at Harold's prolonged silence, his gaze inquisitive and confused. "What?"

"If you appreciated his help, why'd you send him away as though he were no more than hired help?"

Annabelle set down the spoon and rubbed at her forehead, smearing it with powdered sugar. "I can't have these conversations today. I'm too busy."

"When can you have them? When you've torn out a man's heart and tossed it aside as though it were of no significance, you should know the damage you've wrought."

She tugged out a stool and sat across from Harold, her cakes momentarily forgotten. "Did he come to the café to talk with you?"

Harold grunted his disappointment. "I ventured to the livery. My horse is ornery." He speared her with a glare as she giggled, as most recently his horse Brutus had ripped away his pantaloons bottoms in a fit of pique. Besides her ongoing separation from Cailean, his horse's antics were the talk of the town. "And I wanted to see if Alistair or Cailean could find a way to soothe him. I'd read about men out East who put people under a sort of spell, and I wanted to know if they could do that for my cantankerous horse."

He shook his head. "Alistair said there was no hope for a horse as old and set in its ways as Brutus but agreed to work with him for a bit. I followed your husband into the office to tease him about changing professions." His jaw clenched, and his glare intensified. "I've never seen a man brought so low."

Annabelle rubbed at her eyes. "I'd thank you to remember I've been hurt too."

"Don't you sound righteous?" He met her glare with an implacable stare. "Have you found that clinging to your hurts and disappointments has brought you comfort? Does your indignation keep you warm at night?" He paused at her sharp intake of breath. "What more do you want that man to do to show he's repentant?"

Annabelle shook her head. "My sister told me that she wouldn't know what she'd do if she didn't have her resentments to feed."

"Do you want to be like her? Alone? Bitter?" He sighed. "You have the chance for a full life, Miss Annabelle. I know that man of yours disappointed you. But you'll disappoint him some day too. It's the nature of being human. None of us are perfect. We must hope that those we love are brave enough to believe in our love rather than cling to resentments."

He huffed out a breath as she remained silent. "Life is a balance between joy and despair. Those who have a good life find a way to focus on the joy. Don't cling to despair, Miss Annabelle." He rose and stroked a hand down her arm. He slipped out the back door, leaving Annabelle deep in thought.

The next evening, Annabelle woke with a start from her nap. She fumbled as she looked for her watch and stretched with a groan. It was seven, and she hoped it would not be too late to visit Fidelia. Or her husband. She rose, arching her back and moving her neck from side to side. She had done a brisk business of her specialty cookies, muffins, and cakes, and she had decided to take the next two days off.

She slipped on her boots, donned a jacket, and hefted a box before she exited out the front door, locking it behind her. She walked slowly to Cailean's house and knocked on the door. She smiled at Sorcha when she answered. "How is Fidelia?"

"Asleep. She hasna woken much in the past few days. I think that tea is a sedative." She bit her lip as she studied Annabelle's reaction.

"Good. She'd be in too much pain if she were awake as the doctor has nothing else to offer us for her." She fought a frown. "Said he couldn't waste good medicine on a woman like her."

Sorcha gasped. "He never."

Annabelle fidgeted, moving from foot to foot as she held the box. "Is Cailean here?" Sorcha shook her head. "Do you know where he is?"

"She doesna ken," Alistair said from the parlor. "But I do. Why do ye want to see him now? Ye near destroyed him yesterday."

"Please, Alistair. Tell me where he is. I have to talk with him."

He rose and met her in the front hall. "Did ye think it'd soothe yer aches if ye broke his heart?"

She gasped. "No! Of course not. And I refuse to believe I broke his heart."

He bent down and was nose to nose with her. "Why? Is it because ye don't believe he has one? Because he does. And I never thought to see him this low. Not again. Not after Maggie." His eyes shone with anger and concern for his brother.

"Please, let me make this right." She moved to the kitchen and set down the box. She shook her arms as they ached from holding it.

"He's in the livery. In the small office off the stables." Alistair watched her a moment before he returned to the parlor.

Sorcha held open the back door for Annabelle, and she hefted the box again. Sorcha smiled her encouragement to Annabelle, closing the door after her.

Annabelle trudged across the slick pathway between the livery and house, almost dropping the box once. She paused, catching her balance at the last second. After a minute, she edged forward until she reached the door. She set down the box and pulled the barn door open with a grunt. Warm, humid air greeted her, and she grabbed the box, shutting the sliding door behind her by using one hand, her hip and a foot.

The inside of the barn was dark, although a patch of light shone at the far end. She used it like a beacon and made her way there. She tried not to jump as horses whinnied or snorted as she passed.

"Damn it, Alistair. Leave me be!"

She froze at Cailean's wounded voice. She inched forward again and paused at the doorway. He sat hunched over his desk, studying something in front of him while he held a glass of whiskey in his hand. "I'm not Alistair."

He spun, sloshing whiskey onto his pants. "Belle," he breathed. "What are you doing here?"

"Happy Valentine's Day," she whispered. She placed the box on his desk and backed up. "I'm sorry I'm so late. I fell asleep after I closed the bakery today." When he continued to stare at her as though she were an apparition, she flushed. "I brought you something."

He rose, ignoring the box, and dropped his whiskey glass to the floor. His hand shook as he raised it, tracing fingertips down her cheek. "You're really here."

"Yes," she whispered as her throat tightened from unshed tears. "I'm finally here."

He looked at the box and raised an eyebrow. At her nod, he opened the lid, stuttering out a breath as he beheld what was inside. He turned to face her. "Truly?"

She nodded as a tear leaked out. "Yes."

He looked again at the cake in the box with white icing and piped words in pink that read: *You hold my heart.*

She stammered when she spoke next. "I was afraid it was obvious … as the cake is in the shape of a heart." She gasped as he spun to her and clasped her cheeks between his strong hands, holding her in place. "I love you, Cailean."

He swooped down and kissed her. He tasted of whiskey and desperation and her heart's desire. She wrapped her arms around his neck, pulling him close. After a deep kiss, he pulled away. "I don't understand. You said there was nothing I could do yesterday."

"I already loved you. What more could you do?" She stroked a hand over his stubbled jaw. "I was a fool. I was focused on my orders for today. And I didn't want to ruin what I had planned for you today. I never meant to cause you pain."

She squealed as he pulled her tighter, nearly squeezing the air from her. "I thought I'd lost you. That you wanted a divorce."

"No. Never." She pushed until he backed up enough for her to meet his eyes. "I won't lie and say there won't always be some hurt from what happened. I needed you, and you weren't there." She put her hand over his mouth to shush him. "However, since that moment, you've never let me down. You called the midwife on my behalf. You dared God and the devil himself to take me from you." She met his chagrined gaze. "I remember that from my fever-induced haze."

She leaned forward and kissed him. "You stocked my woodpile. You brought me water in the dead of winter. You aided Fidelia, in every way I could have hoped you would." She blinked away tears.

"You love her, and her pain hurts you," he said around her fingers. "I hate to see you hurt."

Tears spilled down her cheeks. "I'm sorry it took me so long to realize I was clinging to my fear with as much fervor as you had clung to yours. And I did as much damage."

"Don't absolve me, Belle. I lost the chance to know the joy you felt at the dream of our bairn. To be there when you became ill." He let out a stuttering breath. "If I hadn't acted as I did, you may never have lost our bairn."

She tried to swallow a sob and lost. She buried her face in his shoulder, crying in his arms again. "I'm sorry. I promised myself I wouldn't cry tonight."

"You're so strong. So independent." He kissed her head as her sobs abated. "I fear you don't need me."

She leaned back in his arms and smiled as tears continued to course down her cheeks. "Of course I need you. Your strength gives me courage. Those few months of harmony were the best of my life. I knew you supported my work and that I could come home, every night, and you would listen and tease and support me. You'd ease my worries about those who aggravated me, helping me see the humor and joy in my day." She looked into his eyes. "Every day with you, before it all changed, you brightened my life."

He made a sound of distress in his throat. "I hate that I ruined it. Give me a chance to make it right. Please tell me that this cake, this declaration, means you're moving home."

She smiled. "Yes. I want to be with you. Forever." She traced a finger down his chest before she blushed. "Before we leave the barn, I was hoping you'd live out a fantasy with me."

He stilled. "What is that?"

She leaned forward and kissed him. "Make love with me in your barn."

He laughed and lifted her, carrying her through the door to an empty clean stall. He set her on her feet and held up a finger, asking her silently to wait, as he marched back into the office. He returned with a blanket that he set on the clean hay. "Everyone thinks hay is romantic. It itches like the devil." He tugged her down with him, and they knelt in front of each other.

He stared into her eyes, the shaft of light from the office illuminating half her face. He cupped her cheek, his thumb tracing over her soft skin. "I can't believe you're actually here with me." He leaned forward and kissed her lips, gently curved up in a smile. "That you are brave enough to forgive me."

She did not allow him to deepen the kiss before pulling back. "I may have moments of weakness. I will need you to work through them with me."

"Aye. I understand those well enough. Mine almost cost us our marriage." He swooped down and kissed her again, deepening the kiss. He eased her backward, leaning over her with his weight on his knees and elbows. He groaned as she arched up into his touch. "I never thought you'd let me touch you again."

"I've missed you." She gasped as he traced fingers over her corset-covered breast. "I've missed this." She held his worried gaze.

"I don't want to hurt you," he whispered.

"I spoke with the midwife today. She came in for cookies, and there was a lull in customers." She gasped as he eased her dress open, his kisses following her parted dress. "There should be no reason we can't enjoy each other."

He leaned back, and his grin was visible in the office light. "Is that what you call making love now?"

She giggled before tugging his shirt free and easing it off his head. She kissed his shoulder and chest. She smiled as his breath hitched at her soft touches. "I love that you react to me as I do to you."

He tugged pins from her hair, loosening it so that it poured over her shoulder. "Until the day I die, I'll want you." He kissed her deeply.

"My Belle." They freed each other of their clothes, rediscovering their passion and love.

～

A while later he smiled as he felt her stir in his arms. She kissed his shoulder before placing her head over his heart. "I love you, Belle. You an' no other."

Her breath hitched at his words. "I understand if you still love Maggie."

He kissed her head. "A part of me will always love her. But she's gone. You're my wife. My future. You'll be the mother of my bairns." He moved so that a shaft of office light lit her face. "Saying *I love you* doesn't seem enough."

She sighed as she arched up to kiss him. "You've shown me your love too, Cailean." She smiled as she pulled a piece of hay from his hair and then giggled when his stomach growled.

"I didn't eat dinner," he said as he nipped at her lips. He stilled as he stared at her. "Is the cake chocolate?" At her nod, he gave a small whoop of joy. He tugged on his pants, wrapped her in the blanket, and carried her into his office.

"I hate destroying your work of art." He stared at the cake reverently.

"There's nothing that a baker likes more than to know that others find her food delicious." She kissed him and smiled as he forgot about the cake and focused on her. When she broke the kiss, she whispered, "And you were smart enough to marry the baker. I can bake you cakes anytime you want."

He laughed and pulled her close. After a moment, when his stomach had growled again, she wriggled out of his hold and reached around him. She pulled two forks out of a small envelope attached to the side of the box. "I hoped we'd have a reason to eat this privately."

He gave her a quick kiss before grabbing a fork and spearing it into the cake. He groaned with pleasure after the first bite. "Heaven," he said between mouthfuls.

She laughed and took a bite. She nodded. "Not bad. I might add a bit more vanilla next time."

After he had devoured one-third of the cake, he groaned and dropped his fork. "I couldn't eat another bite, even if I wanted to." He traced a finger from her hairline to her jaw. "I should get you to bed. You've had a long day and your only day off is tomorrow."

She smiled mischievously at him. "No, it isn't. Tomorrow is Sunday and my normal day off, and I've given myself Monday off, too."

His grin broadened. "Then it will be like two Sunday mornings for us," he whispered. "Finally."

"Finally." She squealed as he picked her up, wrapped only in a blanket, and carried her through the barn, across the yard to the house, and then upstairs to their bedroom where he deposited her in the center of their bed. "That was scandalous."

"Forgive me if I embarrassed you." His gaze was unrepentant as it beheld her, covered in an old blanket from the barn, on their bed. "Let me love you again," he whispered.

"Yes," she gasped, arching up to meet his kiss as his callused palms roamed over her.

In between kisses he whispered, "For so long I've dreamed of you in our bed again." He pulled her tight, holding her close. "Please don't leave me again."

She shuddered. "I won't, love."

He inched away until he could meet her gaze. "And I promise to never treat you like I did last summer and fall, which forced you to leave me." His eyes lit with joy as she nodded her understanding.

She tugged him down to her. "Join me in bed, husband."

He sighed. "With pleasure, my wife." He kissed her neck. "My Belle."

CHAPTER 14

The following morning, Annabelle crept into Fidelia's room. She smiled at Sorcha as she slipped out to grant the sisters privacy. Annabelle grabbed her sister's hand, giving it a gentle squeeze. "Dee, I hope you can hear me. I hope you know how much I love you and that I'll always help you in any way I can."

Fidelia cracked her eyes open, the brilliant blue dulled by pain. "Where have you been?"

"I was busy with orders for Valentine's Day. And then, when I arrived last night, you were asleep. I spoke with Cailean." Her blush intensified at the knowing look in her sister's eyes.

"You reconciled with him. You have the look of a satisfied woman." She groaned as she attempted to shift in the bed.

"Yes. We forgave each other." She pushed back her sister's hair, frowning at the pain she saw in her sister's gaze. "What can I do?"

"You've done all you can. You've allowed me a respite from my life. It's a wonderful gift."

When it seemed she was slipping into sleep again, Annabelle squeezed her sister's hand. "I don't want it to be a respite, Dee. I want you to leave the Boudoir and never return."

Fidelia closed her eyes in resignation. "It's the only work available for a woman like me. I refuse to live on charity."

Annabelle made a sound of distress as she glared at her sister. "Fidelia, you don't have to live on charity. You have a bank account with enough money to survive for years if you are frugal. Why won't you consider a new life?"

"I will never take his money. I've told you that. I'd rather see it rot in the bank than ever touch it." She glared at her sister.

Annabelle huffed out a frustrated breath. "You know as well as I do that allowing your family to aid you is not charity. I want to help you, Dee. You must learn to accept help—as I have." She fought tears. "I can't bear the thought of you returning there. Of that man having the chance to hurt you again."

Fidelia grimaced as she moved. "My choices—and my mistakes— are mine to make, Anna." She opened her eyes and glared at her sister. "Just because you aided me doesn't give you the right to believe you can make decisions for me."

Annabelle swiped at her cheek as a tear fell. "I don't mean to act like Father." She reached forward and touched her fingers to her sister's arm. "Do you know what it was like, being summoned to the Boudoir in the dead of night? Arriving and not knowing if you'd still be alive? And then finding you unconscious in that tiny room, barely breathing?" She shook her head. "I refuse to feel guilty for wanting to protect you, Dee."

She blanched as Fidelia muttered, "You're six years too late."

"I see." Annabelle sat stiffly in her chair, her hand folded on her lap. "No matter what I do, no matter how much I show you that I care, you'll never forgive me." She sniffled as Fidelia's silence was her answer. "You should know, Dee, whatever you believe to be true, know that I love you. And I won't be truly happy until you are free of the Boudoir."

She rose and stumbled out, walking downstairs to the kitchen. She bumped into Sorcha as she moved toward the stove. Sorcha pushed her to the table, and she sat. She barely noticed when Sorcha placed a cup of coffee in front of her.

"What's the matter, Annabelle?" Sorcha asked. She sat across from her and sipped from her cup of coffee.

"Nothing I do will ever make amends for what I did—or failed to do—for Fidelia in the past." She shared a tortured look with Sorcha. "It doesn't matter what I do now. All that counts is what I didn't do."

Sorcha made a disapproving sound in her throat. "She's in pain. She's embarrassed. She'll come around."

Annabelle rubbed at her face. "I don't believe she will. And I can do nothing about it. She told me once how she didn't know what she would do if she couldn't feed her resentments. I never understood the strength of that conviction until now."

Sorcha's fingers thrummed on the table as she stared out the window, lost in thought. Light snow showers had begun to fall, and a gentle wind blew the snow outside.

"What is it, Sorcha?"

"If that is what happens when ye cling to what ye perceive to have been done against ye …" She shook her head as her gaze remained distant. "I dinna want to be like her."

Annabelle focused on her sister-in-law as she attempted to ignore her nagging concerns about her sister. "What happened to you, Sorcha?"

"Nothing happened to me," she whispered. "Except my mum wasna Cailean's mum. Or Alistair's or Ewan's." She flicked a glance through her lowered lashes to gauge Annabelle's reaction. When she saw that Annabelle was not repulsed by the revelation, Sorcha relaxed. "My father had an affair. An' I was the result."

"But you were raised with your brothers?" Annabelle asked. "How wonderful to have still known family. You weren't cast away and forced to live without knowing your father's love. Your brothers' love."

Sorcha shrugged. "My mother … my brothers' mother always resented me. I never understood why."

Annabelle nodded as she thought through conversations with Sorcha and Cailean. "This is why you were so hard on my sister. Because you feared you would be considered like her?"

Sorcha nodded, her gaze drenched with tears. "I was no better than the likes of Mrs. Jameson. I'm sorry, Anna. But I was so ashamed."

Annabelle gripped her sister-in-law's hand. "Rather than focusing on your differences with your brothers, I'd rejoice in how you are alike." She smiled as she met Sorcha's dazed gaze. "And give thanks that they've never seen you as anything but their little sister."

Sorcha smiled. "I've acted like my mother … my adopted mother. Allowing bitterness and prejudice to guide me. I dinna want to be like her."

"What was your mother like?"

Sorcha shrugged. "I dinna ken. She died when I was a bairn, after my birth." Sorcha's gaze sought Annabelle's, as though reminding herself how close her sister-in-law had come to death due to a pregnancy. "Cailean told me how she lit up a room by entering it."

Annabelle smiled. "What a wonderful way to remember a person." She squeezed Sorcha's hand. "You do that too, when you aren't glowering at your brothers."

Sorcha laughed, as Annabelle had hoped she would. "What will ye do for yer sister?"

Annabelle gazed out the window, frowning to see that the snow was thickening. "I don't know. There isn't much more I can do to show her I care. If this isn't enough, then I can't force her to change the way she perceives me." Annabelle took a deep breath. "I must continue to hope that her future will not always be overshadowed by her past."

Annabelle approached Cailean's home, *her home* she reminded herself, pausing to maneuver around a snow pile before walking up the two front steps. Late afternoon sunlight glinted off the fresh snow, enhancing the brilliant blue of the sky above. She came to an abrupt halt when Mrs. Jameson stepped in front of her, bristling with indignant outrage.

"I never thought such a thing would come to pass in this town," Mrs. Jameson said, her voice carrying on the slight breeze.

Annabelle straightened her shoulders to further perfect her posture and attempted an impersonal smile for Mrs. Jameson. "I'm afraid I don't know what you mean."

"Harboring whores outside of their accepted den of depravity. The upstanding citizens of this fine town tolerate their presence because we know we will not have the misfortune of mingling with them. Now. Now!" Her voice rose to a shriek. "Now, to know that to visit the livery, we are aiding a man in his illicit pursuit of pleasure." She shuddered. "Is such vice to be borne in our town?"

Annabelle leaned toward Mrs. Jameson, her chest heaving with her anger. "You consider yourself charitable?" She scoffed as Mrs. Jameson preened at the term. "If I bought you a dictionary, you wouldn't be able to find the term. You're heartless and mean and spiteful. You live off of others' misfortunes in an attempt to feel significant."

"Have you no pride? Allowing your husband's whore to live in your home, along with his wife?" Her gaze filled with pity and superiority raked over Annabelle.

"My husband cares for my sister as his sister-in-law. What you think you know doesn't matter to me. Unlike some women, whose husbands beggared their families from their frequent visits to the Boudoir ..." She raised an eyebrow as she met Mrs. Jameson's shocked gaze.

"How dare you?" Mrs. Jameson gasped.

"I dare because my sister is clinging to life after a man brutally attacked her. She has shown more bravery, more determination, and more refinement of spirit than you will ever understand in her attempt to survive in a world that is cruel to women living alone." Annabelle took a deep breath. "A world you could make easier if you showed kindness rather than contempt."

"Women such as your sister are beneath notice." She shook her head in dismissal. "I will ensure that those in this town who still believe in morality understand that your bakery and your husband's livery are businesses to be avoided."

Annabelle gripped her hands together, turning her fingers white. "I see you in church each week, speaking with the pastor. I'm surprised the building doesn't crash down upon your ears, if this is the measure of your Christian charity." She pushed past Mrs. Jameson to run up her front steps, slamming the door behind her. She leaned against it, shaking with anger and dismay.

That evening she lay in bed, curled on her side as the scene replayed in her head. Cailean joined her, moving to curl around her as he held her in his arms. "Ah, heaven," he murmured as he buried his nose in the hair at her nape. "I'll never tire of holding you."

She gripped his arm around her belly and fought tears. When she sniffled, his arm tightened as though questioning what was wrong. She stroked his arm once before turning to face him.

He frowned as he saw the tears tracking down her cheeks, chasing each one with his thumbs. "What's brought this on, darling?" He swooped forward and kissed her cheeks.

"Oh, Cailean, I'm sorry," she whispered. "I never meant to harm your business."

He frowned as he saw her anxiety mount. "What are you talking about? My business is sound. There are few foolish enough to forego Alistair's abilities with a horse."

She took a deep breath and sniffled. "I had a run-in today with Mrs. Jameson. She accused us of harboring a … a whore and suggested you had your own private bordello." She flushed beet red. "I wasn't kind to her."

Cailean's frown deepened, and he cupped Annabelle's cheek with his palm. "She threatened to have the townsfolk boycott the livery?" At her nod, his lips twitched, and then he burst out laughing.

Her eyes filled with confusion. "I don't understand why you aren't angry."

He watched her with tenderness, a callused finger stroking her cheek. "She's tried, at various times during the past few years, to affect my business." He sobered. "Because I refused to court her daughter."

"Oh my," Annabelle whispered.

"She wanted a successful businessman for a son-in-law, and I think she relished the thought of moving into this house."

"What did you say to dissuade her? Alistair told me a few tales about your curt comments to the women of this town."

Cailean shook his head. "I can't recall, although I'm certain it wasn't perceived as kind." He fought a chuckle. "Imagine her dismay to watch me wed you and then have your sister move in."

Annabelle's shoulders relaxed, and she fell into his arms. "I won't deny that her harsh words sting." She snuggled farther into his embrace. "I trust you will tell me if she could harm your business."

He kissed her head, his fingers playing in her hair. "She cannot. Hell, Belle, she couldn't even hurt your business, and that was far less established than mine. She doesn't have the influence she thinks she does."

He sighed as he kissed her head. "However, I'm afraid some towns-folk already have the same impression she does about Fidelia and me." He paused. "Forgive me, Belle. My visits to the Boudoir last fall have not helped this situation."

"I wonder what they would say if they knew the truth?"

He chuckled at her whispered question. "Few would believe me. Men don't go to the Boudoir for conversation."

Annabelle sighed. "I'd be relieved if my business slowed down a little at the bakery. At least until school is done and Leticia can assist me again. After her wedding of course." She kissed his neck and cuddled into his embrace. "Thank you for welcoming Fidelia here."

"Your sister will always be welcome here, my love."

The following night after dinner, Sorcha was upstairs spinning wool while Cailean had followed Alistair outside on the back porch to smoke his pipe. Annabelle ventured into the parlor to find Ewan reading. Lamps on tables lit the room, lending a gentle glow to the room, while the potbellied stove pumped out heat on this cold evening. "I'm sorry to interrupt," she murmured as she joined him on the settee.

He laughed. "But ye're going to interrupt me anyway."

She smiled. "Yes. I wanted to thank you for helping Fidelia. I should be embarrassed to have seen you at the Boudoir, but I will always be grateful you were there that night."

Ewan smiled. "Cailean canna determine if he'd rather have me there or playin' poker at the Stumble-Out."

"I should think either place is a dangerous endeavor." She smiled as he laughed, refusing to speak about his enjoyment of gambling.

He sobered as he focused on his sister-in-law. "I'm sorry yer sister was abused. No woman, no matter her profession, should be treated in such a way."

"Thank you," Annabelle whispered as she rested her head wearily against the back of the settee.

"I imagine ye're having trouble convincing her to leave the Boudoir." Ewan met Annabelle's startled gaze. "Seems that Madam has a strange ability to convince the girls there that they will only ever have worth as a whore."

"I loathe that woman."

Ewan chuckled and set aside the book before crossing his palms over his stomach. "She's an easy woman to dislike." His amused gaze met hers. "I think she's a woman terrified of poverty."

Annabelle shook her head in disgust. "That may be the case, but she shouldn't brainwash those poor women into believing they could do nothing more with their lives."

Ewan sobered. "Not all are as able as ye, Annabelle. And many will look to others to make their lives easier." He sighed. "An' few are as fortunate to have family like I do."

"Fidelia has family," Annabelle snapped.

Ewan raised an eyebrow and tilted his head as she glowered at him. "Aye. Ye know it, and I know it. But I think she still has trouble believin' it. For some, it takes a lot of time to prove ye're steadfast."

Two weeks later, Annabelle returned from the bakery, entered her home and headed for the kitchen. She stilled when she saw Sorcha and Cailean seated at the table, cups of untouched tea in front of them. Cailean's gaze was guarded, while Sorcha's eyes were red from crying. "What happened?" Annabelle grabbed Cailean's arm. "Has something happened to Fidelia? Alistair? Ewan?" Her increasingly frantic gaze roved between the two of them as they remained silent.

"Sit down, love," Cailean whispered. He waited until she had pulled out a chair before he began to play with her fingers. "I've failed you, and I'm so sorry."

"Cailean, you're frightening me. What's happened?"

Sorcha pushed a crumpled note toward her, and Annabelle frowned. She glanced at it, her gaze focusing as she recognized Fidelia's writing.

Forgive me. I never meant to cause you more trouble. I'm not worth it. Hopefully your business will improve once I'm gone.

Fidelia

"No!" Annabelle screeched. She ripped her hand from Cailean's grasp and raced up the stairs. She barreled into Alistair's room, what she had considered Fidelia's room while she stayed here, and fell to her knees as she found it devoid of any evidence of her sister's presence. "No," she whispered as tears leaked out.

Cailean entered behind her, his soft touch on her shoulder causing her weeping to intensify. "I'm so sorry, Belle."

"How could she leave?" She pounded her fists on the floor before turning and throwing herself into Cailean's arms. "How could she?"

He tugged her until she sat comfortably on the floor in his embrace. He crooned in her ear until she had calmed and held her against his chest even when she tried to ease away from him. "It's my fault. She heard me talking to Alistair about the slight downturn in business at the livery and Mrs. Jameson's threats. I fear Fidelia thought it was because of her presence here."

"Why would she worry herself about a horrible woman's gossip?" Annabelle asked, rubbing her face against his chest.

"Words are powerful, Belle." He sighed. "You know how the Madam controls the women with words as much as with any implied threat from her thug or her clients." He kissed her head. "Ezekial arrived, and Sorcha let him in. She didn't know who he was. Why would she?"

Annabelle shuddered and burrowed farther into his embrace.

"He asked after Fidelia, and, when she joined him downstairs, he didn't have to say anything. She left with him, slipping that note into Sorcha's hand."

"Where were you?"

"In the barn. Sorcha came for me, and I raced after Fidelia. I'm sure that scene will feed the gossips for months." His mouth turned down in disgust as his palms stroked her back. "I couldn't convince her to return here. That she could have a better life here than in the Boudoir."

He shifted Annabelle a bit and pulled another slip of paper from his pocket. "It was as though she knew I would follow her. She gave this to me for you."

Annabelle's hand shook as she grabbed the scrap of paper with *Anna* scrawled on it. She took a deep breath before reading:

I hope you will come to understand and accept that my life is to be lived in the Boudoir. I know you believe you love me, but this is my life, and I will live it my way. Alone and independent, with little need for family. Please don't attempt to visit me or to change my mind. If I want to see you, I know where you are.

Charity

Annabelle dropped the note and fell into her husband's arms as she sobbed. Images of her and Fidelia when they were young in Maine flitted through her mind. Of them chasing waves on a beach. Of them trying to catch fireflies. Of them hiding under a side table as they evaded their father's wrath. She cried as though mourning her sister and her dreams for what could have been.

"I'm so sorry, Belle."

"It's not your fault. She refused to remain here. Refused my care." Her voice broke. "My love."

He tilted back until he could frame her face with his hands. "I wouldn't be so sure about that, Belle. I think your care, your love, is what gave her the strength to return to that life. I think she's terrified of depending on anyone again. Yet she's not the same woman as when you arrived one year ago."

"That horrible man who beats her will kill her. Someday. Somehow. And there's nothing I can do to stop that," Annabelle whispered.

"She might have returned to the Boudoir, but you've shown her your love. If she needs you, she'll seek you out."

"I'm such a fool," she whispered as she fought more sobs, failing to calm with Cailean's soft crooning. "I thought I could love her enough to ease her torments."

"No one can love us better, Belle. And Fidelia must face her own demons and realize she deserves more than the life she leads at the Boudoir. A life that you are willing to help her lead." His hold on her eased as she relaxed in his arms. "Hopefully she will realize that soon."

Annabelle ducked her head. "I know you may think me a fool, but I can't give up on her, Cailean. I will still continue to dream for her, even if she can't dream for herself."

He smiled and kissed her cheek and eased her away to meet her devastated gaze. "That doesn't make you a fool. That makes you brave. And only causes me to love you more." He kissed her forehead, moving backward to stand. He held a hand down to her, helping her up. "Come. Rest a while before dinner. There's no reason for you to worry about everything tonight."

He held her in his arms until she fell into a fitful sleep before joining his siblings downstairs.

The following Sunday, Leticia and Hortence joined them for dinner. Cailean had removed the extra chair that had been brought in from the parlor for Fidelia in the hopes of lessening

Annabelle's grief at the absence of her sister. Annabelle pulled a pot roast with root vegetables simmering alongside it from the oven. She sliced the meat, placed the vegetables in a bowl, and set everything on the table.

When she sat next to Cailean, he squeezed her leg and smiled. "Please, eat while it is hot."

"What do you have for dessert, Miss Annabelle?" Hortence asked. She ducked her head when the adults laughed.

"It's a surprise," Annabelle said with a wink. She accepted the passing bowl of vegetables, serving herself a portion before handing it to Cailean. "How are the wedding plans progressing?"

Leticia groaned. "I would like to wed in late June, but the pastor insists it needs to be early June as he has to attend a convention in Minneapolis and will be out of town from mid-June until August."

"An' I dinna want to wait until August," Alistair said, smiling when his statement provoked a fierce blush in his bride-to-be.

Cailean and Ewan laughed, but it was Ewan who spoke. "You've been mighty patient, Alistair, although Leticia is smart, making you wait until she's good and ready."

Annabelle gave her husband a tap on his arm. "You didn't afford me the same courtesy."

"No, but it all turned out well." He raised her hand and kissed it. "So the wedding will be early June. Hopefully there won't be much rain this year in June."

"Mama says I get a new dress for the wedding!" Hortence said with a broad smile.

"I hope Sorcha is helping to sew it," Annabelle teased. "I'll focus on the cake." She frowned as she noted an undercurrent of unease in Leticia, even though she attempted to feign excitement for her upcoming wedding.

"I will miss teaching." At Leticia's whispered comment, Alistair gripped her hand. "I hate that I must give it up."

"Who have they found to replace ye?" Ewan asked.

"No one yet, but I'm hopeful they'll find someone soon. I'd like to know there will be no interruption in the children's education."

Cailean sighed. "With Mrs. Jameson on the school board, it will be a challenge to find anyone willing to move here to work. She'll scare any potential candidate away."

"My replacement will believe we are all like Mrs. Jameson!" Annabelle said. "Wretched woman!" She flushed as she saw Hortence listening to their conversation with avid interest. "I said no such thing, Hortence. I didn't mean it."

"She's a puffed-up bellows, full of hot air," Hortence said around a bite of soft carrot. "That's what Ephraim, one of the older boys in school, says." She smiled as the adults laughed in agreement.

"Well, don't go repeating what we say. I'd hate for your mother to get in trouble due to something one of us said." Annabelle smiled at Hortence when she nodded her agreement. With Sorcha's help, they cleared the table and left the plates to the side of the sink.

She extracted a round layer cake hidden on a shelf in the pantry and set it on the table. It had white frosting with small rosettes around the top in light green. "I was feeling fanciful and hoping for spring. No one purchased this yesterday, so I thought we might as well enjoy it."

"Irene and Harold would have enjoyed selling this," Leticia said as she handed out glasses of milk to everyone.

"I was tired and didn't feel like baking anymore." She cut into it and caught her husband's delighted smile when he realized one of the layers was chocolate. The other was a white cake. "I hope you enjoy the cake," she said as she cut large slabs.

"And if you don't, I'll eat your piece!" Cailean said with a wolfish grin and a wink to his wife.

Later that evening, Annabelle rested in Cailean's arms, sleep eluding her. When she sighed and rolled to her other side, he chuckled. "You need your sleep, love. You must get up early tomorrow."

"I know. I can't stop thinking about today." She calmed as his fingers stroked over her arm before linking with her hand.

"What worries ye?" he asked, his accent reappearing as sleep beckoned.

"Why is Leticia uncertain about her marriage to Alistair? They've known each other for years. It makes no sense to me."

Cailean snuffled out a laugh into her ear. "You look for a problem where there isn't one. She's worried about giving up teaching." He sighed as his words did little to soothe her distress.

"I think there's more." She tucked her head under his chin. "No matter what I ask or what I say, she's not inclined to speak with me about it."

Cailean cupped her cheek and drew her face up so he could stare into her eyes. Faint moonlight illuminated the room. "Have ye ever stopped to think that she might fear marriage? I've yet to hear much about her first marriage." He shrugged. "If it had been a good union, and she mourned him, I would expect to hear more about him."

"You never speak of Maggie," Annabelle whispered. His sharp intake of breath caused her to frown. "I didn't mean to hurt you."

"You didn't. Not much." He leaned forward and kissed her. "I couldn't speak of her due to a grief too great to voice. I've never had the impression it was the same for Leticia." He ran the pad of his thumb over Annabelle's eyebrow. "Besides, she has a daughter. She should speak of the lass's father at some point."

"But she never does," Annabelle murmured.

Cailean made a noise deep in his throat of agreement. "I think she fears what will happen when she marries Alistair." He paused a moment as though relishing the feel of her in his arms. "We'll help them through their troubles, as they aided us."

"Their wedding should be joyful, Cailean, not traumatic."

He chuckled as he met her gaze. "Thank God we reconciled, or I fear she would have postponed the wedding for fear of what MacKinnon men are like."

Annabelle watched him with a flirtatious smile, pressing into him while her arms snaked around his shoulders. "And what are MacKinnon men like?" she whispered as she kissed his jaw.

"Handsome." He kissed her eyebrow. "Persuasive." A kiss to her nose as she giggled. "Impossible to resist." He laughed as she playfully bit his earlobe.

He rolled over with her, nuzzling her neck before meeting her gaze. "Loyal. Honorable. Dedicated to family." His eyes shone with love as she traced her fingers over his jaw. "I love you, Belle."

She nodded as her fingers tangled in his hair. "I never thought to feel what I feel for you. I didn't know it possible." She pulled his head down for a kiss. "I love you, Cailean."

"Whatever challenges come, we will face them together, Belle." His gentle kiss ended too quickly for her as she arched up, following his lips.

"Yes, Cailean, always together," she whispered, her eyes lit with a transcendent joy.

SNEAK PEEK AT MONTANA GRIT!

 HAPTER ONE

Montana Territory, June 1885

No one expected the wedding to be a disaster. In fact, it had been heralded by many in Bear Grass Springs, Montana Territory, as the wedding of the season. Another MacKinnon brother was to wed, to the dismay of the mothers in the town who had hoped for more than a wandering miner for their daughters. As for the bachelors of Bear Grass Springs, few eligible women lived in town; thus many of the men were equally disappointed to see the beautiful teacher marry the livery owner.

Alistair MacKinnon, the second eldest sibling at the mature age of thirty-four, paced in front of the altar on a bright Saturday afternoon in early June. He wore his best suit and had polished his rarely worn dress shoes three times, although he fought grimacing with each step because they pinched his toes and he longed for his boots.

"Stop fidgeting and sit down. You'll give yourself blisters," ordered Cailean, the eldest MacKinnon sibling by three years. He shook his head in amusement as he watched Alistair.

"Ye were no' any better," Alistair grumbled.

Cailean chuckled as he thought about his own wedding to the town baker, Annabelle Evans, the previous June. Although the two eldest MacKinnon siblings had left the Isle of Skye together over a decade ago, Cailean had worked to hide his accent, while Alistair had never lost his. "I know. But I was always the more emotional sibling."

Ewan, the youngest MacKinnon brother, approached with a flask. "Take a wee nip," he urged the anxious groom-to-be and rolled his eyes as Alistair waved away the offered libation. "Ye dinna ken how much longer she'll keep ye waitin', an' this will calm yer nerves."

Alistair glared at his youngest brother. "I willna meet my bride on our weddin' day through a haze of whiskey." He allowed his brothers to push him onto the front pew.

"Ignore Ewan. You know Sorcha is with Leticia, and our sister will ensure they are not too late." Cailean rapped his fingers on the pew's back as time seemed to crawl. He looked toward the front of the church. "Guests are arriving, and Ewan and I should welcome them." Cailean placed a firm hand on Alistair's shoulder. "Stay here. Think about your bride-to-be, about what's to come." He gave his brother a pat on the shoulder and marched down the aisle with Ewan behind him.

Alistair sat in a daze on the bench, his mind filled with images of his fiancée, Leticia Browne, as he thought about the last few days leading up to the wedding.

As spring would soon give way to summer, and the bear grass that gave the town its name verged on the point of blooming, Alistair breathed a sigh of relief that his long courtship with Leticia was almost at an end. As he squired his fiancée through the newly constructed home they would share in two days' time, he smiled with contentment. The new home had been built on the opposite side of Main Street from where the MacKinnon Livery stood, on a large empty plot near the alley that abutted the rear door of Annabelle's bakery.

"Dinna Ewan create a lovely home for us?" he asked, the hint of Scotland stronger in his voice as he beheld Leticia standing amid the early evening rays in their living room area on the ground floor. Although smaller than the home he shared with his siblings, the basic design for their new home was the same with the kitchen and dining area separated from the living room on the other side by a long hallway. Upstairs were three bedrooms, rather than four.

She smiled at him and sat on the secondhand settee given to them by Irene and Harold Tompkins—a couple who acted as doting aunt and uncle to the MacKinnons and ran the local Sunflower Café. "I love it."

"An' ye dinna mind that the kitchen is small?" Alistair stood over six feet tall, and his brown hair was virtually black in the dimming evening light. He watched Leticia with warmth in his brown eyes.

She laughed. "Do you know what it will be like to have a home that is mine? To decorate as I want, without worrying I'll offend the owner? To build a home with you?" She rose, smiling broadly as she wrapped her arms around his waist. Her thick blond hair, pulled back in a bun, loosened as his fingers tugged at the pins holding it in place.

"I'm fighting my impatience," he whispered as he pulled her close. "Two days seems an eternity."

She shivered and squeezed her arms tight around him. "It will pass faster than you imagine."

He sniffed her lilac scent and smiled. "Aye, I know. After waiting years to marry, I fear ye'll find another reason we should wait."

"No," she whispered as she traced a pattern over his lower back. "No more waiting, not after two days from now."

He groaned, bending his head to kiss her. She sighed softly, arching up to meet his impassioned kiss. After only a few moments, he broke their embrace, wandering the room. "I canna be trusted to touch ye just now." He shared a rueful smile with her, his smile broadening as he saw her pleased blush. He broke his gaze from her delighted blue eyes and looked around the room. "Ewan did a good job."

She chuckled as she ran a hand over her light-blue dress that nearly matched her eyes. "He did a masterful job, as you knew he would. He was determined to build a beautiful home for his brother." She traced the fine trim on the sill around a side window. "I can envision a vase of flowers here, with curtains blowing in the breeze."

He sat on a windowsill at the front of the house, maintaining his distance from her. "I can see us curled on that settee, warming each other on a cold winter day while Hortence plays on the floor."

She laughed as she thought about her six-year-old daughter. "You'll be on the floor playing with her."

"Aye, I probably will. Although 'twill be a tough choice. Canoodle with my wife or play with my daughter?" He frowned as he saw Leticia fight tears. "What is it, darling?"

She watched him through eyes drenched with adoration, love, and wonder. "I will always be humbled by how you have accepted Hortence as your own."

"She's an easy lass to love." He rose and outstretched his hand to Leticia. "Come. Let's explore our home." He laced their hands together as they wandered to the sparsely furnished kitchen and dining area, although it had a top-of-the-line Great Majestic stove. They continued upstairs, poking their heads into the three rooms before returning downstairs. "I ken I'm supposed to wait until after the ceremony to give you my wedding present, but this is all I can offer."

She fought a mixture of laughter and tears as she threw herself into his arms. "Oh, Alistair. I could want for nothing more than to marry you in two days' time and to live here with you and Hortence."

"An' ye don't mind that wee Hortence will spend a few days with Cailean and Anna?" he whispered into Leticia's ear, provoking a shiver.

"I'll miss her. I've never spent a day apart from my daughter." She arched away, meeting his worried gaze. "But I want time with you, Alistair. Time for the two of us."

He moved as though to swoop forward and kiss her but then backed up with such speed he bumped into a door. "Aye, 'tis good to know." He cleared his throat. "I dinna think we should linger here alone for much longer."

"Yes, you might damage the schoolteacher's reputation, retiring at twenty-eight to wed," she teased. Her latent anger eased at being forced to give up her teaching position as her wedding day approached. She followed him outside, looping her arm through his elbow.

"'Tis a good thing the schoolteacher taught her final class last week," he murmured.

They walked the short distance to the house he shared with his siblings, where his sister, Sorcha, helped mind the house with his sister-in-law, Annabelle. As the town baker, Annabelle did the majority of the cooking for the family, while Sorcha preferred to embroider, mend the clothes, and spin wool. The MacKinnon house sat next to a large livery and the nearby paddock where Alistair worked with his eldest brother, Cailean.

While Alistair and Leticia walked arm-in-arm through town, they smiled, nodded, and spoke to all they passed. As co-owner of the local livery established four years ago, Alistair knew most men in town, and, as the former schoolteacher, Leticia knew all those with children. The engaged couple ambled up the boardwalk, past the bakery, the bustling café, and the Odd Fellows Hall.

Bear Grass Springs sat toward the apex of a large valley with the Obsidian mining camp in the tall granite-peaked mountains above it, while a creek gurgled past the edge of town. Down the rolling hills, a broad valley opened up for as far as the eye could see, providing the perfect habitat for large herds of cattle. The green hills heralded a wet spring, although summer's heat would soon turn them a golden brown.

The couple turned as gunshots sounded, and raised voices floated on the wind from the opposite side of town. "Seems the good times have already begun at the Stumble-Out," Alistair said wryly as he looked at the saloon down the street that sat across from Betty's Boudoir, the town brothel.

"There's nothing to worry about as I'm sure Ewan is home," Leticia soothed.

Alistair squeezed her arm and turned for the family home. "For now." He inhaled deeply, then shook his head. "Stay for supper with us. Annabelle's cookin' tonight, so I know we'll eat well," he said with a wink. When they arrived at the MacKinnon home, they found his sister, Sorcha, the youngest MacKinnon sibling at twenty-four, on the parlor floor, playing with Hortence.

Hortence saw her mother and rose, hugging her around the waist. After her warm welcome, she ignored her mother, dropping to her knees to play with Sorcha again. "I have an aunt!" she proclaimed with a triumphant thrust of her fist upward, as though she had won something.

"Aye, in two days ye'll have two aunts and two uncles," Alistair said as he sat on the floor near her. "Ye're a lucky girl." He smiled as she giggled.

Her giggles faded as she ducked her head a bit and smiled at him. "I'll have a papa too."

He tugged her to his lap and held her tight. "Aye, technically ye will." When she stiffened in his arms, he stroked a hand over her head. "I already consider ye mine, Little Bug. The weddin' just makes it official." He grunted as she flung her arms around his neck and gave a small whoop of joy. He laughed as she kissed him on his cheek. Another grunt followed when she scampered off his lap, her knees and feet digging into his legs. He rose and joined Leticia on the settee, content to watch his sister and his daughter play.

"I love your nickname for her," Leticia murmured.

He smiled as he watched Hortence's exuberant play. "We found a ladybug on one of our rambles, an' she proclaimed it her favorite bug because it was part red and pretty." He shared a long look with Leticia. "I told her that she was my Little Ladybug, but that's a long name, ye ken?" His gaze softened further as he continued to focus on Hortence. "So she's my Little Bug."

"She's been teased terribly about her red hair."

Alistair tensed next to her. "I hate the cruelty of others but especially when directed at children."

She kissed him on the cheek. "And I love how you want to protect her."

He held his fiancée's hand and sighed with satisfaction as she rested her head on his shoulder. When Annabelle called out that dinner was almost ready, they rose, washing their hands before sitting at the round table set for seven with a small bouquet of wildflowers at its center.

"Who brought you the flowers?" Cailean asked Annabelle.

She flushed. "One of the miners has a sweet tooth but can't afford a cookie. I gave him a few of the cookie pieces a couple days ago, and he brought the flowers today as a thank-you."

"And you gave him more sweets today," Cailean said matter-of-factly. He laughed as his wife blushed. He raised her hand and kissed it as she paused by his side in her movements about the kitchen. "I'm glad you're soft hearted, Belle. Not everything can be about profits."

She served them all large bowls of venison stew and set a plate of sliced bread on the table. After pulling a small slab of butter from the icebox and placing it alongside their meal, she sat next to Cailean.

"Did ye hear what Mrs. Jameson has proposed?" Ewan asked as he paused in wolfing down his supper. At their curious stares, he set aside his spoon. "She read a story about rules for schoolteachers and is intent on enacting them for the next one."

"What sort of rules?" Leticia asked.

"Ones to prevent *illicit behavior.*" Her soon-to-be brother-in-law wiggled his eyebrows at her.

"Illicit behavior? When did I ever do anything illicit?" She shot a worried glance at her daughter, Hortence, but everyone appeared as confused as Leticia was.

"Seems she wants to forbid the walking out with gentlemen and to enact curfews. Female teachers should be home each night by eight, should refrain from wearing any form of scent or any provocative clothing."

Annabelle choked back a laugh. "Is she serious?" At Ewan's nod, she shook her head. "This is her petty way of declaring that Leticia was an unfit teacher, simply because she was courted by an honorable man while she taught."

"'Tis more than that," Alistair murmured. "Mrs. Jameson wants to strike out at us because she's bitter that her daughter willna be Mrs. Alistair MacKinnon." He leveled an intense gaze at his youngest brother who had just turned thirty. "I'd be careful, Ewan. She's intent for Helen to be a MacKinnon, an' ye better have yer wits about ye so that ye don't get trapped by one of her schemes."

Cailean chuckled as he played with a ruffle on his wife's collar. "That's one of the reasons she was irate that Annabelle had *lured* me into marriage." He winked at his wife as she rolled her eyes. "After Mrs. Jameson overcame her delight in spreading gossip about us, she realized she'd lost me for her daughter."

His siblings laughed. "Helen wouldna have had ye!" Ewan said. "Not after ye told her that she looked worse than an overripe raspberry about to burst at the previous Founders' Day party. She couldna stand the sight of ye."

"The same could never be said for her mother." Cailean frowned. "All Mrs. Jameson cared about was that I had a good business and a large house."

"Now that she sees ye happily wed, it only makes her envy greater," Sorcha murmured. "An' she's delusional enough to believe her daughter would have been equal to Annabelle."

Cailean squeezed his wife's hand. "For me, Annabelle is incomparable. As Leticia is for Alistair." He raised his glass of water in a toast. "To the lucky couple, who, in two days' time, will end the longest courtship in town history."

They raised their cups before *clink*ing them.

Annabelle giggled. "Yes, this family will have the longest and one of the shortest in town history."

"As long as we are wed, I dinna care how many years it took us to arrive at this place," Alistair said with a loving gaze into Leticia's eyes.

~

Available March 2018!

ALSO BY RAMONA FLIGHTNER

Are you yearning for more time in Bear Grass Springs? The next books in the series are coming soon!

Coming Soon:

Montana Grit (Bear Grass Springs Book Two)- **March 2018**!

Montana Maverick (Bear Grass Springs, Book Three) **April 2018**!

Montana Renegade (Bear Grass Springs, Book Four) **May 2018**!

Banished Saga:

The Banished Saga Books 1 &2 (Banished Love and Reclaimed Love)

Undaunted Love, Part One (Banished Saga, Book 3)

Undaunted Love, Part Two (Banished Saga, Book 3.5)

AFTERWORD

As most often occurs, the idea for this novel came to me as I sat by a river a few summers ago as I took a break from fly fishing. I had been toying with the idea of starting a new series, but had put it on the back burner as I was busy writing novels in the Banished Saga. However, the words, "I'm not marrying a whore," popped into my head and I immediately wanted to know who said them and why. Thus, this new series was born.

I had forgotten the challenges inherent in creating a new series. From new characters, to places, to settings, and I tried to talk myself out of attempting a new series while in the midst of another one. However, I soon found the joy in research and creating something new. I hope you love the MacKinnons and the people of Bear Grass Springs as much as I do, and I can't wait to share the next novels in the series with you.

Happy reading,
Ramona

ACKNOWLEDGMENTS

Thank you to my wonderful first readers who helped me enrich the story and sense of place. Your ideas and aid was invaluable.

Thank you to my fantastic editor, DB. You are an essential member of my team, and I don't know how I'd do this without you!

Jenny Q—you make gorgeous covers, and I'm so excited to work with you again on this new series. Thank you for another beautiful cover.

Finally, I couldn't do all of this without you, my amazing reader! Thank you for all of your support!

Made in United States
Troutdale, OR
05/13/2024

19843133R00159